Deceptive Valor

Clay Warrior Stories
Book #9

J. Clifton Slater

Deceptive Valor is a work of fiction. Any resemblance to persons living or dead is purely coincidental. I am not a historian, although I do extensive research. For those who have studied the classical era and those with exceptional knowledge of the times, I apologize in advance for any errors.

The large events in this tale are from history but, the dialogue and action sequences are my inventions. Some of the elements in the story are from reverse engineering techniques and procedures. No matter how many sources I consult, history always has holes between events. Hopefully, you'll see the logic in my methods of filling in the blanks.

I need to thank Hollis Jones who kept the story on track and grammatically correct with her red pen. Without her, the project would have wandered far from my plan. And my writer friends and support group who keep me sane. You are much appreciated.

J. Clifton Slater
Email: GalacticCouncilRealm@gmail.com
Website: www.JCliftonSlater.com

Deceptive Valor

Act 1

"First, I shall indicate the causes of the war between Rome and Carthage, known as the Hannibalic war, and tell how the Carthaginians invaded Italy, to break up the dominion of Rome. And cast the Romans into great fear for their safety and even for their native soil… while great was their (Carthage's) own hope, such as they had never dared to entertain, of capturing Rome itself."

Polybius of Megalopolis, Greek Historian

"…while the Carthaginians conveyed most of their army to Sardinia with the intention of attacking Rome from that quarter. They would thus either drive them out of Sicily altogether or would render them weaker after they had crossed over there. Yet they achieved neither the one object nor the other. The Romans both kept guard over their own land and sent a respectable force to Sicily with (Consul) Postumius Megellus and (Consul) Quintus Vitulus."

Cassius Dio, Roman Historian

Welcome to 262 B.C.

Chapter 1 – Tharros

The Qart Hadasht warship cut through the waves of the Tyrrhenian Sea. After an open water crossing from Agrigento in Sicilia, it made a brief stop in Sulci on the southwest edge of Sardinia. Once resupplied with water, grain, and fruit, the exhausted crew rowed out before first light heading north. By last light, the crew dropped the sail, lowered their oars, and rowed towards land.

At 130 feet in length and 20 feet wide with a top deck only 7 feet above the ocean, the swift warship could deliver a killing blow with her bronze battering ram to the side of an enemy ship. Or, bring one hundred eighty knives employed by powerful oarsmen to a fight and provide ten heavy infantrymen to a land battle. The purpose of this specific trip required none of these.

On the broad beach at Tharros, a town located halfway up the coast of Sardinia, the flat bottom of the warship ground on the sand. One hundred oarsmen jumped to the beach and grabbed the hull. They carried and dragged the trireme out of the surf and up onto the beach. Once completely out of the water, a man dropped over the side and marched inland. He wore the thick soled military boots favored by the Iberian army, a blue tunic, and slung on his shoulder was a leather satchel. The man and the messages in the leather pouch were the reason for the hurried pace of the sea voyage.

***

Lieutenant Noguera stumbled and found he had to concentrate on placing his feet. An Iberian engineering officer, he could march or sit a horse for a week without issues. But after five days of sea travel, his knees wobbled, and his legs moved as if he had been indulging in good Iberian beer. Where the trail changed to a rocky surface and began meandering between trees, the odd feeling left, control returned to his legs, and he picked up his pace.

Noguera had a lot of work ahead of him. In a month, 13,000 heavy infantrymen would arrive at Tharros.

2

Although the plan called for them to stage briefly on Sardinia, his Iberian commanders would expect housing, food, beer, wine, and drill fields while there. He stomped on the hard ground and began calculating…

A blinding pain shot through his head, his mind closed to blackness, and his body went limp.

***

The Iberian engineer crumpled to the ground.

"I thought you were here to observe," the Sardinian fisherman whispered. "Not start a one-man war."

"I was observing. That's why I clubbed him," Alerio Sisera whispered. The Legionary slid his gladius into the sheath, grabbed the Iberian Lieutenant's ankles, and pulled the unconscious man into the trees. "Look at the crew on the warship."

The fisherman raised up on his toes and, in the fading light, he peered between trees at the shoreline.

"The warship has a crew. Yup, you're right," the Sardinian mumbled. "Not really surprising, is it? They just rowed her ashore."

"Not at the crew. At their state of exhaustion," Alerio corrected while reaching down and relieving the Iberian of the satchel. "They have pushed through a long journey. And for what?"

"Only half have made it to the beach. The rest are collapsed on the deck," the fisherman commented. "They do look beat. Why the rush and what do you think they're hauling?"

"Him and this leather bag," Alerio replied with a nudge to the ribs of the Iberian with the toe of his boot. "I can't carry him or take time to question him. But I can take the satchel."

"Kill him," the Sardinian instructed. "and let's get moving."

"He's not worth it," Alerio replied as he moved away.

"Another Qart Hadasht mercenary," the fisherman spit out while drawing a short, sharp knife used for gutting fish. As he stooped over the body, the fisherman bent down and slid the blade across Lieutenant Noguera's throat. "Now there's one less."

The two men faded back into the trees, then turned and ran for the edge of Tharros.

***

In the dark following sunset, Alerio and the fisherman circled the town, located the road heading north, and fell into a steady jog. About a mile outside of the settlement, they moved off the trail and crept into the woods.

"The ponies are here," Alerio announced when he saw the animals.

"Not ponies, Legionary," the fisherman scolded. "Those are Giaras horses. Small and tough like us Sardinians."

"They look like ponies to me," Alerio insisted as he untied his mount. "But if you want our rides out of here to be horses, then they are horses."

The two men nudged the animals back to the road. Once on the hard surface, they trotted away from Tharros.

***

In the middle of the night, Alerio and the fisherman arrived at Bosa. No lights glowed in the windows of the small homes or on the streets of the coastal village. From

4

the top of the bank, the two men looked out over rolling waves. Closer in and on the beach, all of the village's fishing boats rested upside down in case of rain.

"I could have used a hot meal and a good night's sleep," complained the Sardinian. "But you had to stir up a mess."

"I needed the pouch," offered Alerio. "But it was you who killed him."

"I did but you just had to have that pouch," responded the fisherman. "Now instead of relaxing, we get to launch, paddle out, and lower the sail. Come on."

"After a week of sneaking around Sardinia, this was the first interesting thing we came across," Alerio said in his defense. "And soon you'll be free of me."

"The Republic pays me handsomely for guiding spies," the fisherman exclaimed while sliding off his mount. "It pays better than fishing and occasionally I get to kill a Qart Hadasht mercenary. "

"Do you do this often?" Alerio questioned as he rolled off the horse and followed the fishermen to the boats on the sand. "I mean guiding not the killing."

"Whenever there's a rumor that the Empire's planning an invasion of the Republic."

"You don't sound convinced they might try," Alerio suggested.

"Twice a year for three years now, the Legion sends over a scout," the fisherman explained while gripping the side of his boat. "I paddle them around and show them the Qart Hadasht towns and fortifications. In every case, there is no new construction or new marching camps. I collect the fee, send the spy home, and everyone is happy."

"It sounds boring," Alerio admitted.

"Except, like I said. Every once in a while, I get to kill a mercenary."

"Why not a Qart Hadasht citizen?" Alerio asked.

"Only two types visit Sardinia," the fisherman stated as the boat flipped over and rocked on its keel. "High ranking military commanders and rich merchants. In both cases, they never travel without a school of little fish swimming around and bodyguards."

Alerio took the opposite side and helped lift the fishing boat. Together, the two men walked it into the surf.

***

Deep into the night, the land gave up its heat and the wind blew out to sea. The fisherman positioned the flat sail to catch as little of it as possible. By morning, the sea breeze reversed, and the fisherman woke just long enough to shift the sail to keep them from being driven ashore. Then he curled up in the bow of the narrow boat, pulled a cloak over his head, and went back to sleep.

"I'm not sure but these look like bear claws to me," Alerio said. He held the rear oar with one hand. The other he used to extend the brim of his Petasos to shade his eyes against the morning sun.

"Sail around the fingers of land and into the strait," the fisherman ordered from under the wrap. "Wake me when we get to the fishing village at Torre della Pelosa. Or, if you have any problems."

Alerio tilted the rear oar and guided the fishing boat around the broken shoreline. The wind hit the sail and the fishing boat made wakes as it entered the channel. Sardinia rose on one side and a long strip of land that made up the remainder of the island climbed from the water on the other.

The land peaked at about sixty feet, just enough to block the wind. From an exhilarating rush across the water, the fishing boat languished. To compensate for the limp sail, Alerio pushed the oar back and forth turning and propelling the vessel towards a collection of fishing huts.

"Is the trading ship here?" inquired the fisherman.

"I don't see anything larger than a fishing boat."

"Take us in and let's find lunch and lodgings," suggested the Sardinian. "You'll probably have to wait here for a day or so."

"And where will you be?"

"As far away from you as possible."

"Why?" Alerio inquired.

"Because Legionary, you killed an Iberian and there will be a price on your head."

"Correction, you killed the mercenary."

"You know it and I know it," the Sardinian offered. "But the Qart Hadasht commanders don't."

***

Alerio and the Sardinian sat away from the huts and dined on baked fish and vegetables while sharing a skin of wine. The fisherman sat on the sand with his legs crossed and the Latian used his bedroll as a low chair.

"What do you suggest we do while we wait for the trader?" Alerio questioned.

"That's not my problem," the fisherman replied. He stood, patted the pouch of coins Alerio had given him, and started to stroll towards his fishing boat. "I'm heading home, Corporal Sisera. May Fortūna smile on you. Although a blessing from Dolos may be better. Which do you favor, luck or cunning and deception?"

The Sardinian guide kneed the rail on his boat to get it started. Once moving, he ran it into the water.

"I'm not sure about your meaning," protested Alerio. "The Qart Hadasht control the coastline to the south. Why do you think I'll have a problem on the northern end of the island?"

"Because, Legionary," the fisherman said as he hopped into the boat. Once standing and gripping the rear paddle, he added. "the Republic isn't the only one with a big coin pouch and loose purse strings."

Alerio stood on the beach and watched the fisherman work the rear oar. The boat tracked along the shoreline until it vanished behind the land features and left the channel. Once alone, Corporal Sisera walked to the satchel and his bedroll. He picked them off the sand, turned away from the village, and marched off.

The Centurion and Optio, who trained him during the harvest every year at his father's farm, had an expression for situations like this - Perfututum Beyond All Recognition. With that unhappy thought in mind, Alerio Sisera hiked east along the shoreline. It was a long way to the Capital and across half an ocean but, at least, he was heading in the right direction.

Chapter 2 – Beyond All Recognition

Late in the day, Alerio jogged along the flat ground at the top of the beach. Following the curvature of the Gulf of Asinara, he reached the town of Porto Torres with daylight to spare.

To the experienced Legionary, the run felt to be about fourteen miles. That estimate and the sun's position allowed him to enter the streets of Porto Torres and nonchalantly stroll to a pub. If the turncoat farmer alerted Qart Hadasht command to his whereabouts, they would start with Torre della Pelosa. By the time they moved to search Torres, he would be long gone.

"Goat meat, cheese, bread, and vino," he ordered. Then added. "And I'll need a couple of wineskins of water for the road."

"Traveling far, Latian?" inquired the serving lass.

"I'm here to explore your lovely island," Alerio lied. "I'm heading inland and don't know where the watering holes are located."

She lifted her eyes and scrutinized the intersecting streets.

"Where's your horse?" she asked.

"I just got off a boat. Do you know anywhere I can buy a Giara?"

"My husband has an old mare around back," she offered. "I'm sure he'll sell her cheap."

"Cheap? What's wrong with the animal?"

"She is barn sour," the server described. "Leave her untethered or untied and she'll come back to her stable. And so…"

"And so, she's cheap because I probably won't have her long," Alerio said finishing her thought. "Bring the horse around after I eat, and I'll have a look. And don't forget my water bags."

Later, with a full belly and the bedroll, water bags, and the satchel tied to the Giara, Alerio tapped her with his heels and the animal moved southward. The tavern owner and his wife stood outside the pub waving and smiling. Alerio wasn't sure if the smiles were gratitude for his business or for the steep lease rate for a horse that would bolt at the first opportunity.

Once out of sight of the hamlet, he tugged on the reins and guided the horse to the left and back to the shoreline. Legionaries run and can easily jog twenty miles, take a break, and do another ten miles. Heavy infantrymen were required to do it but, Alerio only knew a few who enjoyed spending the day in continuous motion. Much preferable was sitting on the back of a tough mountain Giara and letting the horse do the miles.

Comfortable on the back of the animal, he wouldn't stop until late into the night.

***

"Good morning, grandma," Alerio greeted the old horse. "You're facing the wrong way and it doesn't look pleasant."

During the night or perhaps early in the morning, the homesick Giara had shuffled her tethered legs around until they straddled a thick thorn bush. Compounding the discomfort, her lead line was tied to a tree behind her. There had been enough length for the animal to munch on green grass. But not enough for her body and head to face homeward. Her neck twisted back, and one ear rested against her shoulder.

"I'll make you a deal," Alerio promised while pushing out of his bedroll. "You get me to a dock where I can catch a ride home. And I'll turn you lose so you can go home."

At the word home, the Giara stomped her front legs. The rapid movement caused thorns to penetrate her skin. She stopped and shuddered at the pain.

"Whoa there, old gal," Alerio cooed. He pulled the long-handled custom swords from the ends of his bedroll. Holding them down at his sides, the Legionary strolled around the horse studying the trapped animal. "Five barbs have drawn blood. And from the looks of it, Mistress, at least that many more are posed to join them. This is going to require drastic measures."

Reaching under his woolen workman's shirt, he extracted a roll of black silk. Some might consider it an expensive piece of cloth and it was. But to Alerio, it served as a bandage when necessary. In this case, it had a different purpose.

"Hold still, you do not want to see this," he explained while wrapping the dark silk around the animal's head. Once sure the horse couldn't see, Alerio stepped back and raised both blades to waist level. Then he began to chant.

And the stories are told
By the old men and the sages
Of the Sherden and the Tjekker
The ancient Sea People
Raiders and life takers
Men who shunned civilized cages
Retold by narrators down through the ages

Of the Sea People and their rages

The sharp blades alternated hacking at the heart of the
thorn bush. Branches with thorns collapsed inward, falling
away from the horse's legs and belly. With the sounds of
the chopping covered by the singing, the Giara stood still
while the steel edges trimmed away the spikes.

From the morning mist they come
Oars plunging and sails undone
Horned helmets above eyes of malice
Round shields over hearts that are calloused
And standing with legs askew
The Sea People raise their great iron swords
On they row
Through shrouds of history
Through the tales of old
Of the Sea Peoples' crews
Who are coming for you

With the bush flattened, Alerio tossed the swords over
to the bedroll. Then he gripped the lead line in one hand
and, with the other, pushed and prodded the horse
around. She hesitated when he stopped singing. Despite
the low stature of the Sardinian horse, it was muscular
and wouldn't budge. When the Latian started singing
again, the horse began moving.

They came for the wealthy town on the shore
Fortified against raiders
With armed men barring the doors
They rowed from the sea as told by lore
Bold-hearted and cold-hearted
The warships from the mist
Brought the Sea People

And despite the will to resist
The walls tumbled into grist
And the treasures vanished
As the Sea People rowed away

Guiding the horse, Alerio walked her away from the spikes. In a grassy area, he retied the lead. Again, he stopped singing. The Giara spun and pressed forward against the Legionary's shoulder.

"Is that a request for more," he asked. "Or are you trying to get by me and head home. Let me remind you, we have a deal."

They came for the city on the Egyptian coast
Blessed by the gods
With Pharaoh's army as their host
They appeared from the fog as if ghosts
Equal valiant and insolent
They eyed the temple's gold
Respecting no deity
The Sea People battled and stole
They slew the soldiers eightfold
And to the beach they strolled
Then the Sea People rowed away

As he sang, he tied the water bags, rolled, and packed the bedroll, and fixed the satchel on the horse's back. Then he swung up and nudged the animal eastward towards Isola Rossa.

By high noon, Alerio was feeling proud of the distance he had put between him and any agents searching Torre della Pelosa for him. Then the God Nemesis punished his arrogance. Far out in the bay, a Qart Hadasht warship rowed by heading for Isola Rossa.

Alerio put heels to the animal's sides, urged it up the slopes, and off the shoreline. When he had a view of the coastal city's beach, the Legionary hopped down. He and the horse shared water while watching the warship spin then row backward to shore.

***

The trireme barely touched the sand when the one hundred eighty oars stroked forward and halted the rearward momentum. Two figures leaped from the deck, landed in knee high water, and splashed ashore. Under the rowing, the trireme shot away from shore, spun as if a toy boat, and powered away to deep water.

"Only two," Alerio commented to the Giara. "If I can locate them, you'll be heading home before you know it."

With a jerk of her head, the horse attempted to pull free and head west.

"Not yet," the Legionary scolded. "I need to be fresh when I get to the city."

On the beach, four men rushed to meet the newly arrived agents.

"Six is a little different. Maybe I can reach a Republic trader before they find me," he pondered while climbing onto the horse. "This really is perfututum beyond all recognition."

From the morning mist they come
Oars plunging and sails undone
Horned helmets above eyes of malice
Round shields over hearts that are calloused...

Chapter 3 – Agents and Mayhem

Alerio and his mount ambled into Isola Rossa. On the beach side of the city, the six men paired up, fanned out and began their search. On the landward side, Corporal Sisera was also searching.

"Citizen. Where is the cloth seller?" Alerio inquired from atop the horse.

"The best is near the docks next to the sail maker," a man replied. "If you don't care for quality and I can see by your dress that you don't, you'll want to see Giuanne. His clothing is less."

"Less coins or less quality?" asked Alerio.

"Both," the man answered while pointing to a row of merchant stores in a district with rundown huts. "You'll find his establishment halfway into that sector of the city."

"Thank you," Alerio said as he nudged the horse in the flanks. The animal remained standing as the man walked away. *The Sea People raise their great iron swords. On they row, through shrouds of history."

Only while he sang did the horse move in the direction of the rundown section of Isola Rossa.

***

A middle-aged man stood at the door to a building, his eyes following the stranger riding up the street. On either side of him, racks held used cloth. Mostly clean, but definitely secondhand and frayed.

"Are you ill?" the man questioned.

"No. Why do you ask?" Alerio responded while sliding off the horse. Once the reigns were securely tied, he asked. "Are you Giuanne?"

"I am and it sounds as if there is something wrong with your throat."

"My voice is a little scratchy," Alerio admitted. "Singing is the only way to keep the horse moving east. And I've been crooning to her all morning."

"Sounds like a hard week of choir practice," Giuanne offered. "Come in and tell me what I can do for you."

They entered the shop and Alerio glanced at the back wall expecting to see a wall and an exit. There was no wall, and the Legionary could see directly into the rear compound. Only one employee occupied the space. Alerio knew the man was a worker because his wrinkled old hands trembled as he cut a piece of cloth.

"You don't seem to be very prosperous," Alerio observed.

"My cloth isn't rich fabric. For that you'll want to find the sail maker and go next door," Giuanne said defensively. "where you will overpay for mediocre craftsmanship. But if you want a fair price and good stitches, I can help you. But don't waste my day, decide quickly."

"I need sticks, course thread, woolen trousers, a woolen pullover, a felt Petasos, and a red cloak," Alerio told the cloth maker.

"Other than the cape, you just described what you're wearing," Giuanne observed.

"Exactly," Alerio remarked. "Can you fill my order?"

"I can. When do you want to pick up the goods?"

Alerio looked at a patch of light on the floor tiles. Moving to the edge of the light, he stepped off a pace and a half. There, he rubbed the edge of his boot on the tile marking a line.

"When the sunlight reaches there," he answered. "Is that a problem?"

"No. Your purchases will be ready."

"Good. Now there are a couple of other things," Alerio informed him. He handed the cloth maker several silver coins, then as he leaned in, he added a couple of gold ones. "Here's what I expect for the over payment."

***

The two local thugs strutted down the back street. With their chins jutting forward and chests raised, they attempted to give off the impression of violent and capable men. What crumpled their façade, caused their feet to stumble on the stones, and their bodies to hesitate wasn't the way the man dressed.

He stepped from an alleyway wearing a petasos with the brim pulled down low over his eyes. They expected the hat, in fact, it was one of the identifying articles. And it wasn't the red cape or the messenger's satchel slung over one shoulder. They knew about both as well as the hobnailed boots and the woolen workmen's clothing. All of those items had been described by the two agents from the warship.

What threw the local muscle off their stride was his steady gait and the fact he didn't pause at the sight of two men pulling swords as they came at him. Both ruffians had served as Qart Hadasht irregulars and weren't afraid of a fight. But neither had faced an outnumbered and unarmed opponent who sang while marching into a confrontation.

***

"And the stories are told," Alerio warbled. Three paces from the thugs, he tossed back the cloak exposing two sword handles jutting over his shoulders. In another step, he reached up, wrapped his fists around the hilts, and drew the custom blades. *"By the old men and the sages."*

The local heavies split apart in an attempt to flank their prey.

"Of the Sherden and the Tjekker," the Legionary sang. His blades swung to his left in parallel, mirroring each other while rotating towards the gangster on that side. *"The ancient Sea People."*

Seeing two steel tips coming at him, the thug shuffled two steps back and brought his sword up into a guard position. While he offered a stationary target and a duel for the spy, his companion edged in from Alerio's rear.

"Raiders and life takers," Alerio chanted. He parried the man's blade while bending his knees and lowering and cocking his head to the side. With the left-hand sword engaged, Corporal Sisera allowed the tip of the right sword to drop towards the ground. *"Men who shunned civilized cages."*

Had the ex-soldier on his left charged forward and crowded the Legion weapons instructor, the man sneaking up behind Alerio might not have been crippled and scarred for the rest of his life.

"Retold by narrators down through the ages," Alerio's right sword cycled low enough for the edge to throw sparks as it struck the stone road. Once passed the lowest point in the arc, the tip and leading edge of sharp steel rose. The ruffian on the right screamed as the blade severed the fingers on his sword hand and peeled the

tissue from the back of his wrist. Blood drawn by the blade splattered up and over the Legionary's head creating an arch. While the injured thug sank to his knees, Alerio's sword finished crossing the sky. It fell, splitting the forehead of the man on his left. *Of the Sea People and their rages.*

Spinning on the wounded man, Alerio reached down, cupped the man's jaw, and lifted a face painted in agony.

"Hurts," the man whimpered as fat tears rolled down his cheeks. "It, it hurts."

"If you didn't want Algea's blessings, you shouldn't have been playing with sharp objects," the Legionary offered. "There is one benefit to a visit from the Goddess of Pain."

"What's that?"

"You know you are alive," Alerio commented while placing a blade on the bridge of the ex-soldier's nose. "I have some questions. Answer them truthfully and you'll be free to find a physician. Lie to me and you'll be disfigured for the rest of your life. Refuse to answer and I'll leave pieces of your body spread all over the road."

"We were told you didn't have the stomach for a standup fight," he moaned.

"Someone lied to you," Alerio acknowledged then demanded. "When is the trireme coming back?"

"The warship was going to drop men at Vignola Mare and Capo Testa, then return to pick up their soldiers," the bleeding man stated. "The trireme should be back long before sundown. They will leave instructions with men in each town to be on the lookout for you.

"How will they recognize me?"

"The satchel's stitching is special," the wounded man replied. "Plus, they will know you by your hat or the scar on your head when you take it off."

Hopefully, Alerio's former Sardinian guide would enjoy the Qart Hadasht gold. He certainly delivered a wealth of information to earn the traitor's coins. Alerio promised himself if he ever returned to the island, he would pay the fisherman a visit.

"There are four others in town looking for me," Alerio explained. "What would you do if you spotted me?"

"We would, or rather, should have shouted ajo-ejo-ajo," he answered. "It means, let's go, yes, let's go."

"Thank you. Now go find a doctor," Alerio urged. He lifted the sword from the man's nose and slid it into the back sheath along with its twin.

"That's it? You are letting me go?"

Alerio moved a hand towards one of the hilts.

"I can remove a few body parts if that will make you feel better."

"No. No," the thug pleaded while crawling to his knees. "I just thought. Well, I know you are in Isola Rossa. How can you be sure…?"

"You really do want me to take an arm or a leg, don't you?"

The man scrambled to his feet and staggered up the street. While he moved inland, the Legionary trotted in the other direction. A block down and in a crossroads where he could see a section of the beach, Alerio shouted.

"Ajo-ejo-ajo! He is running towards the edge of town, ajo-ejo-ajo," he warned. "Follow me."

His shouting brought the sounds of four pairs of feet running. Before he saw any of the hunters, the Legionary jogged to a pile of boxes on a wall at the intersection.

"They came for the wealthy town on the shore. Fortified against raiders, with armed men barring the doors," he sang. The sounds of pounding feet drew closer, but Alerio maintained his place behind the boxes. *"They rowed from the sea as told by lore. Bold-hearted and cold-hearted."*

At the crossroad, two men sprinted into view and stopped. They faced away from one another, obviously, searching up the street for the escaping Legionary and their companions. Taking advantage of their preoccupation with the search, Alerio lowered his shoulders and plowed into their backs. Both toppled over and sprawled on the street. Alerio vaulted over their bodies and sprinted up the street.

"It's him," one of the men screamed while jumping to his feet. "Ajo-ejo-ajo, ajo-ejo-ajo."

The two men collected themselves and chased after their target. At the next block, the other pair joined them.

"He's just turned that corner," one reported while pointing to a cross street.

Although the four men lost sight of the spy, they were confident in the direction he was heading.

"The warships from the mist, brought the Sea People," Alerio crooned as he raced around the corner. *"And despite the will to resist. The walls tumbled into grist."*

***

With a burst of speed, the Legionary reached the shops and the old Giara who stood tied to a post. He slung the satchel off his shoulder and rapidly tied the messenger pouch to the horse. Then Alerio walked the mount for a few steps until they came abreast of an alleyway.

"Go home, lass," he said loudly while swatting her rump. "Go home."

Between the word 'home' and the slap, the horse leaped forward and raced down the street. Without waiting to watch the horse leave, Alerio dove out of the street and into the alley. Using a rope, he climbed to the roof and hoisted up the line.

"*And the treasures vanished,*" he sang softly while squatting down to watch the trail leading out of town. He rested his arm on the bedroll with the messenger's paperwork inside. "*As the Sea People rowed away.*"

On the street below, the Qart Hadasht agents and the local thugs came around the corner.

"Can you see him?" one of the agents asked.

"There. He's riding out of town," the other agent pointed out.

Far down the street, a felt Petasos bobbed, and a red cape flared back as a figure in workman's woolens and a horse trotted out of the city. Without hesitation, they took the trail westward.

Alerio wasn't worried the Giara might stop and reveal the fake man on her back. The mount was in such a rush to get to her stable, she continued to trot even after leaving civilization far behind.

Chapter 4 – Signal Fires

No one paid any attention to the man dressed in the tattered cotton toga with the strip of cloth wrapped around his head. The only luggage carried by the unkept man was a bedroll that appeared to be in better shape than the hunched over man and the rags he wore. Once the transport Trionis beached, her Captain jumped down and took notice of the shabby dress.

"I don't do charity, beggar," Captain Forus warned. He added a shooing motion with his hand as if to wave off a pest. "Stay away from my ship."

The dirty vagabond limped off the grass and shuffled down to the beach. As the beggar neared the ship's officer, Captain Forus balled up his fist preparing to enforce his declaration and defend his position.

"And stay away from me and my crew."

A crowd of people from the city trudged onto the beach hauling goods or wheeled carts with items to trade. They filled the space between the beggar and where the Trionis rested. Among the towns people seeking trade was the poor clothing maker.

"Giuanne. I'm sorry. I have no used fabric for you this trip," the Captain informed the tailor.

"What do you have?" Giuanne responded with a smile. He held up two gold coins. "Wool, cotton, fur, or maybe silk?"

"I see your fortunes have turned, my friend," Forus offered.

"Indeed, they have, Captain. Trade with the others for anything except the cloth. I will pay for it all. Afterward, I have a favor to ask."

The citizens of Isola Rossa huddled around the aft planks of the transport. Each person looking for barter stepped up and showed their merchandise. Forus made offers. If accepted, the Captain called up to the deck where crewmen pulled items from the cargo hold. For most of the morning, materials were handed up to the deck and finished goods were passed down to the beach. All the while, Giuanne stood close by observing the transactions. The beggar also watched the proceedings but from the edge of the crowd.

When the last citizen left, Giuanne stepped up. Forus looked up at the crewmen on the transport.

"Bring down the fabric. All of it. The clothing maker is back in business," the Captain ordered. He looked at Giuanne and added. "The cloth is worth four or five gold coins in trade. I'm letting it go for two. However, I want first choice to buy the finished products."

"I appreciate this," Giuanne stated while handing Forus the two gold coins. Then he dropped a third into the Captain's hand.

"What's this for?" questioned Forus.

"The drifter requires transportation to Roccia del Coccodrillo," explained Giuanne.

"There's nothing on that island except scrub trees, salt grasses, and rocks," Forus exclaimed. "Who would want to go there?"

"I'll let him explain."

Giuanne waved the beggar forward and went off to find porters for the cloth. Forus expected to have his nose assaulted by the unwashed vagabond but was surprised when all he detected was the aroma of fresh dirt.

"I am Corporal Sisera assigned to the Southern Legion," the beggar whispered. "And I need to get off Sardinia as soon as possible."

***

The Trionis wallowed in the tide fighting to maintain a heading in the rough seas.

"Stroke," bellowed Forus. "Stroke. Just a few more steps lads and we'll be in the cove."

"You call that a cove, Captain?" one of the crewmen inquired.

"It's better than the rocks on the shoreline," Forus replied.

The transport bobbed before riding a wave between the points of stone and entering the calmer waters.

"Port side, back it down. Starboard, power ten, stroke," Forus shouted.

The two oars on the left side of the ship reversed as the sailors walked backwards. While their counterparts on the right-side dipped their oars and completed ten long steps driving the oars deep. In response, the Trionis' bow swung around and ended up facing the open sea.

"We can't hold her for long, Corporal Sisera," Forus advised. "Get off now. Or you'll have to swim back."

"May Poseidon keep the seas calm, the monsters in their depths, and the birds flying along your route," Alerio said as he placed a foot on the aft rail. Just before jumping, the Legionary added. "Thank you, Captain."

Then Alerio sailed over the rail and splashed into chest deep water. Holding his bedroll overhead, he waded to the shallows, and up onto a white sandy beach.

"Together, stroke," Forus ordered his four crewmen. He didn't bother looking aft at his former passenger. The Captain focused on steering the Trionis between the rocky points guarding the small cove. "Stroke, stroke."

Corporal Sisera climbed off the beach and up on the rocky shoreline. After dropping his bedroll and a pouch, he began collecting dry branches and twigs. By the time the transport rowed behind the island and vanished to the south, Alerio had a large pile of tinder. Using loose stones, he created a structure resembling an open-faced oven. Then he sat down and pulled cheese and bread from a pouch and began eating.

***

The day before, a Republic warship had rowed out of the Legion beach at Ostia. She began her crossing of the Tyrrhenian Sea long before daylight. After a full day and night of sailing, the trireme beached at Budoni. The first order of business was a sacrifice to the God Favonius for the steady but, mild west, wind. Then the crew spread out on the beach, ate rations, and napped.

By early afternoon, the Centurion ordered his three Principales and the Optio to awaken the crew and prepare to shove off. Now that the ship was on station, she would begin hunting pirates along the east coast of Sardinia. Besides protecting commerce heading to and from the Republic, the Legion trireme was tasked with keeping an eye on the activities of the Qart Hadasht fleet.

"Optio. Standby to launch," Centurion Atylidae instructed from the rear steering platform.

Located midship but down on the rowers' walk, the Optio called forward and up to the Third Principale, "Stand by for launch."

The junior officer leaned over the bow rail and looked down at the water then scanned the horizon. With no ships or rocks in sight, he waved back to the steering platform. Per regulations, he replied verbally to the ship's NCO. "All clear, Optio."

The Sergeant bellowed, "All clear for launch. Machine, run out your oars."

From both sides of the Optio, the eighty most powerful oarsmen on the warship shoved fifteen feet long fir oars through holes in the hull and pinned them in place. Up on the steering deck, the First Principale acknowledged the wave from the foredeck officer and walked to the aft rail.

"Second Principale, stand by to launch," he called down to the beach.

The warning order was shared by the officer standing on the ground, "Stand by to launch."

"You heard the officer. Place your delicate hands on the wood, brace your shoulders, and prepare to get your dainty feet wet," the First Oar shouted. "Standby for launch."

The remaining one hundred oarsmen leaned against the hull and replied, "Standing by, First Oar."

Before Centurion Atylidae could issue the order for the ship to be pushed off the beach, a priest came racing from the city of Budoni. The trireme's senior officer indicated for the First Principale to meet the celebrant.

Responding immediately, the junior officer dropped over the side, landed on the beach, and jogged to meet the messenger. When he reached the priest, he exchanged a few coins for a letter. Then turning, he ran to the warship and, using three oar-holes as footrests, scampered up the side of the trireme.

"Centurion. The letter was dropped off four days ago," the First Principale explained. "The temple priest forgot about it until he noticed us getting ready to leave."

The ships commanding officer unfolded the parchment and scanned the words. Then he spoke to his steering and navigation specialists.

"Immunes. We have a new course and mission," Centurion Atylidae informed the two Legionaries. "We have a Legion NCO to pick up."

"Where is he, sir?" one of the navigators inquired.

"A place called Roccia del Coccodrillo," the ship's senior officer replied. Then down half the length of his one hundred thirty feet ship-of-war, he ordered. "Optio. Launch."

"Third Principale, we are launching," the ship's NCO called to the bow officer while alerting the eighty rowers. "Prepare to stroke."

Across the steering deck from the Centurion, the First Principale bent over the rail.

"Launch," he called down to the officer of the second deck.

The trireme slid off the beach. Due to the angle and the weight of the ram on the bow, the ship nosed downward.

"Machine, stroke," the Optio ordered.

While the rest of the oarsmen and the Second Principale scurried up the sides, the center rowers dipped their blades and in one powerful stroke, propelled the warship out of the shallows and into deep water. The surge brought the ram up and leveled out the ship.

***

On the morning of the sixth day, Alerio crawled out of his bedroll and went in search of firewood. All the readily accessible branches had been collected and burned in the campfire. If he didn't scrounge up more, he'd have to rob from the signal fire's supply. In addition to the trouble of having to trek away from his camp to locate firewood, the Legionary's rations were low. Mentally, he went over his gear while jumping from rock to rock. Unfortunately, his kit lacked thread and a hook or a net. Spear fishing was out unless he could find a straight shaft among the twisted limbs of the trees growing on the small island.

With hunger pains gnawing at his gut, Alerio carried an armload of wood back to his camp. After blowing the embers to life in the campfire, he stacked branches in the bottom of the signal structure. Taking the last piece of bread, he stabbed it with a stick and held it over the fire. If he couldn't eat well, at least he could eat food that smelled cooked.

Out on the ocean, a fish broke the surface, splashed down, and disappeared below the waves.

"You are lucky Master Swordfish," Alerio said while taking a nibble of the toasted bread. "If I had a boat and a spear, you and I would have quite the match."

As if to challenge the assertion, the large fish breached the waves again. This time, it twisted and flexed violently in the air before crashing to the surface in a spray of seawater.

"Point taken," Alerio remarked. "In Neptune's world, you are a king. In mine, I'm only a hungry Tesserarius. Leap up here so we can discuss how delicious you are."

Alerio let his eyes roam the horizon to get his mind off of food. As he swept south, a white shape appeared in the distance. Several moments later, the shape became a sail above a ship-of-war. Rapidly, the Legionary stacked stones in front of the campfire flame. Once the fire was hidden, he shuffled back into a gully.

The warship sailed closer and Alerio remained out of sight. Only when he recognized the armor of the officers and the shields along the rails did he raise up, toss flaming ember from the campfire into the signal structure. Burning embers set the dried and stacked firewood on fire. With the signal beacon roaring, Alerio raised both arms and waved.

When the sail raised and sailors strapped it to the cross beam and oars jutted from their holes, Alerio lowered his arms and began rolling his bedroll.

***

Once Alerio was on board, he marched to the Centurion.

"Sir. Corporal Sisera. I'm detached from the Southern Legion," he reported.

"Tesserarius. I assume there is a reason, you were lounging around an uninhibited island off the coast of Sardinia," Atylidae offered. "I'd like to know why."

"I'm in possession of Qart Hadasht dispatches."

"Are they important?" the ship's senior officer questioned.

"I don't know," Alerio admitted. He reached into the bedroll and pulled out an oiled piece of folded lambskin. "Sir. I can't read Phoenician."

Alerio offered the waterproof package to the Centurion.

"You're telling me you allowed yourself to be stranded out here and don't even know why?"

"It seemed like a good idea until I ran out of food, sir," Alerio declared.

"Optio. Who in the centuria can read Phoenician?"

"I believe we have a number of readers in the crew, sir. But the best educated is Gibbus, the Third Principale," the ship's Sergeant responded.

"Gibbus. To the steering deck," Atylidae called to a young officer who was supervising the sailors as they lowered and tied off the sail. Then the ships officer ran his eyes over the sun baked and gaunt Corporal. "Optio. While we get this sorted out, find Sisera something to eat."

"Yes, sir."

Alerio and the ship's NCO stepped down off the platform and moved to a cabinet. As the Optio pulled out oatcakes and cured ham, the junior officer walked by on the left cover deck. Before the Third Principale reached the platform, Atylidae spoke to the helmsmen and the navigators.

"Immunes. Turn the ship south, maintain a tarda stroke rate, and set watchers. We still have a job to do," he explained. Then as the junior officer mounted the platform, the Centurion handed him the oiled skin package. "Principale. Here are some dispatches from the Qart Hadasht Navy. Give them a look and see if they contain any useful information."

"Yes, sir," Gibbus agreed while unwrapping the protective cover. He lifted out the first piece of parchment.

"They have a new Admiral taking over the Sardinia and Sicilia region. Admiral Hanno the Elder. I'm sure the Senate will want to know about that."

"Less politics, Principale. More reading," growled the Centurion.

"Yes, sir. This is interesting. A General Hannibal Gisco is taking over the ground forces for the region," Gibbus exclaimed while reading another message. Suddenly, he blurted out. "Good, Mars."

"What promoted you to invoke the God of War?" Atylidae questioned.

"The Qart Hadasht Empire has gathered and staged fifty thousand troops," the Principale explained.

"Corporal Sisera. Did you see any sign of fifty thousand mercenaries?" the Centurion inquired.

"No, sir," Alerio replied with his mouth full. "I was all along the west coast and didn't witness any troop build ups or large land bases."

"Not on Sardinia, sir," Gibbus corrected. "At least not yet. The fifty thousand are staged at a city in Sicilia called Agrigento."

"What do you mean, not yet, sir?" Alerio questioned the deck officer.

"The mercenaries are scheduled to be shipped to Sardinia once camps and facilities are constructed," Gibbus read.

"It seems the Empire is going to war with the Sardinians," suggested Atylidae.

"No, sir. According to these last messages," the junior officer stammered. "Sardinia is a stopping off point. The target for General Hannibal Gisco and his fifty thousand mercenaries is Rome."

A chill ran through the crewmen at the stern. Rapidly, the conversation was repeated until the entire crew grew silent waiting for more information. Calmly, Atylidae took the messages from Gibbus and indicated for the junior officer to return to his station.

"Immunes, standby for a change of orders," the Centurion announced. "Helm, turn us towards the Republic. Navigators get your land fixes quickly. Second Principale, we're making for Ostia, and I need every man pulling hard."

"Yes, sir," the deck officer exclaimed. "First Oar. What's the record for crossing the sea?"

"Dawn to dawn, Principale," the First Oar answered.

"Can we beat that?"

"If the great Gods Vulturnus grants us a steady east wind."

"And if the God is sleeping?"

"Then we'll row the crossing," the First Oar declared. "Oarsmen. Stand by."

"Standing by, First Oar," replied the one hundred eighty rowers.

"Sir. The centuria is with you," the deck officer reported.

"First Principale, set a medietas stroke rate until we judge the wind offshore," Atylidae instructed. "Sailors, oarsmen, take us home."

The trireme shot forward as the oars dug into the water. Alerio had to grab the edge of the platform with one hand to keep from falling over. With the other, he shoved a third slice of ham into his mouth.

Act 2

Chapter 5 – Republic Navy Base Ostia

The sun had yet to reach its zenith when the coast of the Republic appeared on the horizon. To the Centurion's satisfaction, the rowers pulled them through spells where the God of the east wind deserted them. All during the dark hours, they made up for the limp sail with muscle and tenacity.

"Navigation, find me Ostia," he ordered. "Optio. My complements to the oarsmen on a job well done."

While the senior NCO moved along the center walkway talking with the rowers, the First Principale conversed with the navigators. After listening to their reasons for the heading, the deck officer stepped away and faced the helmsmen.

"Make for a southeast direction," he announced. "Musician, medietas stroke rate, set it by your pipes."

During the passage, the keeper of the stroke beats had used the drum. In the night, it was feared the melody of the pipes would draw monsters from the deep. In the daylight, there was less fear of sea creatures, and the pipes were entertaining as well as functional.

The trireme cut through the waves with the oars plunging and rising at a mid-tempo. Soon the land climbed higher and fishing villages appeared on the shoreline. Cruising down the coast, the only thing faster than the gliding warship was a horse at full gallop or a bird in flight. One had a limited distance before being overtaken by exhaustion and the other was swift enough to outpace an errant arrow and reach its destination. But the ship-of-war neither vacillated from exhaustion nor reached its terminus quickly. Rather, she maintained the movement created by a light breeze on a square piece of cloth and one hundred eighty broad-shouldered oarsmen.

"Tesserarius Sisera, when we reach the naval base, you will accompany me and Third Principale Gibbus," Atylidae instructed. "I'm sure the Fleet Praetor will have questions."

"Yes, sir. But then I'll need a horse," Alerio informed the Centurion. "I have to report to my Tribune in the Capital."

"Once the Praetor is done with you, Corporal," Atylidae assured Alerio while emphasizing the Legionary's rank as an NCO. "I'm sure he'll provide you with whatever he considers necessary."

**

"Centurion Atylidae, why am I seeing your face?" questioned Praetor Zelare Sudoris. He had glanced up, recognized the ships' officer, and went back to the dispatches on his desk. "If you've been blown off course, I'm too busy to point out the direction to Sardinia. If you've sunk your ship, the Capital is due north. Go find someone else's day to ruin."

The Republic's Navy was small with only thirty triremes for defending the entire coastline against pirates. Thirty warships, if the older ones weren't in dry dock for major repairs or beached while new boards were installed to replace the rotten ones. The Republic had other vessels in the form of river and ocean patrol boats, but they were attached to Legion commands in specific regions. This left the Praetor of the Fleet doing two jobs: controlling the placement of warships to combat seaborne piracy; and campaigning with or against factions of the Senate for a budget to build more warships. Both tasks kept the Praetor busy.

"I believe you'll want to read these," Atylidae stated. He unwrapped the oiled skin, placed it and the exposed Qart Hadasht messages on his boss' desk.

Zelare Sudoris sneered at the pieces of mismatched parchment. Then his eyes landed on the seal imprinted on the lower edge of the top one. His hand shot up and he spread the documents revealing the same seal in the same place on each.

"I recognize the mark, but I don't read Phoenician," Sudoris declared. "Explain these."

Atylidae stepped to the side while extending an arm and inviting Gibbus to step forward.

"My Third Principale is proficient in the language," the Centurion offered.

The junior officer marched to the desk, saluted, and put a finger on one of the messages.

"This report lists fifty thousand mercenaries quartered in Sicilia," Gibbus reported. He shifted the finger. "This one instructs the Qart Hadasht garrison to prepare a base in Sardinia for the army. And this one is the order of march for attacking our Capital."

Praetor Zelare Sudoris leaned back in his chair and peered up at the ceiling. Lost in thought, he ignored the two ship's officers standing in front of his desk. Finally, a tight smile formed on his lips, and he lowered his chin. As his eyes dropped, he noticed a third person standing in his office.

"Who is that?" he demanded.

"Sir, Corporal Sisera," Alerio replied with a salute. "I was on assignment in Sardinia and captured the dispatches. With your permission, I'd like to ride to the Capital and report to my Tribune."

"Centurion. Take your Third Principale, gather your crew, and launch your ship," Sudoris ordered while folding the oiled skin and covering the messages. "I want an early warning picket line far out to sea."

"Sir. My crew is exhausted. We made the crossing overnight after…"

"Centurion Atylidae. I gave an order and I expect it to be obeyed," the Fleet Praetor exploded. "And take the signalman/spy with you. For his own protection."

"I am an infantryman, sir. I don't need protecting," Alerio protested. "What I need is a horse. I have a duty to report to my Tribune, sir."

"When did you get elected Consul?" Sudoris questioned.

"I didn't. I'm not a Senator," Alerio stammered. "I'm not sure why you asked that. sir."

"Because, I am the Praetor of the Republic's Navy," Sudoris shouted. "And unless you are a Consul, a Senator, or a Legion officer, I just gave you an order. Need I say more?"

"No, sir," the Legion NCO responded by turning about and following the ship's officers from the office.

Behind them, the Praetor bellowed for his aide. The Tribune rushed from his desk passing Atylidae, Gibbus, and Sisera as he made for his boss' office.

What none of the men were privy too was the broad smile on Zelare Sudoris' face. For over a year, he had been begging and pleading with the Senate for funds to build up the fleet. Today, an undisputable reason landed on his desk. For pride and political reasons, he needed to be the one to sound the alarm. Soon everyone of importance in the Capital would be thanking the navy for saving the Republic. That at least ought to be worth ten or more additional triremes.

***

"Centurion. I really need to report to my Tribune," Alerio pleaded as they walked to the beach. "He will not be happy at the delay."

On the roofs of the buildings, covers were removed from ballistae. Along the shoreline and docks, infantrymen jogged to defensive positions and the onager covers were pulled back. And ahead of the three men, two warships launched from the beach.

"Corporal Sisera, I have a crew that pushed through the night to reach Ostia," Atylidae explained. "Now I have to kick them awake and have the navigators, helmsmen, sailors, and oarsman take us back to sea. That's two hundred men who will not be happy."

"Make that two hundred and one, sir?" Alerio suggested.

'Exactly. Optio. First Oar. Get them up and our ship off this beach," the Centurion called ahead. "Principales, take your positions."

They were at the top of the slope before dropping down to the sand and gravel. Alerio stopped and looked back at the Legion fortifications.

"There's something missing, Centurion," the Corporal observed.

"I see bolt throwers to guard the mouth of the Tiber and Legionaries on the shore to repel an invasion. And out in the bay, you'll notice transports are being lashed together to block the entrance to the river," Gibbus remarked. "I would say the route to the Capital is pretty well defended, Corporal Sisera."

"All that is true, Principale," Alerio commented to the deck officer. "But I don't see any cavalry."

"Gibbus stop worrying about horses," the Centurion scolded not giving the deck officer an opportunity to reply. "You aren't to bother yourself with anything that doesn't have rowers on its flanks and a sail midship. And in case you missed it, that was your hint to get to your section."

"Yes, sir," the junior deck officer acknowledged before racing down to the beach.

"Sisera. I'm going to the steering deck and direct the launch," Atylidae explained. "It's a confusing time with men climbing onto and off of the ship."

Foregoing additional dialogue, the Centurion of the trireme quick marched down the slope without looking to either side. Realizing the officer had abandoned him, Alerio spun on his heels and sprinted to the first building.

While Alerio made his way to the Legion stables, Zelare Sudoris was halfway to the Capital. With the

Praetor were the Qart Hadasht messages and a large cavalry escort. They were driving their mounts hard.

Chapter 6 - Locations of Conviction

Alerio didn't know about the firestorm the captured messages started in the Capital. As he guided the horse up Esquiline Hill, intimate meetings of important men were taking place in selected areas of the city. He located the dark entrance of Villa Velius and hopped off the exhausted mount. At that moment, neither the Tesserarius nor his Tribune were aware of the political capital being traded among power brokers possessing knowledge of the Empire's dispatches.

The Legion NCO marched up the walkway, rapped on the front door, and stepped back. The door opened behind iron bars, and in candlelight, an ancient, lined face peered out between the bars.

"We do not accept deliveries after dark," an old servant informed Alerio.

"I have no delivery. But I must speak with Tribune Velius, immediately."

"In my experience, young man, issues described as requiring instant meetings usually are less important in the morning," the servant advised. "Come back then. Master Cassiel Velius is bathing before turning in for the night."

The servant began to close the door.

"At least tell him Corporal Sisera is camped on his doorstep," Alerio offered. "I'll be here waiting for him to finish breakfast."

"You would sleep on the stoop?" inquired the house manager. "What will you do when the city guard finds you?"

"I am a heavy infantryman. It will not go well for the guard," Alerio assured the servant. "And their commanders will have questions for you for allowing one of Tribune Velius' spies to sleep outside the Villa. But I will."

To prove the point, Alerio sat, then leaned back and stretched out his legs. He tilted the Petasos down over his face and crossed his ankles. The door closed leaving the Legionary on the front porch in the dark.

Alerio had just dozed off when the door reopened.

"Corporal Sisera, I assume your trip to Sardinia was interesting," Velius, the old spymaster, guessed.

"Tribune Velius. Good evening. I apologize for the state of my dress," Alerio said while standing. "I came straight from Ostia. But I don't have the Empire dispatches anymore."

"Dispatches? As in Qart Hadasht military communications?" inquired the head of Southern Legion's Planning and Strategies Section. "Not, anymore, implies that you once possessed such items. I'd like to know why you don't now. And, how you came by them should be a good story. But more importantly, what did you learn from these vanishing dispatches?"

"The Empire..."

"Not on the stoop. Come in," Velius offered while opening the iron security gate. As Alerio stepped in, the spymaster leaned back and commented. "Your personal aroma tells me you came directly here from Sardinia."

"Yes, sir. Not long ago, I was on the trireme that plucked me off an uninhabited island," Alerio remarked. "I could go and wash, but the news is significant."

"Now I'm more intrigued. But not enough to suffer further attacks on my nose," Velius stated. "You bathe and I'll have the cook fix a platter."

"Both sound good to me, sir," Alerio admitted.

***

Later, with a clean and stuffed Corporal Sisera reclining on a couch, Cassiel Velius asked another question.

"Was there a timeline mentioned for the attack?"

"Not that Principale Gibbus mentioned," Alerio replied then a yawn escaped his mouth. "I'm sorry, Tribune. Other than the mercenaries already bivouacked on Sicilia and waiting for Sardinia to prepare for them, there was no date. If I may ask, sir, why did Praetor Sudoris take the dispatches and attempt to send me out to sea?"

"Politics, Corporal Sisera," Velius answered. "Have some more wine. I'll be back in a few moments."

Cassiel Velius pushed to his feet with a grunt, straightened and stretched his back, then shuffled out of the room. Alerio poured wine into his mug and closed his eyes.

"Sisera. Sorry to disturb your nap but it's time to leave," Velius instructed.

Alerio looked at the mug of vino cupped in his hand and balanced on his thigh. He didn't know how long he dozed but the level in the mug matched the last pour.

"Yes, sir. If you need me, I'll be at the Chronicles Humanum Inn," Alerio responded while shaking his head to throw off the sleepy feeling.

"I'm sending two house guards with you," Velius informed Alerio. "You will proceed to Senator Maximus' Villa. I can start the gears of the Legion turning but politically, I'm limited. Spurius Maximus is better situated to manage that front."

"Why two bodyguards?"

Cassiel Velius pressed a sealed letter into Alerio's hand.

"You are the anchor to the report, Corporal Sisera. Having the Qart Hadasht dispatches and knowing what they contain are two incomplete aspects," described the spymaster. "Skeptics can dispute their authenticity. Knowing how the letters came into the Republic's possession is the pedestal for the debates. You, Alerio, are the source and need to be protected."

"Debates, Tribune?"

"The guards are waiting at the stable," Velius stated without answering. "Hurry, it's late in more ways than you may realize. By the way, excellent work Tesserarius Sisera. You are dismissed."

***

Three horses trotted out of the Velius compound and onto the empty street. They moved down Esquiline Hill rapidly which required the riders to pull back on the reins to slow their mounts. Then they hit the flat land, reined left, and let the mounts pick their own gaits. The horses must have sensed the tension in the riders as they stretched out on the avenue. Several blocks from the senate building, the trio turned left. A couple of blocks later, they pulled the horses to a stop at a high wall.

Alerio jumped down, marched to the compound's door, and hammered it with his fist.

"Deliveries at dawn at the west gate," a voice called from the far side of the wall.

"I'm Corporal Sisera on a mission for Tribune Velius," Alerio shouted. "I need to speak with the General."

"It's the middle of the night," the man replied.

"Really. I am envious of your grasp of the segments of the day," Alerio stated. "Now, listen up Legionary. Get Belen out here before I dismantle this wall and come over there and kick the living merda out of you."

Voices arguing on the far side were followed by a pair of feet running away. Alerio smiled at his outburst and the result. All of the Senator's house guards were former Legionaries and understood the passion of an angry Tesserarius.

Not long after the threat, a voice called from the other side.

"Corporal Sisera, is that you?" Belen, Senator Maximus' secretary, inquired.

"It is and I know it's early morning," Alerio assured him. "But this can't wait until dawn."

The door opened and the Greek stood on the far side holding a lantern. Flanking him were men armed with naked blades.

"Tesserarius Sisera, in the future I would appreciate you adhering to a civilized schedule," Belen said. Then to the house guards, he added. "Put away your steel."

Belen turned and headed for the house. Alerio rushed over the threshold, caught up with the secretary, and fell in beside him.

"How have you and the General been?" Alerio inquired.

"I was sleeping," Belen replied. "As is the Senator. But apparently, not for long."

"This is important," Alerio assured him.

"It always is, Corporal Sisera," Belen uttered while ushering him into the main room. "Wait here."

***

Moments later, former Consul and General Spurius Carvilius Maximus appeared from the direction of his bed chamber. Even wrapped in an old robe with his hair uncombed and sleep in his eyes, Spurius Maximus gave off an air of command. While crossing the great room, he indicated for Alerio to follow. The Senator didn't speak until they entered his office and Maximus plopped down in a chair behind his desk.

"Tesserarius Sisera. I have to be at the Senate before dawn," the Senator stated while placing his hands on the desktop and drumming his fingers. "Which means, I could have slept a little longer. Why am I out of bed other than to avoid Epiales?"

"General Maximus. I'm afraid what I bring is a nightmare. But not from the spirit Epiales but, from the Qart Hadasht Empire," Alerio said using the Senator's military title. He placed the letter from Velius on the desk. "I intercepted dispatches while on assignment in Sardinia and the Tribune decided that you should be alerted."

Spurius Maximus pulled a Legion pugio from under his robe and sliced open the letter. It made Alerio wonder if the General slept with the weapon. The thought struck him as odd seeing as the Senator lived in the Capital, had house guards, and traveled in civilized circles.

"A man can be surrounded by Legionaries and still have to defend himself," Maximus offered when he noted the puzzled look on the young NCO's face. "Let's see what Tribune Velius has to add to this late-night intrusion?"

While the Senator read and Alerio waited, Belen came into the room with a tray. On it was a pitcher of watered vino, a bowl of fruit, and a large plate with slices of bread and salted beef on it.

"The General doesn't eat early," the secretary informed Alerio. He poured a mug and placed it at Maximus' elbow. Then, he rested the tray on the corner of the desk. "If I remember correctly, you do."

"Thank you," Alerio offered while snatching a piece of meat and a chunk of bread from the platter. He started to cram the food in his mouth. But he thought of his mother and her scolding about manners. With her in mind, he took polite bites and chewed with his mouth closed.

"I wanted those dispatches," the Senator exclaimed. Releasing the Tribune's letter, he let it float down to the top of the desk. Then he slapped it with the flat of his hand as if the parchment was a bug attempting to fly away. Alerio flinched at the sharp report, but Belen stood calmly watching his boss. "The most important intelligence we have ever laid our hands on, and it's snatched away by a partisan."

"I don't understand, sir," Alerio inquired. "Will Praetor Sudoris suppress the knowledge from the messages?"

"No. But he will give them to Gaius Duilius. And Senator Duilius by now will have used the missives to build a coalition," Maximus explained.

"What difference does it make, General. If in the end, the Republic is warned about the threat?" Alerio asked.

"What action should we take, Corporal Sisera?" the Senator inquired. "Based on your knowledge of the situation."

"March on Agrigento and crush the Qart Hadasht army."

"Spoken like an infantryman, straight forward and direct," the Senator gushed. "Excet you'll need the Senate to approve the plan and fund the expedition."

"It seems clear to me, sir. It's a threat to the Republic and needs to be stomped down."

"Belen, send word to Tribune Velius and ask him to be my guest at the morning session. After that, find appropriate clothing to make Corporal Sisera presentable while hiding his identity," Maximus instructed. Then he looked at Alerio. "You are not wrong, and this would be easier of you had delivered the missives to me. But there are many interests in the Senate and, more often than not, they pull in different directions. The struggle to reach a workable solution can get messy."

"I tried to get the dispatches to the Tribune, sir," Alerio offered. "But I was out ranked."

"I know," the Senator said as he stood. "Stay and finish your breakfast. I'm going to walk in my garden and think."

When General Maximus and Belen left the office, Alerio popped a fat grape in his mouth. While he chewed, he pulled a chair up to the desk. Then he lifted a big chunk of meat from the platter and a slice of bread. Both were shoved indelicately into his mouth. He was alone, it was the middle of the night, and the Corporal was hungry.

Chapter 7 - Accords and Resolutions

One thing in the Capital was beyond dispute. No matter the exact turns of the sand dials, the crowing of various roosters, skewed visions of seers, or calls from experienced night watchmen, the rising of the sun was undisputable. Nevertheless, some always contested the daily event.

"Gentlemen. We would like to start the session," Consul Otacilius Crassus called out.

Several of the Senators lingered on the wide marble porch while a few more walked rapidly across the lawn or up the pathways heading for the stairs. All of them held their heads down and kept their eyes on the ground, as if to deny the bright orb climbing over the roofs of Rome.

"I was taught the Senators were pious men who honored Sol Indiges," Alerio whispered from under the hood of the gray robe. "It's why they begin the day when the Sun God first appears in the sky."

"They are men, and all men have flaws," Cassiel Velius informed him. The Tribune also wore a robe, but

49

the Legion officer's cloak was red and the armor under it ornamental and impressive. "And some men are more flawed than others."

As if to highlight the point, a group of late arrivals came through the door carrying a covered table. At first, they moved towards the dais, but another Senator stood and waved them to the aisle beside his seat.

When they had placed the table, three of the porters shuffled to their seats. The fourth looked up at the gallery before bending to speak to the Senator issuing orders. Alerio recognized Praetor Sudoris.

"Who is the Praetor speaking with?" Alerio inquired.

"Gaius Duilius. He's a Senator from the coast with fishing and farm concerns," Velius offered. "It seems Duilius is Zelare Sudoris' patron."

"Is he associated with one of the partisan groups, General Maximus mentioned?"

"Indeed, Tesserarius Sisera, Gaius Duilius is the leader of a faction."

On the floor facing the tiered and curved seating of the Senators, Consul Otacilius Crassus rapped the dais with a cane.

"The Senate of the Republic is called to order," he announced. "The first order…"

"I wish to hold the floor for a matter of grave importance," Gaius Duilius blurted out. He shot to his feet and raised two fists into the air. Maintaining the pose, he peered around as if daring another Senator to challenge him.

Alerio scanned the Senators. Most appeared shocked at the abrupt interference while some appeared to know

50

the reason. They were the men seated in the immediate area of Senator Duilius. Further away and on the other side of the hall, Senator Maximus sat with his legs crossed and a bored look on his face.

"Gaius Duilius has requested the floor," Consul Crassus stated. "If there are no objections? Senator Duilius, the chamber is yours."

"We have discussed the need for funding to enlarge our fleet," Duilius began. Groans and laughs could be heard scattered throughout the senate chamber. Gaius Duilius ignored the reaction to the topic and pushed on. "For too long, the Republic has depended on the sea to keep us safe. Well, that is no longer the case."

The Senator reached out and snatched the cover from the table. Alerio could make out what he believed to be the original messages plus a few extra pieces of parchment. The distance was too great to be sure.

"What I have beside me are official dispatches from a Qart Hadasht courier," Duilius exclaimed. "In a moment, I am going to invite all of you to come to my side and examine the documents."

"What about those of us who can't read Phoenician?" asked a Senator located not far from Duilius.

Alerio chuckled. The theatrics were so blatant that if this was a public play, the audience would begin tossing radishes at the Senators. Despite the planned question, Gaius Duilius paused as if pondering it for the first time. He had possession of the dispatches and had orchestrated how to reveal the information. There was little doubt he hadn't considered the language barrier.

"For those of you who lack the Phoenician letters, I have provided transcripts of the messages in Latin," Duilius announced. "But let me sum up what's contained in them. The Empire has hired a mercenary army of fifty thousand soldiers."

Mumbling and angry words populated the chamber. Duilius let it build and, before the protests died completely, he spoke again.

"Currently, the army is camped on the west coast of Sicilia in a city called Agrigento," he explained. The chamber settled as Duilius described the situation. "From Agrigento, the army will sail to Sardinia. Shortly after arriving on the island, the fifty thousand soldiers will board transports and sail to their ultimate destination."

Gaius Duilius reached over and plucked a piece of parchment from the table. Ignoring the questions being hurled at him, he focused on the sheet. When the Senators were roaring for an answer to where the mercenaries were going, he placed the sheet on the table and stopped to smooth it out. When he stood straight, he raised his fists into the air.

"There is one element in the Qart Hadasht plan that we can control," Duilius stated. "They will move by sea. With a bigger fleet, the Republic can stop them."

"Where is the mercenary army headed?" shouted a Senator on the far end of the chamber.

"Gentlemen, the army of fifty thousand mercenaries are heading for us," Duilius bellowed. "Right here to our Capital. Come, read the dispatches for yourselves."

Gaius Duilius dropped his arms, uncurled his fists, and made a gesture as if offering the table to the assembly. Not all of the Senators rushed to review the messages.

"I would think that everyone would want to read them," Alerio remarked.

"It's not necessary. Every voting block has a representative or two who will do that for their faction," Velius explained. "That's interesting. Postumius Megellus has been in a conference with Senator Maximus since Duilius finished his soliloquy."

"What's interesting about two Senators talking?" questioned Alerio.

"Postumius Megellus is a leading candidate for Consul," the Tribune advised. "He is not Maximus' first choice. At least, he wasn't."

The Senators gripped wrists in parting and Postumius strolled to the crowd around the table. He picked up a sheet, held it out, turned it over, and laid it back on the tabletop. Alerio assumed he would return to his seat and report to his block. But the candidate for Consul walked to the front of the room, stopped, and faced the other Senators.

"I have concerns about the authenticity of these so-called dispatches," Postumius Megellus announced. "To the best of my knowledge, Qart Hadasht commanders do not leave official communications sitting around unguarded. Just how did you come across these Senator Duilius."

A smile came across Gaius Duilius' face as if the question led to another opportunity to push his agenda.

"They came into my possession via our fleet. If we had a larger number of warships, we could not only sink the army that's headed our way, but we could better defend our shores."

"That wasn't an answer to my question," Postumius Megellus observed. "How did the fleet come to have these messages?"

"Praetor Sudoris. Standing at the back of the room brought them to me," Duilius responded by pointing to Zelare Sudoris who stepped away from the wall and saluted. "The future is warships, gentlemen. Triremes and quinqueremes to rival the Qart Hadasht fleet. Or, mark my words, we will be vanquished from the seas."

"That is still not an answer to my question."

Another voice chimed in. Senator Duilius and Praetor Sudoris appeared uncomfortable. And Postumius Megellus stepped back out of respect.

"I as well would like to know how Praetor Sudoris came to have those messages," Manius Dentatu questioned.

"He'll have to address the issue now," Tribune Velius informed Alerio. "Dentatu is one of the old guards. He was Consul thirteen years ago. The man has seen every kind of political game and subterfuge you can imagine."

"I can't imagine anything political here, sir," Alerio offered.

"Then you might want to brush up on some of the finer points," Velius instructed.

Before Alerio could ask about the statement, the ancient senator slammed his fist into a chair and slammed his right foot into the tile floor. Alerio smiled. He recognized the Legion stomp then tried to visualize the Senator as a young man. Suddenly, he saw a fit and muscular Manius Dentatu. Under his robe, Corporal Sisera saluted a former infantry officer.

"Praetor Sudoris. How did the dispatches come to be in your possession?" Manius Dentatu inquired. Slightly stooped and frail, the old Senator held the Praetor with his gaze while waiting for a reply. The years may have stripped away the physical, but the Legion spirit lived. "I require an answer, Praetor."

"Senator Dentatu. One of our triremes brought them back from Sardinia," Sudoris said.

"As a result of an action at sea? Perhaps our ship gouged an Empire warship with its ram?"

"No, sir. They picked up a Legion spy off a deserted island and rowed overnight to Ostia," Sudoris explained.

Alerio started to take a step forward, but Velius placed a hand on his arm.

"Senator Maximus will let you know when it's time to reveal yourself," the old spymaster said. "For now, let the drama play out."

"Materialize this Legion spy," Manius Dentatu directed. "I'd be interested in his story."

"That's not possible Senator. He is out on the trireme on patrol," Sudoris offered. "It will take several days to locate the ship and bring him to the Capital."

"And the Navy shows it true colors," a Senator bellowed. "I have a solution to the Qart Hadasht army. Station Legions along our coast. Fortress Republic is the answer. Stop them on the beaches."

Alerio leaned in but Velius anticipated the question.

"Lucius Libo. He and his faction are against expansion," the Tribune explained. "They vote against Sicilia or expeditions to the north on every occasion. To their way of thinking, the Republic is big enough."

"Why not just build a wall around our country," another Senator challenged. "We know where the mercenaries are. Direct action is the best approach. Send over six Legions and stomp them into the soil before they reach ours."

Alerio tried to follow the debate but, to his ears, the voices talking and yelling over each other sounded like a beehive. All buzz, with no discernable logic. But the longer he listened, the more he understood.

There seemed to be four schools of thought. Prop up the coastal defenses and put most of the funding into building a fleet. Or, assemble Legions along with troops from allies and march directly to Agrigento on Sicilia. Or, build permanent fortifications along the coast and station Legionaries there to stop any invaders. And do it all fast, unless the dispatches were fake. In that case, the fourth concept was to do nothing drastic.

Alerio finally understood the General's earlier remark about there being many ways to resolve the situation. About then, the General stood up and signaled for silence.

"My esteemed colleagues. Let me take one issue off the table," Senator Maximus alerted the chamber. "The messages were taken from a Qart Hadasht officer by one of Tribune Cassiel Velius' agents."

"Maximus. That's also a secondhand tale," Manius Dentatu barked. "An answer no better than Gaius Duilius' shift to Praetor Sudoris."

56

Alerio stifled a chuckle. In his younger days, Senator Dentatu probably had a different title. Based on his no-nonsense approach, Centurion Dentatu must have been a fine infantry officer.

"And you would be correct, Manius Dentatu," Maximus acknowledged. "Except, the man who killed the Empire officer, took the dispatches, and fought his way to a deserted island, is standing beside Tribune Velius. His name is Alerio Sisera, and he will be available to answer questions about the mission after the debate."

"Sisera, show yourself," Dentatu shouted. His voice cut across the distance as it must have cut through the din of combat in the old Senator's glory days. Sharp and clear it was an order that could not be ignored.

Alerio tossed back the hood, stepped forward, saluted, and shouted back, "Here, Centurion."

The senate chamber exploded in laughter at calling the old man by a military title. But several didn't find humor in it. Especially Manius Dentatu who returned the salute along with a smile.

"Alright, Senator Spurius Maximus. Show us what else you have," ordered Dentatu.

"I propose we march on Agrigento with four Legions. A fixed enemy with designs on the Capital can't be allowed to live," the former General stated. "That being as it is, we do need a stronger fleet. I am suggesting we begin funding an expansion. Due to the threat, some of the funding will go to coastline defenses until we deal with the Empire's mercenary army."

"Senators Duilius and Vitulus, can you live with those compromises?" Dentatu inquired. When both nodded their approval, the old man turned to the other Senator. "Lucius Julius Libo. You cannot stop progress. Consul Crassus, the floor is returned to you for senate business."

***

Alerio and Velius made their way out of the gallery and along the hallway. At the back of the chamber, they crossed and took the steps down towards Senator Maximus' seat.

"I do feel a little put out," Alerio confessed.

"Why is that?" the Tribune inquired.

"The Senator didn't introduce me by rank. I know it's minor but, being a Legion NCO is a big part of who I am."

"Alerio Sisera. You sound positively introspective. Have you been studying the Greek mysteries?"

"No, sir. I must be more tired than I thought. Sorry to verbally vomit on you."

As they reached the Senator, Alerio caught Zelare Sudoris staring at him. The look on the Praetor's face wasn't of appreciation or fondness. It was more the glare of a bird of prey observing his next meal. Thankfully, Alerio was Legion heavy infantry, and he wouldn't have to deal with the fleet officer.

Belen intercepted Alerio and pulled him away from Velius. They continued passed where Maximus was holding court. Finally, the secretary installed him beside Consul Otacilius Crassus's dais.

"Answer questions about the mission," Belen instructed. "Make it a good story. But evade any mention about you, your rank, or other missions the Legion has sent you on. Is that clear?"

"I'm a one mission Tesserarius," Alerio promised. "I've been introduced to the senate before. Maybe a few would like to know I've been promoted."

"Alerio Sisera. No rank. And believe me, no one in this chamber knows you or cares about your promotion or career," Belen informed him. "Keep it simple and follow the rules."

Over the secretary's shoulder Alerio spotted the Praetor. That's one angry officer, Alerio thought. Then Manius Dentatu shuffled up with three other senators.

"Where were you when you killed the Qart Hadasht officer and captured the dispatches," the old Senator demanded.

***

By mid-day, the Senators broke into working groups to decide on the funding for the expedition to Sicilia, extra Centuries to defend the coastline, and the initial budget to begin building the fleet. Like any good Legionary, Alerio remained at his post next to the dais even though no additional Senators came by to question him.

Velius walked over from Maximus' group with two letters in his hand.

"Sisera, you are relieved from duty," the Tribune informed him. Velius held out a letter. "You've been assigned to Megellus Legion East. The Battle Commander is Colonel Gaius Claudius. I believe you know him."

"Yes, sir. The Colonel and I have been in some merda together," Alerio commented with a knowing smile. "Is General Maximus' Century with that Legion? I hate the thought of settling in with a new unit."

"I have no idea and the Senator is busy," Velius remarked after a sideways glance towards Maximus. The old spymaster handed Alerio the second letter. "It doesn't matter anyway. Here's a letter of promotion signed by three Senators. It's their way of saying thank you and repaying you for your service to the Republic."

"Optio Sisera. Optio Sisera. I like the sound of Optio Sisera," Alerio stated. "It'll make my father proud."

"Perhaps you should read the letter before getting so excited," Velius suggested.

Alerio unsealed the letter, glanced down, and noted the seal of the senate on the parchment. There were three signatures, Senators Spurius Maximus, Gaius Duilius, and Manius Dentatu. The signatures on the letter made Alerio smile, then his hand shook, and his lips quivered.

To all concerned. This is a warrant issued and verified by the Senate of the Republic. From this day forward, Alerio Sisera shall be recognized as an officer in the Legions of the Republic with the rank of Centurion.

Alerio looked up into the smiling face of Tribune Velius.

"Congratulation, Centurion Sisera," he said. "You'll be assigned to Planning and Stratagies, not to an infantry Century. We need you in a fluid assignment."

"I don't know what to say, sir. Why the promotion?"

"Senator Maximus was angry that his protégé had the dispatches taken from him," the Tribune explained. "When he asked why, I reminded him a Tesserarius has little power or authority to resist an officer's orders."

"So, he put together a faction and promoted me to Centurion?"

"Oh, there was no coalition for that. The Senators volunteered to sign the warrant. It seems, you do have fans among the Senators."

Act 3

Chapter 8 – The Last Circus

"Centurion. Sir. Centurion," the sailor called out. When the officer didn't react, he stepped over the Legionaries sprawled on the top deck, made his way to the Legion officer, and tapped him on the arm. "Sir. The ship's Centurion would like a word with you."

Alerio felt the pressure on his arm. Coming shortly after the hailing, he realized the sailor was calling him.

"Sorry. I got lost in the view," Alerio lied. In fact, he didn't identify as being a Centurion and had ignored the sailor.

"Yes, sir. The ship's officer wants to speak with you."

As the sailor had done, Centurion Sisera stepped carefully between and over the infantrymen sitting on the deck. Off to the sides of the trireme, oars lifted and dug into the blue water while the huge piece of cloth snapped in the wind. To Alerio, the warship felt as if it was just skimming the surface. He ducked under the sail and continued to the aft.

"Centurion, you wanted to see me?" Alerio asked once he reached the steering platform.

"Feri," the ship's officer replied.

"Excuse me, sir?" Alerio questioned.

"My name is Feri," the Centurion informed him. "It's customary to say your name in response."

Legion officer Sisera wasn't adjusting well to his new rank. Every time he said Centurion to an Optio, he expected to get dressed down and be brought up on charges for impersonating an officer. At the Legion transit office in the Capital, the speed of finding transportation surprised him. It seemed they wanted officers in Sicilia as soon as possible. And apparently, Centurion Sisera was one of them.

He had boarded the trireme with nineteen infantrymen just out of basic training. Fresh faced and hauling new gear, the Legionaries followed the crew's direction and divided. Then, for the most part, they stayed on their assigned side of the ship to keep it balanced.

"Sorry, my mind was on Messina. The name is Alerio Sisera."

"Well, Sisera, my mind isn't that far ahead of us," the trireme's Centurion remarked. He pointed off to the right. "We have a ship coming from the west. If it's a Qart Hadasht warship, I'll need you to get these green Legionaries up and dressed for war."

"I can do that. Just give me the word."

"One more thing. If we ram the warship, keep the Legionaries on their sides," Feri instructed. "All of them on one side will tilt us over and the oars on the opposite side will be rowing air."

"Let me go tell them."

"Thank you. Be sure they understand."

"Not a problem," Alerio assured the warship's commander.

Centurion Sisera walked one side of the top deck. At each Legionary, he stood the infantryman up, told him to respond when given the order and explained the importance of remaining on the assigned side of the ship. Once he impressed on the Legionary the gravity of the situation, he moved to the next man. At the bow, he crossed over and spoke with the Legionaries on the other side. Eventually the circuit returned him to the steering platform.

"What did you say to the Legionaries?" Feri inquired.

"I told them when I shouted for them to arm up, they better be dressing," Alerio reported. "Or I would personally reach down their throats, pull out their guts, and feed them to the fish."

"And about crossing to the other side of the warship?" Feri asked.

"The same," Alerio said.

"You must be a Century line officer," Feri guessed. "because you certainly know how to talk to infantrymen."

"I've never filled that position," Alerio confessed. After a few moments of thought, he offered. "I suppose, I'm a cartographer."

The strange ship coming from the west angled north once its crew sighted land. Feri and Alerio remained on the platform discussing maps until they entered the Messina Strait. Shortly after, the trireme rowed into the harbor and the city of the same name.

***

The harbor at Messina churned with vessels, both warships and shore traders, and boats ranging from fishing to patrol. All of them ferrying Legionaries and their gear to Sicilia. With Qart Hadasht quinqueremes and triremes prowling the strait and the seas on either end, the Republic needed to be creative. Replacing a few big, slow-moving transports carrying many, the Senate settled for many ships hauling a few Legionaries. It's how Alerio ended up on an overloaded trireme with nineteen inexperienced infantrymen.

When a shore trader pushed away, Feri's trireme performed a half circle. With the aft facing the beach, the Centurion ordered 'back it down' and the warship rowed backward until the rear of the keel ran up on the beach.

"Stand up, line up, march to the aft," Feri shouted, "and get off my ship."

The infantrymen jumped up, began marching to the aft, and just before reaching the platform, they jumped to the sand. Based on the speed of their exit, it was apparent the Legionaries wanted off the warship as much as the ship's Centurion wanted them gone.

"Where are you headed now?" Alerio asked.

"We'll patrol up the east coast of the Republic to Crotone," Feri answered. "There we'll pick up another load of heavy infantrymen or Velites and carry them to Sicilia."

"Sounds mundane," Alerio offered as the infantrymen filed passed him.

"It pretty routine unless I can find a pirate or an isolated Qart Hadasht warship," the ship's Centurion described. "then we'll give them some love with our huge bronze ram."

"Even if it's a quinquereme?" Alerio teased knowing the warship with five banks of oars towered over Feri's three-banker.

"A trireme is built for one thing," Feri bragged. "Not as a platform for artillery and archers, or a transport for the Legionaries. This ship and my oarsmen are an intelligent arrow with a broadhead for hunting. She's built to take down anything that floats, then back off, and do it again."

"That doesn't sound boring at all," Alerio acknowledged.

"Rumor has it the Senate is funding more warships," Feri advised. "We could use a good Centurion to command a trireme."

"Feri. I'm an infantryman," Alerio stated as he adjusted the bundles of his gear. "I'll stick to the mud but, thank you for the ride."

***

Alerio vaulted to the sand and joined the line of newly arrived Legionaries marching up the beach to the docks. Where the docks ended, he stepped in front of a table near a warehouse.

"Optio. I'm assigned to Megellus Legion East," Alerio said. "Can you point me in the general direction?"

"Yes, sir. Megellus Legion East is the last circus to the south. Do you need directions?"

"No thank you, I've been to Messina before."

Alerio pushed into the crowd where the Legionaries were crushed together as they passed through the alleyway between the warehouses. On the far side, as if water poured from the mouth of a pitcher, they spread out.

"You there, Sons of Mars," Alerio called to a group of rough men watching the Legionaries walk by.

"We are. And what business is it of yours, Centurion?" one replied.

"I didn't see his ship in the harbor," Alerio mentioned. "Is Captain Frigian in port?"

66

"Who wants to know, rooster?" another of the men demanded.

If the crude reference to the horsehair comb on a Centurion's helmet wasn't a clear enough challenge, the man rested his hand on the hilt of a sica. Alerio smiled, pulled two infantrymen out of the flow, and steered them towards the men.

"Bringing help?" another of the Sons of Mars sneered.

"In a matter of speaking," Alerio replied while handing his gear to the pair of Legionaries. With his hands free, the Centurion faced the group of locals. He selected the mouthy one and leaned forward. "Let's try this again, pirate. I'll ask it slow so the followers of Coalemus can follow along. Is Captain Frigian in port?"

"And I'll ask this again. Who wants to know?"

"Stupid. Just as I feared."

The Son's hand wrapped around the hilt of the sica and began to draw the blade. Alerio's left hand clamped over the man's knife hand trapping it against the sheath. In a natural reaction, the pirate reached over with his left hand to help free the blade. Halfway across his body, the Legion officer intercepted the hand. Their intertwined hands shot up and off to the side. With a clear path, Alerio leaned in further and smashed his forehead into the man's undefended nose.

Bleeding and staggering, the pirate's knees buckled. But he didn't fall to the ground in that location. Alerio caught him and tossed him off to the side. The Son landed like a moaning sack of grain, leaving a clear space between the other Sons and the Legion officer.

67

The remaining three reached for their knives and Alerio had his gladius partially drawn when a voice rang out.

"What's this? Hold there."

Everyone looked towards the voice to see a massive Son's oarsman moving along the edge of the newly landed Legionaries. Among those just arrived were three squads from Second Century Velites. The veteran skirmishers shifted out of the flow to see if the Centurion required assistance.

"Hold there," the huge rower begged again. Raising both hands, he moved forward showing he was unarmed.

Reaching the man on the ground, the rower used one big hand to snatch the bleeding man into the air. Then, with the pirate dangling helplessly off the ground, the big oarsman used his other hand to turn the man's body as if inspecting a prize piglet.

"What are you doing?" the man asked in a nasally tone.

"Checking you for holes and broken bones."

"He didn't stab me, you fatuus. He broke my nose," the pirate complained. His feet hung above the ground and the pirate kicked the air. "Put me down."

The giant lifted him higher, did another visual inspection, then suddenly dropped the man. Sprawling at first, the pirate attempted to stand but the rower pushed him down with a foot.

"Thank you for sparing him, Captain Sisera," the oarsman said. "Some Sons have short memories."

"I was simply asking after Frigian," Alerio explained.

"The Captain isn't due back for a few days," the oarsman reported. "I will inform him you have joined the Legion."

"Thank you," Alerio said. He turned and took his gear from the Legionaries. "Good job you two. Dismissed."

While the Centurion and the infantrymen joined the movement of Legionaries traveling away from the harbor, the skirmishers waited to see if the injured man challenged the large Son of Mars.

"What did you do that for?" the man shouted once the pressure from the foot allowed him to stand. "And what was that nonsense about checking me for holes."

"That was Captain Alerio Sisera, you idiot. He trained the Sons heavy infantry when King Hiero came calling," the oarsman answered. "I've seen him take two men to the ground and not leave a mark. Or take on four Hoplites and leave all of them dead in five strokes with his swords. He is not someone you want to fight. Besides, he's a friend of Captain Frigian. Now, if you still want to come at the man who just saved your life, have at it."

"No. Peace brother," the man said backing down from the oarsman.

Another of the Sons commented, "That was Sisera? I heard he was a demon in a fight and a priest afterwards. Legionaries have a nickname for him."

"Death Caller," the oarsman offered. "The Legionaries call him Death Caller."

The Velites hoisted their gear and exchanged glances. Unspoken, the question of who and what was a Death Caller passed between the skirmishers. They joined the crowd and drifted with the tide of Legionaries into

Messina. Most of the infantrymen made directly for the southern gate. This seemed like it was going to be a lengthy operation and the veteran light infantrymen took a different route.

"Long campaigns shouldn't be set upon dry," squad leader Clathri declared. "It goes against the Goddess Adiona."

"What does the Goddess of safe returns have to do with us lingering in the town?" Hortatus the Decanus from Third Squad questioned.

"Her temple over looks two important landmarks in Messina," Clathri explained. "From the hill, she gazes upon the harbor and from yonder pub, we will gaze upon her temple. While gazing, we shall salute her with mugs of wine and ask her blessing for a safe return."

"I'm convinced," Hortatus acknowledged. "And I'm thirsty."

The three squads left the main thoroughfare and headed for the pub.

***

Alerio departed the city through the southern gate and hiked the road passing three Legion marching camps. Each was the size of a small town. A ditch three feet deep and five feet wide surrounded them forming squares and defining the camps' outer limits. Inside the ditches, palisades ran along the straight sides and curved around the corners to form walls. Any enemy seeking to attack a bivouacked Legion would not catch the Legion, their supplies, or their animals out in the open.

At the fourth camp, he turned off the main road and approached the entrance ramp.

"Is this the last circus?" Alerio asked the guards.

"Sir, that would depend on how the march to the west coasts goes," the Lance Corporal replied.

"Isn't that the truth," Alerio remarked as he strolled into the camp.

He didn't need to ask where the headquarters tents were located, or the animal pens, latrines, or the supply tents. Everything in a Legion camp had a location as proscribed by military doctrine. Every afternoon during the trip across Sicilia, an advance team would survey and place stakes for the exact same placement. And every night after hiking twenty miles, Legionaries would dig the ditch and set the palisades creating a temporary Legion fort.

Alerio strolled down well-defined roads drawing confidence from the familiar surroundings. If he could find his Century and move into an NCOs' tent, he would be on firm footing. Then he reached a crossroads and his stomach soured. What he wasn't accustomed to sat at the end of the intersecting road. After inhaling deeply to calm his nerves, Centurion Sisera squared his shoulders and trudged towards the headquarters' tents.

Chapter 9 – Detached by Request

"Name and division, sir?" requested the guard from First Century.

The gates were wide open and supply wagons, infantrymen, skirmishers, and servants moved freely in and out of the Legion camp. Despite the apparent lack of security, each area had sentries posted to watch their supplies and equipment. No area was as blockaded off and protected as the headquarters tents.

It wasn't so much the headquarters as the senior men working there. But not all of the men. First Century was tasked with guarding the General and the Battle Commander. Even with Consul Megellus still at the Capital and not in residence, the Century took the duty of defending Colonel Gaius Claudius seriously.

"Centurion Alerio Sisera of Planning and Strategies," Alerio replied to the sentry.

"Yes sir. They are expecting you. Go right in," the Legionary responded with a salute.

Usually when Alerio reported to a headquarters division, he was in trouble, or the Legion was. This time, it was simply an assignment. Alerio returned the salute and marched towards the tents.

Just before entering the biggest one, he wondered if the servants had set out bowls of fruit and cheese for the staff. Then, a realization hit him. He didn't have to ask permission before taking a piece. As a member of the command staff, he could take fruit or cheese at his leisure. The thought struck him as humorous and, compounded by nervousness, his emotions reached a bursting point. As he pushed through the tent flap, the pressure exploded in a robust self-abasing laugh.

The loudest part of the snort reverberated around the interior of the command tent. Legion officers standing at a map table snapped their heads around and drilled Alerio with their eyes.

"What's so funny, Centurion?" Colonel Gaius Claudius demanded. Then his brow creased in recognition. "Centurion? Sisera?"

"Yes, sir."

"Gentlemen. If we are overrun, I suggest you locate Centurion Alerio Sisera and hide behind his shield," Gaius Claudius offered. "I've had the pleasure of watching him work defending me with a shield and gladius. No offense to your infantrymen, Bruno."

"None taken, Colonel," Bruno Sanavi the Centurion for First Century responded. "In a catastrophe, we welcome any body able to hold a scutum to protect the Colonel and his staff, no matter how clownish."

"Gentlemen, we have a mission," Gaius Claudius said calling the meeting back to order. "If what the Consul says is true, we need to be in Agrigento within a month."

Alerio stepped in between a Tribune and a Centurion and examined the map spread over the tabletop. The Legion's route cut north of Mount Etna, dipped south, and reached the Valley of Symaethus west of Centuripe. From there, the marked path followed other valleys in a more or less westerly direction. There were few details on the map.

"Colonel. A month will be too late," Alerio stated. "By then, we'll need to turn around and force march back to Catania."

"Why would we return so quickly?" the Tribune beside him questioned.

"By then the mercenary army will have passed through Sardinia and be on Republic soil, sir," Alerio declared. "The Legion will be needed to defend the Capital."

73

"Do you believe the Empire dispatches?" the Tribune asked. "Although I don't see how you could have an opinion based on what has to be third hand information."

"Sir, I didn't get your name?"

"Senior Tribune Myrias Pompeius," the staff officer replied. Then, he put force behind his words in a display of power designed to put the young Centurion in his place. And maybe prevent the junior officer from mouthing off in the future. "I'd like to know why you're so confident."

"Be careful of ambushes, Myrias," suggested Gaius Claudius. "I've seen Sisera operate when we took Messina."

"Colonel, I'm just trying to make a point about young officers attempting to influence policy with rumors," replied Myrias. The senior staff officer shifted his attention to Alerio. "We are waiting for an answer Sisera."

"I do believe the dispatches, because Tribune, I took them from the Qart Hadasht officer and brought them back to the Republic," Alerio reported. "As far as rumors, I can assure you the messages weren't planted, doctored, or created by special interest Senators."

Gaius Claudius cocked his head, cracked his neck to relieve the tension, and looked at the Centurion on the other side of Sisera.

"Senior Centurion Lembus, how many of our heavy infantry Centuries have reported in?"

"Thirty-two Colonel. The other four should be in route," the senior line officer reported. "The problem is, we don't know when they'll arrive."

"Centurion Qualis. Same question," Claudius inquired.

"Seven of my ten Veles Centuries are in camp," the senior officer of skirmishers answered. "As Senior Centurion Lembus pointed out, we don't know when to expect them."

"Tribune Numitor. Where do we stand with your command staff and our junior Tribunes?"

"We're thin as the junior Tribunes come late to any campaign," Numitor answered. "But the noblemen can catch up before we reach Agrigento."

"Centurion Ephoebias, same question for you and your cavalry?" Claudius inquired.

"I only have about seventy-five in camp, Colonel," the cavalry officer stated. "As challenging as transporting Legionaries has been, moving our horses across the strait has been a bigger issue."

"They will catch up. Until the Tribunes arrive, I'll need twenty-five of your mounted Legionaries to act as messengers," Claudius explained. He stood still and his eyes seem to go out of focus almost as if he was looking into the future. Finally, he lifted an arm and pointed two fingers at the map. "In the morning, I will offer a sacrifice to Jupiter for blessings on our operation."

All the officers looked down on the map at the spot indicated by the Battle Commander's fingers. There was no mistaking the location. Gaius Claudius pointed directly at the city of Agrigento on the west coast of Sicilia.

"Colonel, for clarity are you ordering a breakdown of the camp?" Senior Tribune Myrias Pompeius asked.

"Senior Centurion Fratris Lembus, break camp before dawn. Centurion Tapeti Qualis, I want five Centuries of skirmishers in the vanguard. Centurion Caenavi Ephoebias, give me flank protection and patrols in the space between the Velites and the main columns," Claudius ordered. Then he closed the meeting. "Gentlemen, go prepare Megellus Legion East to march at dawn. Our Legion will engage the enemy on these shores and not on home soil. Dismissed."

***

Alerio followed Tribune Numitor out of the tent. When the head of Planning and Strategies for the Legion noticed it, he stopped.

"This will be easy duty for you, Sisera. You can draw a mount from the headquarters herd. The cook prepares the evening meals. You are on your own for breakfast, but the pantry is open to staff officers," Numitor informed him. "Is there anything else I can do for you?"

"The map of our route looks a little lean on details," Alerio stated.

"It is slim on features. The Republic hasn't had time to survey Sicilia," the Tribune admitted. "It's one of the reasons we were planning on a slow march. Until you opened your mouth."

"I want to be assigned to the vanguard, Tribune," Alerio stated. "I won't need a horse, but I will require a mule and runners."

"What are you proposing Centurion Sisera?"

"I'm going to map water sources, trails that require patrolling, and the best route of march," Alerio described.

"The Legion can travel better if you know what's up ahead."

"That's not what I expected from a Tesserarius jumped up to a Centurion," Numitor confessed. "I'm impressed you don't want to cling to the easy life of a staff officer."

"Don't get ahead of yourself, sir," Alerio cautioned. "I'm going to raid the headquarters' pantry before I leave with the skirmishers."

"Your maps will help. After the day's march, I'll make a copy and send it to the Legion following us," the Tribune stated. "I wasn't sure what to do with you but now I do. You are the cartographer for Megellus Legion East. Pack you gear. I'll alert the Colonel."

"Very good, sir," Alerio acknowledged. "But I haven't unpacked. And I do have a question. Where do I sleep?"

Chapter 10 – Good Count, Good Days

As the sacrificial bull's front legs collapsed and he fell to the ground, the mighty animal bellowed. Echoing the bull, Centurion Tapeti Qualis roared.

"Velites of the vanguard, move out," the senior skirmisher officer roared.

His order quickly spread among the five waiting Centurions, NCOs, and Centuries. Before the priests finished smearing the bull's blood on their naked flesh, the forward element of the Legion jogged out of the camp.

Tucked in between the third Century and the fourth, a man wearing a beaver Petasos and leading a heavily laden pack mule, jogged easily along with the skirmishers.

"Who's the merchant?" one of the Velites asked.

"Don't know," a squad mate replied. "but he'll soon figure out we don't roll as slow as the supply wagons. "

"Or march pretty like the fat lads in the heavy infantry," another squad member offered.

Centurion Sisera heard the remarks but ignored them. The skirmishers failed to take into consideration that the heavy infantrymen not only marched with their gear, but they ran with it as well. With the bulk of his gear stashed on the mule, Alerio knew he was the equal of any but the fastest Veles.

It was a pleasant day and the units moved easily down the broad path. Five miles out from the camp, they left the road, dropped into a walk, and dispersed from their marching columns. Spreading out into an arrowhead formation, one Century moved up front and two shifted to flank the lead unit. The final two Centuries stacked in the center as reserves and reinforcements.

"My Centurion said you needed a squad," a Lance Corporal of the light infantry reported.

"Give me two men of equal height to march in front of me," Alerio directed. "The other six I'll want ranging ahead looking for likely ambush locations, possible enemy approaches, green grasses, and water sources."

"We just left camp," the squad leader complained. "The Legion won't need water or grazing fodder this far into their march."

"Sir," Alerio mumbled.

"What?" asked the Lance Corporal.

"Let me start over. I am Centurion Sisera," Alerio stated. "Are there any more question?"

"No, sir. Two in front and the rest scouting."

"Make sure the pair are the same height," Alerio added.

Two skirmishers separated from the squad and jogged to Alerio.

"Orders, sir?"

"You are my counters. The land is too rough, and we don't have the luxury of properly surveying the route," Alerio explained. "in order to mark the distance, you two will count paces. Every thousand steps, I'll mark a mile on the map. Easy?"

"Best duty we've had in weeks," one replied. "When do we start."

Alerio glanced around until his eyes fell on a rock formation off to the right and a crop of trees on the left. He reached into a saddle bag and drew out a flat board, a square of pressed bark, and a dull bronze nail.

"When we reach a spot between those trees and those rocks," he explained. "begin your count."

They reached the location and the two Velites counted while they marched. At one thousand steps, Alerio etched a mile marker and tapped identifying features into the bark matte. It was the first of many miles he would etch on the march across Sicilia.

***

At midday the next afternoon, with the sun touching the top of the sky, a messenger rode up to the main body of the skirmisher's formation. When the Legion camped the night before, the skirmishers pushed on and spent the night on the trail. Later in the trek, and closer to disputed territory, they would sleep in the protection of the Legion's marching camp.

"Centurion Sisera?" the mounted messenger inquired as he reined in his mount.

"Over here," Alerio call while rolling a series of bark parchments. "Take these to Tribune Numitor."

"Yes, sir," the rider acknowledged.

The hooves beat the earth heading back to the Legion. A few of the skirmishers behind Centurion Sisera watched the horse and rider pass them. Then one turned to his squad mates.

"He's not a merchant," observed the Veles from Forth Century. "Just another headquarters staff officer."

"What was your first clue," another man inquired. "The messenger or the squad assigned to him?"

"Neither. It's the mule."

"Mule?"

"If he wanted, he could be riding a horse," the original Legionary responded. "Instead, he's walking a pack mule."

"And that's better than riding a horse?"

"Sure is. If he rode a horse, he'd be a target for an arrow, or a spear, and we'd look to him for directions. By walking, he gets low and, as would any headquarters officer, he dodges responsibilities. Plus, he has a pack animal to carry his gear."

"What are you talking about?" his squad mate asked with a shake of his head. "At the first opportunity, I'm making a sacrifice to Muta to have the Goddess silence you."

"Why? I'm only making an observation."

"If you people have finished solving the problems of the world," their Optio growled while trotting up the line.

80

"How about you get to the left flank before I put my large hobnailed boot up your collective cūlī."

"Move out," the Decani ordered.

Unlike heavy infantrymen who moved as a block of shields, armor, and steel creating a powerful front, light infantrymen were fluid. Fourth Century broke from the center of the formation and jogged off to the left. Their loose, field formation allowed them to flow rapidly around clumps of trees and rocks that would require the heavies to break their line of march. Soon, all eighty men of the Century scrambled out of the flatland and vanished in the trees and brush of the hills.

Alerio watched them go then peered to the heights of Mount Etna. While it was cool in the valley and the chilly nights required a blanket or a cloak, high above, snow coated the rim and peaks. Thankfully, the home of Vulcan's smithery and forge remained cold and silent.

A single Legionary jogged out of the trees from the opposite side of the path.

"Sir. There's a wide game trail coming up on your right," a Legionary reported. "My Lance Corporal said it could be used as a fast approach for a hostile force."

"Good find. Please pass on my thanks to your Decanus," Alerio complimented the light infantryman. Then he asked his pair of pacers. "What's the count?"

"Four hundred twenty-five," one replied. The other hesitated, then echoed the count. It was why he had two pacers. In case one forgot what number stride he had taken.

While walking beside the mule, Alerio tapped the map with the point of the bronze nail. Details appeared in the surface with an arrow pointing to the trail on the right and a note of warning. Armed with the information, Senior Centurion Lembus would know to place squads at the mouth of the trail when the main body of the Legion marched by. With heavy infantrymen in position, there was little likelihood of an ambush from that direction.

The day passed with reports of land features marked on maps and messengers collecting the parchments. Alerio didn't fool himself. The appearance of cavalrymen was more to check on the progress of the vanguard than to collect his maps. Still, the riders sought him out to collect the maps and it felt good to be valued.

***

"We're almost at twenty miles," Alerio alerted the skirmisher Centurion riding from the front of the column.

The officer reined in his horse and flashed a grin at staff officer Sisera.

"Scouts from the Second Century have the town of Randazzo in sight," the line officer for First Century replied. Then, before kicking his mount forward, the grin transformed into a broad smiled and he informed Alerio. "I think we'll set the perimeter guards beyond the town. Our scouts spotted a lake down there."

The Velites within hearing distance cheered. While rivers were fine for filling water skins and amphorae and adequate for cleaning clothes and a fast dip, the water ran cold making for a chilly plunge. But the surface of a lake when warmed by the sun allowed for swimming and a soak for the tougher Legionaries. Fast or slow, after two days of marching through mountain valleys, everyone appreciated a chance to bathe.

Randazzo had walls but not defensive walls. A man could easily leap the structure. But it provided a barrier for the goats, cows, and children. Once the citizens realized the four hundred Light Infantrymen and their officers and NCOs posed no threat, several came to the wall with goods to sell. Soon the fresh fruit, vegetables, cheese, and eggs were exchanged for coins and the buyers marched happily to the lake while the citizens hurried to their huts to count their good luck. And it was good luck, because the Velites could have easily stormed the town and taken what they wanted.

Alerio thought about the good sense of leaving the citizens unmolested. Having a friendly town along their line of retreat, if it came to that, was prudent. His pacers called out steps beyond one thousand and at three miles, they arrived at a small lake. Guiding the mule to a crop of trees, Alerio began untying the loads.

"Orders, Centurion," the Decanus of the current squad assigned to him asked.

"Report back to your Century. And thank you for being my legs and eyes."

The Lance Corporal collected his squad and, as they marched away, all eight were puzzled. Never in their time in the Legion had a staff officer thanked them for anything.

"I'm going to get you some grain, mule," Alerio said as he took a handful of leaves and rubbed the animal where the bundles pressed down the hairs on the mule's sides. "Then I'm going to jump in that lake and wash off the travel dust."

***

The five Centurions of the Velites met on the west side of the lake.

"Three on guard and two in the water," Nodatus, the most senior of the officers, suggested. "We'll rotate before the Legion arrives."

"Works for me," the Centurion for Second Century offered. "My lads have been out front pushing since dawn. They deserve to bathe first. Any problems with that?"

"No. Call them in and get them wet," the other line officers agreed.

Although the bulk of the Legion wouldn't arrive until late in the afternoon, three of the skirmisher Centuries spread out and created a picket line further west, north, and south of the lake. They would ensure the advance unit from the Legion arrived to find a secured location. And, the advanced Legionaries would be protected while they laid out the gridlines for the marching camp. Plus, the overwatch allowed the light infantrymen from the Second Century to clean up without worrying about posting guards.

"I'm hungry and tired," an infantryman from Second Squad complained.

"I'm telling you, lad, a swim then a relaxing meal and you'll feel like a new man," Lance Corporal Clathri announced as the squad approached the lake.

"Decanus, the guy in the water," another squad member pointed out. "Isn't that the Centurion who was going to fight the Sons of Mars?"

In the water, the staff officer swam across the lake using smooth, yet powerful, strokes.

"Hortatus. Isn't that Death Dealer or something like that?" Clathri called to the other squad leader.

"Yes. The staff officer is the one they nicknamed, Death Caller. That's what the oarsman said," the Decanus of Third Squad corrected. "He sure swims pretty for a headquarters' officer."

"Probably has never been in a real fight in his life. Some people take on names to impress the lasses," Clathri offered. "He's too young and, truthfully, map making can't be that dangerous."

The infantrymen of the Century stripped down and as the men waded into the lake, on the far side, the staff officer reached the shoreline and stood up. Three of the squads stopped in water up to their thighs and stared. Across the calm water, the young Centurion turned as he scraped his limbs clear of water with the dull edge of a knife. It wasn't the knife holding their attention, it was the unexpected battle scars on the body of the staff officer.

Raised ugly marks on his right shoulder were double tracks down the deltoid muscle. Lines of scars ran over his right hip, on the back of his left arm, up both forearms, plus a scar etched a line over his left eye, and another formed a half moon on the crown of his head. Further evidence of the Centurion's battles were arrow wounds in one thigh and in his side. When he turned and faced away from them, the light infantrymen got a closer look at what froze them in the water. Compounding the evidence of blade and arrow wounds, whip scars wrapped his back in ribbons of welts.

"Death Caller?" Clathri questioned. "He's more like Death Survivor."

"And obviously, a veteran," Hortatus added. "Do you think he needed our help with those Sons of Mars in Messina?"

"I don't think so," Clathri stated. He ran a few steps, dove below the surface, and came up spewing water. "Considering the scars, I would have liked to see the Centurion fight."

***

Alerio poured a handful of wheat into the iron pot, leaned back, and watched the grain boil. A shadow fell over him as a horse approached, then several artichokes and stalks of celery landed beside him.

"You've made an impression on my infantrymen," Nodatus said while securing the strings on a sack. He pointed to the artichokes and stalks on the grass next to Alerio's thigh. "They wanted to share the Century's vegetables with you."

"I don't understand, sir. But I'll take them," Alerio replied while picking up the gifts.

"Save the sirs for the Tribunes, Colonels, and Generals," Centurion Nodatus advised. "Between line officers, it's unnecessary."

"I understand, sir," Alerio said.

Nodatus laughed. "You treat my people with respect. That's rare for a staff officer."

The skirmisher officer tugged the reins and guided his horse around in a half circle.

"If you need help learning to be in command, come see me," Nodatus offered before putting his heels to the mount's flanks and riding off.

Alerio dropped the vegetables into the pot, stirred the mixture with a wooden ladle, and leaned back to let them cook. His challenge wasn't with commanding Legionaries. He understood that aspect of the job. His issue was talking casually to officers and thinking of himself as their equal. To Centurion Sisera, navigating policies felt like a bigger task than managing a knife fight.

Later in the afternoon, the advance unit rode in and began placing lines on the flat ground north of the lake. Before the first Centuries of heavy infantrymen arrived, the men designing the marching camp were at the lake and soaking off the road dirt.

Chapter 11 – Lures and Lucky

The vanguard traveled basically in a westward direction and over the next two days the terrain changed as did their duty. Along the route, the land transformed from steep sided gorges to broader river valleys. Beyond screening for enemy forces, their scouting mission also changed. Where they had reconnoitered for passes through the mountains, they now began testing rivers for crossing points. Fording locations required a solid bottom, a widening of the river where the current slowed, and graduated sides to allow access for the supply wagons. By day four, the river was the Dittaino and locating the ford took part of the day before the Velites located the crossing and marched to the town of Cuticchi.

Alerio ordered his pacers to walk the distances from several features on one side then they waded to the opposite bank and performed the same tasks. The work to get the extra details for the map caused the three to arrive late at the proposed marching camp site.

"Tomorrow, we'll pass under the cliffs of Enna," Centurion Nodatus informed Alerio. "From that point forward, I'm putting three squads with you."

"To protect the mule?" Alerio teased as he pulled the bundles off the animal's back.

"No, Centurion Sisera," Nodatus stated. "To hold our center when we're attacked. Because west of Enna is Qart Hadasht territory."

The line officer walked away to speak with his Century. In response to the warning, Alerio unwrapped his shield, armor, and gladii. After eating, he rubbed them down with oil and honed the blades.

On the far side of the Velites area, the skirmishers not on guard were also cleaning equipment and eating.

"Get a look at that," Lance Corporal Hortatus suggested.

"At what?" Clathri asked.

"The staff officer's shield and armor."

"That, my friend, is not ceremonial armor," Decanus Clathri observed. "It's heavy infantry gear."

"Now we know where he got the scars," Hortatus added. "And it wasn't in cartography class. Unless the map making discipline is more demanding than it appears."

To the light infantrymen, staff officer Sisera's equipment proved to be a curiosity. When he picked up two gladii and began running sword drills with both, they were amazed.

"It seems the Centurion is a heavy infantryman," Lance Corporal Clathri declared. Then after watching Alerio drill, he guessed. "And a weapons instructor."

"That explains the scars but, who fights with two gladii?"

"It seems Centurion Sisera is proficient with two blades," Clathri said. "I wouldn't want to be on the receiving ends of those blades."

Alerio realized he had an audience. Increasing the speed of his arms, he wove intricate patterns with the steel, moved his feet back and forth rapidly, and put on a show for the light infantrymen. He had ended the drills and stowed the gear long before the Legion marched in and began digging the trenches, placing the barriers, and erecting the tents.

***

The cliffs of Enna towered above the landscape to the north. From the road, Alerio judged the heights to be taller than eight men standing on each other's shoulders. Adding to the natural defenses of the city, short walls ran along the top of the plateau. The only reason for the walls, it seemed, was to prevent sheep and children from falling off the bluff. Or possibly to give the city militiamen a place to sit while watching an attacking force attempt to ascend the steep sides. Centurion Sisera decided the latter because armed men sitting on the walls waved and gestured as the vanguard formation passed below them.

"What do you think they're saying, sir?" a Legionary inquired.

"The Enna city guards are wishing us luck," Alerio suggested.

Around him, the three squads of light infantry maintained a defensive formation while marching.

"I don't believe that's the meaning of the hand motions, sir," Decanus Clathri said.

"Tell you what, Lance Corporal," Alerio offered. "You have my permission to climb up there and request an explanation."

"If it's all the same to you, Centurion," the squad leader pleaded after a glance at the imposing heights of the city. "I'll take your word for it."

"Fair enough. Pacers, what's the count?"

***

It began to rain, and the marching boots of the infantry churned the dirt into slop. When the road turned south, the skirmishers left the muddy trail and followed a stream bed westward through the hills. Eight miles beyond Enna, the deluge continued and the now fast running stream flowed into a swollen creek.

"We need to find ways to cross," Nodatus informed Alerio from under an oiled goatskin wrap. "Two Centuries will check up stream and two will move down. You wait here with the three squads from my Second Century."

"Is dividing your forces in a rainstorm while marching in hostile territory, a good idea?"

"Centurion Sisera. Being a Legion officer for the light infantry is not a good idea to begin with," ventured the Centurion for First Velites. "Facing Colonel Claudius and Centurion Qualis and explaining why we didn't patrol the woods, the rock formations, and the hills on the other side of this troublesome water feature, is also not a good idea."

"I believe I understand, Centurion."

"We are Velites, Sisera, first in, every time. First to fight, first to bleed, and first to shove our mentula into the wasp's nest. We are, as always, the first to offer our lives for the Republic," Nodatus spoke with passion and vibrated with conviction. While he talked, pooled water fell from his poncho and spilled down on Alerio. Enthralled and surprised by the creed of the skirmishers, he stood in the waterfall out of respect. "We don't have bad ideas. As a matter of face, Sisera, Velites never have ideas. We are the Legionaries of action. Is there anything else, you'd like to question me about?"

"No, Centurion," Alerio responded.

Nodatus wheeled his horse around and shouted instructions to his Optio. Once organized, the Centurion trotted into the pouring rain followed by his ten squads. Soon the last skirmisher vanished in the gloom leaving Alerio, his mule, and three squad of light infantrymen standing in the rain.

"Orders, Centurion?" Decanus Hortatus inquired.

"Let's move closer to the creek," Alerio directed. "Then, we'll stand watch and wait."

"I hate waiting," Clathri complained. Then he remembered who stood by the mule. "Sorry sir. No offense meant."

"None taken, Lance Corporal. Guide us down to the bank."

***

Wet and chilled, Alerio and the twenty-four skirmishers were close enough to the bank to separate the noises of the overflowing creek from the pounding rain.

"We noticed you drilling with two gladii, sir," Hortatus commented. "The consensus is you're a weapons instructor. Or a pit fighter. There are coins on that occupation as well."

"Weapons instructor," Alerio answered.

From the curtain of rain, a figure crawled out of the flowing water and onto the sand and gravel. Three light infantrymen drew their gladii and rushed to the shape.

"It's First Century's Optio," a skirmisher shouted.

"Bring him up here," Clathri instructed.

The squad leaders reached down and pulled the NCO up the bank and onto the grass. Spitting and gasping, the Sergeant glanced around with unfocused eyes.

"Optio. Report," Alerio demanded while dropping down beside him. "Pull yourself together and tell me what happened."

"Heavy. Heavy infantry," the NCO choked out. "They hit us near a rock formation. On the far bank. Came at us on-line."

"Where is Centurion Nodatus and the rest of the Century."

"They ran for a canyon," the Optio stated. "I hung back to collect the ones just wading out of the water. A second Iberian unit swept the riverbank. A shield knocked me into the water. I tried to swim back but ended up here."

"What are we going to do, Centurion?" Lance Corporal Hortatus asked.

"We should fall back and find a defensible spot," Clathri suggested.

Alerio reached for the mule's back and untied three bundles. From one he pulled his armor, from another he lifted out a dual gladius harness, and from the last, he extracted his Centurion helmet.

"Select your fastest men and send them after the Centuries," Alerio ordered. "Tell the Centurions to cross the creek and execute a pincer maneuver on our location."

"Sir, we'll do anything you want," Hortatus commented. "But you do realize that we are light infantry. In a shield-to-shield meeting, the heavies will win."

"I'm aware, Lance Corporal. Get those runners moving," Alerio directed while slipping his arms through the harness. "Who are your best swordsmen? I need the top four."

"Centurion Sisera. We don't have enough bodies to form two lines, let alone a three-man combat line," Clathri pointed out.

"While you are wasting time telling me what we can't do, Centurion Nodatus and the First Century are fighting for their lives," Alerio challenged. "We are going to cross the creek and help the Century. Clear?"

"Yes, sir," the Decanus responded. "I'm one of your swordsmen."

"As am I," Hortatus announced.

"Select two more men with gladius skills and follow me," Alerio said as he settled the helmet on his head. "Trust me. I'm not planning on dying today. Or getting Legionaries killed."

A leap off the riverbank landed Alerio on the gravel. As he splashed into the water, the three squads jumped off the bank and rushed to join the Centurion.

***

Lance Corporal Hortatus kicked through the swiftly moving water barely keeping his balance and the Centurion's helmet in view. Expecting the officer to wait for the squads on the far shoreline, the squad leader slowed to allow the Velites behind him to catch up. But Sisera didn't break stride.

In a single leap, Alerio vaulted out of the water and onto the bank while drawing both gladii. Not far away and a little blurred by the rain, a row of shields waited for him.

The heavy infantrymen of the Qart Hadasht mercenary force caught the movement. But they had watched the light infantrymen earlier in the day and didn't expect mere skirmishers to attack a formation of heavies.

Two of them shifted into defensive stances and dropped their spear tips in response to the one crazy Latian climbing the embankment. The other eight twisted their heads to watch the entertainment. All ten mercenaries and the Velites wading through the rushing water heard singing. It was scratchy, off key, and barely recognizable, but it was a song.

Poor, pathetic Damocles
He had no future, he barely had a past
And when he asked the girls to dance,
All they did was laugh

Alerio hurdled the embankment, rose high into the air, and threw out his arms. As if attempting to fly higher than the infantrymen were tall, he stretched and reached towards the sky. The spears elevated anticipating the height at which the Latian would come down and impale himself on the steel tips.

Damocles the hopeless
His enemies cried
Don't sign the parchment
Don't take the Republic's coin

The eyes and brains of the mercenary pair misinterpreted the distance. Tucking at the top of his jump, Centurion Sisera fell forward but under the spears. The shafts lowered too late to stop him. Alerio flew under the spears, smacked into the mud, and hacked both the legs of both soldiers. Wounded they fell, landing hard on the wet ground.

Be a crook or a coastal fisherman
You can't qualify, so why apply to be
A Legion's light infantryman

Alerio flexed his stomach muscles and, in a move resembling a fish out of water, he flopped onto his back. Both gladii blades smacked into the mercenaries' helmets, burying their faces in the mud.

You're healthy and spry
You are too young to die
And carry possessions on your back
or meager rations in a sack

Another exaggerated wiggle brought Alerio's legs under him. From a squatting position, he charged forward, and bull rushed towards the end of the heavy infantry line.

Toting a gladius, javelin, and shield
Across a battlefield to make contact

95

One infantryman staggered to the side, being driven by Alerio's churning legs. That mercenary collided with another who stumbled into a third. With half the formation off balance, the mercenary squad leader shouted for his men to back up and reform.

Then to run right back

Dodging arrows, it's wacked

Damocles the bleak, choose another craft

The five upright heavy infantrymen stepped back and away from the mud wrestling match. To their surprise, one man, now down in the mud with three of their companions, had disrupted their solid line. They wanted to laugh at the sight. Before a chuckle escaped their lips, twenty-two Legion light infantrymen leaped over the embankment. All of them singing.

Damocles the meek

Pick somewhere else to be

Except in the Legion's Light infantry

No sane skirmisher would charge a solid infantry screen. Their armor lacked the mass, their shields the size, and their headgear the strength. That being true, tempt Velites with a distracted and out of formation heavy infantry line and they would attack.

The mercenaries found themselves surrounded, separated, and in melee fight - the preferred combat style of tribal barbarians and highly skilled Legion light infantrymen. Twenty-two against seven sealed the fate of the Qart Hadasht forces.

"That was fun," Decanus Clathri exclaimed to his squad and the other Velites. "And almost too easy. We could have left half of us on the other bank."

"Lance Corporal. I'd like to point something out to you," Hortatus advised.

He indicated Centurion Sisera who stood, sheathed his blades, and straightened the officer's helmet. Four dead mercenaries lay at the officer's feet. Obviously, it wouldn't have been so easy if the Centurion hadn't weakened the line.

"Death Caller," Clathri whispered. "Now I understand."

Decanus Hortatus dipped his head in agreement.

"Give me a spread of scouts," Alerio directed while indicating a radius further west. "There's a force out there who trapped an entire Century. Find them for me."

"And what will we do when we locate that many heavy infantrymen, sir?" the third squad leader inquired. "We only number twenty-two light. And those are Iberian infantry. We got lucky."

"We are going to lure them into the open," Alerio replied. Then he held out both hands, palms up as if offering the dead on the ground to the Lance Corporal. "And kill them."

After sending out five scouts, Alerio noticed Hortatus pull the stopper from a wineskin and pour a healthy portion of vino onto the damp earth. The squad leader's lips moved as the deep red liquid stained the mud.

"What's that you're doing?"

"I'm praying for a marriage, Centurion," Hortatus stated.

Alerio assumed the Decanus was thinking about a fiancée at home and plans for the upcoming nuptials.

"Just before the start of a fight?" Alerio asked. "Keep your mind on the present and the future will care for itself."

"That's what I'm praying for, sir, the present," Hortatus informed the Centurion. "A wedding between Sors and Spes."

"I couldn't think of a better moment for the God of Luck and the Goddess of Hope to join together," Alerio admitted.

Then out of the rain, two of the scouts sprinted into view. Both had horrified looks on their faces.

Chapter 12 – All in for the Distance

"First Century has set a defensive line in the back of a short box canyon," one scout reported. "Our lads are putting up a fight, but they can't last."

"Against how many?" Alerio questioned.

"It looks like two Companies of Iberian Infantry," the other scout replied. "I don't see how we can help."

"They have fifteen shields set at the entrance as rear security," the first scout added. "When they finish off the First, they'll come out in formation."

"Orders, Centurion?" Hortatus asked.

The light infantrymen stared at the staff officer waiting for him to decide. Attacking a fixed line of heavy infantry would be honoring Furor and embracing the God's blessing of insanity. Skirmishers don't attack infantry screens, stationary or mobile. Their other choice was to retreat across the stream, stay fluid, and wait for the Legion's heavy infantry to arrive. By then however, the strings of the eighty men in the First Velites would be cut and their bodies growing cold.

"We're going to draw their rear security force out of position," Alerio announced. "and catch them in the open."

"When I was a wee lad, my cousin knocked a hornet's nest out of a tree," Clathri offered. "I was standing under it looking up. When it fell, I instinctively reached out and caught the nest. I sort of feel the same about your plan, sir."

"What makes you think the Iberians will desert a defensible position?" Hortatus asked, while ignoring the negative attitude of his fellow squad leader.

"Because, we are going to make them angry," Alerio promised.

"Sort of like the hornets," Clathri suggested. Absentmindedly, he scratched at his face.

"Yes, and just as unorganized," Alerio assured the Velites. "Bring the squads on-line. Let's go annoy some heavy infantrymen."

***

Twenty Legion skirmishers scrambled up the hill attempting to keep pace with the staff officer. Out front, Centurion Sisera and the two scouts adjusted so the light infantrymen lined up with the Iberian shields. The closer they came, the more obvious it was the heavy infantrymen understood discipline. There were no errant shields or unleveled spears.

"That's death I'm looking at," a skirmisher commented.

"Then do as you were told," Hortatus directed. "I'll be in the center with Death Caller. You and the rest of the squad stand back. Make the Iberians come out after you."

"I know. And sing loud," the Legionary said. "What does the Centurion expect? We're going to frighten the heavies to death with our voices?"

"Care to trade places with me?" Hortatus challenged.

"No, Decanus. You go right ahead and attack their middle with the crazy officer," the Veles stated. "The squad and I will do our part."

The same type of conversation rolled through the three squads. At a spear's throw from the enemy screen, the scouts sprinted for the ends of the Legion line. Alerio slowed and allowed the Velites to catch up.

"It's a good day for the Goddess Nenia," Alerio mentioned. He folded in between Lance Corporals Clathri and Hortatus and peered after the repositioning scouts. Rain limited his vision to a few feet beyond the ends of his line. Then he added. "The Goddess will come for souls today. For whom she comes depends on when the rest of our Centuries get here."

"We could wait," Clathri suggested.

"Listen carefully and you'll understand two things," Alerio instructed.

Clathri and the other swordsman on Alerio's left cocked their heads. Hortatus, on the right, and the fifth man in the assault unit did as well. They all listened. Above the din of the pouring rain, they heard the crack of steel on steel, the smack of blades and spear tips on wet shields, and the grunts and cries of men in combat.

"Centurion Nodatus and First Century don't have the luxury of waiting," Clathri ventured.

Four steps from the enemy's fortified screen, Hortatus inquired, "What's the second thing, Centurion?"

"Our approach will give First Century heart and the will to keep fighting," Alerio answered. He reached up to his shoulders and drew both gladii. Then he sang. *"Ah Desperate Damocles, taking the Legion's pay."*

The advancing skirmishers raised their voices and joined Centurion Sisera.

Ah Desperate Damocles,
Taking the Legion's pay, he sealed the deal
Signed his name, averted his eyes,
And slinked away

Although the Iberians held their shields high, hiding their facial expressions, Centurion Sisera saw joy and a twinkle in their eyes. Unseen, but no doubt there, were the smiles at the absurdity of lightly armored Legionaries attacking a fixed position of heavy infantrymen.

Alerio decided to wipe the smile off of two of their faces. Crossing the gladii, he held them to his front, positioned below his waist. The Legionary officer stutter stepped at the tips of the spears, powered his blades outward while stepping between the shafts.

Damocles the recruit
The instructors cried
Eat dirt, bury your sigh

Both blades impacted the shafts knocking the spears off to the sides. The Iberians weren't worried. While withdrawing their spears to reposition them, they braced their shields maintaining the hard point in their defensive line. When Alerio slapped the spears out of his way, Clathri, Hortatus, and the Legionaries on either side of the squad leaders dueled with the flanking Iberians, keeping them occupied so they couldn't target Centurion Sisera. While the center of the lines dueled, further out, the Legion skirmishers stopped just out of spear thrust distance and hammered aside any steel tips that extended towards them.

It was a classic mismatch between heavy and light infantry. With each passing moment, the fighters settled into roles and the battle lines became static. Then, Alerio lifted his right knee and cocked his leg, preparing to change the dynamics.

Mile after mile until you tire
And when you think you'll die
An angry Optio appears at your side
Asking for your infantry pride

Centurion Sisera drove his right foot towards the ground. As the foot moved, Alerio doubled over at the waist. Following the hobnailed boot as it slammed into the mud, he planted the knuckles of both hands in the muck, and kicked his heels over his head, flipping forward in a controlled airborne tumble. Upside down, the staff officer whipped his legs over the tops of the Iberian shields and pounded the enemy infantrymen's helmets with the heels of his hobnailed boots.

Both soldiers fell back, tripped, and crashed to the ground. A dangerous gap opened in the defensive screen. The pairs of Legion swordsmen beside Alerio pressed forward hacking and slashing. Despite shouts from their Sergeant the Iberian infantrymen couldn't come together to close the break. Stretching out to either side of the fighting, the Velites took a half a step to the rear and barked the next verse as if they were insulting the Iberians.

A sniveling rodent beats feet
You are a slimy slug so creep
And an ugly grasshopper it leaps
Or locusts they swarm

Alerio looked up to see Lance Corporals Clathri and Hortatus battling infantrymen trying to keep the Iberians from moving in and closing the gap. The most dangerous position in combat was lying on your back on enemy shields in the middle of a fight. Chancing a delay, Centurion Sisera bridged his back, lifted his gladii overhead, and cracked the downed infantrymen in their heads, again. Then he drew in his legs, planted his boots, and leaped to his feet.

Toting a sandbag, shield, and javelin
You are becoming a battle platform
Run as an avenging storm
Dodging insults, it's wacked

The Legion line resembled an archer's bow under tension. Solid in the center with five men fighting shoulder to shoulder as if the bow's hand hold section. The Iberians were only engaged in the center and on the ends of their screen. To their Sergeant it was an untenable formation. He wanted all of his swords in the fight.

"Attack," the Iberian NCO ordered. "Watch your line. Close the gap."

As the heavy infantrymen stepped forward, Alerio and the four swordsmen hopped back. They scrambled to the rear as did the ends of the Legion line. Soon, there were two straight rows. But while the Velites shuffled backwards, the Iberians marched forward trying to engage the Legion light infantrymen.

Damocles the weak, choose another craft
Damocles the leek
Lift your head and knees
Skirmisher, Veles trainee

"We got them mad and moving," Hortatus pointed out. "What do we do with them now?"

"The hornets didn't work out either," Clathri suggested.

"Spread the squads," Alerio ordered. "It's time to go on the attack."

***

The thirteen Iberian infantrymen marched away from the mouth of the canyon. They planned on a quick slaughter of the skirmishers before hoofing it back to resume the blockade. That was their mind set. The Legion Velites had a different outcome in mind.

Alerio shouted nonsense words and carved patterns in the air with his blades. Distracted by the antics, the Iberian NCO shouted for the gap to be closed and focused on the crazy Latian. In the chaos, Decanus Clathri rolled up the squad members on his side and shoved them to the end of the line. On the right, Decanus Hortatus herded the other half of the light infantrymen to the other end.

As if the Goddess Theia directed the Iberians' eyes, the Sergeant only saw an isolated, undefended Legion officer. Fixated on the Centurion, he failed to notice the skirmishers at the ends of his formation stop retreating.

104

From backing away and to the side, the skirmishers gang rushed and overwhelmed the ends of the Iberian shield wall. When two of his infantrymen were hacked to the ground, the Iberian NCO woke to the danger.

"Withdraw," he shouted. "Withdraw."

But his eleven remaining soldiers faced twenty-two swarming Legion skirmishers. Any knowledgeable betting man would happily place his coins on the Velites. The Iberians collapsed their line, put their backs together, and huddled in a defensive formation.

"Hortatus. Gather your squad," Alerio ordered. "We're going into the canyon."

"Us against two Companies of heavies?" the Lance Corporal questioned while pulling his Legionaries away from the circular fighting. "More singing, sir?"

"Absolutely," Alerio assured him.

The Legion officer, Hortatus, and seven skirmishers jogged through the rocky opening of the ravine. No sooner had they entered the mouth of the canyon then they dug in their heels, churned mud, and reversed course. Coming the other way was a flood of Iberian soldiers.

"Fight or run, sir?" Hortatus asked while they sprinted back to where the other Velites did combat with the Iberian squad.

"There are bad odds and chancy moves," Alerio replied. "We survived chancy. But these odds are really bad. Pass the word, we run."

They reached the fighting and began plucking skirmishers back from the circle of infantrymen.

"Do you think we helped the First Century?" Hortatus inquired.

"I hope so, Lance Corporal, I hope so," Alerio said in resignation. He raised an arm, indicated the stream, and began to announce the retreat.

Damocles the man
Bulky thighs, calloused hands
Infantry qualified with a war cry
and skills to survive

Singing Legion voices drifted on the wind from three directions. Downhill and off to the left, from the box canyon itself, and finally, the last of the singing voices came from above and beside the canyon.

At the mouth of the ravine the first wave of Iberian infantry appeared. Then, from the rising sides of the entrance, Velites from the Fifth and Second Centuries dropped onto the soldiers. Soon all one hundred thirty skirmishers were in the close quarters fighting.

Damocles the Veles
Your fate is sealed
between the walls of shields
Skirmishers tread the land of the dead

"Decani. Finish off those pieces of merda and sort out your squads," Alerio called to his Lance Corporals. "Then let's get into that fight."

While the Centuries battled, and Alerio's squads fought the eleven soldiers, Fifth and Third Centuries raced up the hillside. The Centurions saw Alerio and his unit and angled towards him. But, when they spied the battle at the mouth of the ravine, they changed direction, and picked up the pace.

First in, first to taste the fire
First to bleed and first to expire

Dread the Legion's spearhead

The one hundred and sixty Velites slammed into the leading edge of the heavy infantrymen. Ordered lines of shields and spears were the preferred formation of battle for the heavies. Conversely, brawling and chaos fit the skirmishers in temperament and training.

Whistles blew and units of the Iberian infantry circled around their officers. Slowly, infantrymen separated from the battle line and joined the mass. When enough had grouped together, the densely packed Iberians began to creep out of the box canyon.

The ladies seek affection
When faced with rejection
In light of the infantryman's perfection
And his enemies tremble

The battle boiled into the open as the two hundred and ninety Legionaries fought the one hundred and eighty Iberian soldiers. If the heavy infantrymen had been on-line, it would have been different. But the melee favored the skirmishers. Then a disturbance at the back of the Iberians drew Alerio's attention.

It's not infantry steel bringing might
It's the spirit and heart delivering fright
Like Wolves, skirmishers assemble
Dodging compliments, a delight

From deeper in the box canyon, a Centurion came into view. Half the comb on his helmet had been sliced away but, there was no doubt he was in command. Nodatus pointed and directed the remainder of the First Century. And with a vengeance, his skirmishers chewed into the disorganized heavy infantrymen.

Damocles the Veles, there is no other craft
Damocles the Veles
Where else would you rather be
Then in the Legion's light infantry

The end started when the Iberian officers broke free on open ground and began reforming ranks of shields. From attacking at will, the Velites began hesitating rather than charging into ranks of spear tips. Once the two sides divided, the fighting stopped and became a staring contest.

"Iberian infantry, step back," a Captain ordered. "Back. Back. Back…"

The mercenary heavies moved further away separating the opponents by more and more space. Behind the stationary Velites line, the Centurions gathered to discuss the situation. Alerio helped organize the wounded before strolling to the infantry officers.

"Orders, sir," Alerio asked Centurion Nodatus.

Splatters of mud melted in the rain and as the smears flowed down the officer's armor some of the blood was washed away. Not enough to hide the signs of battle.

"We have too many wounded for the day. We'll let the Legion heavy infantry deal with the Iberians later," the senior officer replied. "Where are we, Sisera?"

"About nine miles from Enna," Alerio informed him.

"We'll treat our injured, then we'll move out," Nodatus instructed. "Because…"

"You can't tell Colonel Claudius and Senior Centurion Lembus that you weren't all in for the distance," Alerio suggested.

"You're beginning to sound like a Veles officer, Sisera," Nodatus teased. "I may draft you for one of our Centuries."

"No can do, Centurion. I'm heavy infantry," Alerio boasted. "Although, right now, I'm a cartographer and a staff officer."

"For a staff verpa, you handled the Iberians like an experienced infantry officer. And the loud off-key singing allowed the flanking Centuries to locate the box canyon. Very clever," Nodatus explained. "If you ever get sick of politics, let me know."

Alerio flinched at the insulting reference to many officers assigned to headquarters. Excusing himself, he left the Centurions and ambled back towards the stream and his mule. Obviously, his current posting came about from favors by men of influence. Connecting the logic between Nodatus' statement and his position as a staff officer brought a realization to Centurion Sisera. All the Centurions and Legionaries in Megellus Legion East saw him as a bootlicking sycophant and not an experienced heavy infantry Legionary. That's why the squad leaders questioned his orders. He reached the stream, kicked at the water, and waded across.

Chapter 13 – Truth for the Ages

Fifteen miles out of Enna and five miles short of the days standard march, Centurion Nodatus halted the vanguard's forward progress. Runners sprinted to the flanking Centuries and a third messenger backtracked all the way to the center of the column. The courier hopped between the porters hauling the wounded and headed for Centurion Sisera.

"Sir. The forward element has reached Caltanissetta. Centurion Nodatus requests that you use the available Velites and begin digging a defensive ditch. As fast as you can," the skirmisher informed him. "There's something blocking our path."

After etching another mark in the sheet of bark, Alerio inquired, "What's blocking our way, Private?"

"An old Greek fort with Iberian infantry on the walls," the runner explained. "They're the reason for the trench."

Alerio paced off the layout of a ditch and organized the available light infantrymen to begin shoveling dirt. Once the process was underway, he hopped over the trench and jogged towards the front to have a look at the Greek fort.

***

Caltanissetta occupied the foothills north of the rough road. The town had a low fence surrounding a handful of stone and wood planked homes. Beyond the hamlet, the land was muddy. But not muddy from the recent rain. Dotted with domes of dried mud as if the Goddess Tellus had puked up chunks of her earth, the landscape resembled the bank of a river next to a waterfall. Washed and smoothed by consistent rain and not by a single storm. It wasn't pasture for sheep or soil rich enough for farming.

"Why settle here?" Alerio commented as he stopped beside Nodatus.

"Where there are soldiers, there will be people to take the warrior's coins," the Centurion replied. He lifted an arm and pointed a hand at a hill on the other side of Caltanissetta. "It's a truth for the ages. Build a fort and a town will grow beside it."

Alerio's eyes rose from the road ahead, up a steep hill to a stonewall. Peering over the wall were Iberian infantrymen.

"I take it that's what's blocking our path?"

"And block us it does. I'll not march light infantrymen under the spears and arrows from those heights. Or leave an enemy between the vanguard and the Legion," Nodatus explained. "No matter what Lembus or Claudius think about making twenty miles."

"We dig in and wait for our heavies?" Alerio asked.

"That we do, Centurion Sisera," the infantry officer assured him. "Send a note back with the next mounted courier. Tell headquarters the Velites have found an enemy."

"That's all?" Alerio questioned feeling the message was incomplete.

"Do you expect me to deliver a battle plan to the command staff?" Nodatus asked. "Senior Tribune Pompeius and Tribune Numitor wouldn't like me telling them how to do their job."

"But you wouldn't be. You'd be providing them with information," Alerio remarked. "It'll help them form a battle plan."

"Despite the Centurion title and political connections, you really are just a heavy infantry NCO aren't you, Sisera?" Nodatus said with a twisted smile. "Here's another truth for the ages. Stepping forward into a wall of egos is more dangerous than a shield wall. And courage in the face of adversity at headquarters will not win you a breastplate full of medals. Now go prepare the message. And Sisera…"

"Yes, Centurion."

"Keep it short and to the point."

***

Late in the day, cavalrymen trotted their mounts into the Velites camp. Riding with them was Senior Centurion Lembus.

"Nodatus. What are we facing?" the Legion's senior line officer asked as he slipped from the animal's back. "This better be a good reason to halt your march."

"A hill fort controlled by Iberian mercenaries," the Velites officer reported.

"How do you know they aren't tribesmen?" demanded Lembus. "Or even hostile?"

Nodatus spit on the ground, straightened his helmet, and squared his shoulders.

"Look around you, Senior Centurion," he challenged. "I have five dead, ten serious, and fifteen walking wounded. If the Iberian hadn't been heavies, my men would have lined the road with their graves."

"Show me," Lembus instructed. The two Centurions had reached the defensive ditch when the Senior Centurion glanced back. "Sisera, come with us."

Alerio caught up with the officers, hopped into the bottom of the trench, crossed the five-foot distance, and scrambled up the three-foot step to ground level. Once out of the defensive ditch, the three Legion officers jogged forward.

***

Smoke rose above the fort from several locations. One column in particular billowed puffs into the air. High above, the balls of black smoke blended in with the smoke from the other fires to create a single smudge against the cloudy sky.

"That's an ugly climb," Lembus declared after examining the slope. "But the walls aren't high. A couple of Centuries should have the fort by nightfall."

"There's something odd about the smoke," Alerio offered.

Lembus and Nodatus snapped their heads to the side and stared at the young staff officer.

"Is he an idea man?" Lembus questioned.

"Unfortunately, Senior Centurion, he is," Nodatus informed the senior officer. "I've tried to warn him but so far his over exuberance hasn't diminished."

Both officers spoke as if Alerio wasn't standing between them.

"But there is something," Alerio insisted. Feeling as if he needed to defend his observation, he added. "We can count the rising smoke. It will give us an idea of how many Iberian's are in the fort."

"He's not wrong, Senior Centurion," Nodatus suggested. "Do you want to tell him or should I?"

Nothing sends tremors through the ground like the jogging of heavy infantrymen. The ground shook in a steady tempo and the Senior Centurion turned to looked back at the defensive ditch.

"You tell him. I'm going to speak with the Centuries," Lembus stated. "I'll set the assault and we'll get this over with."

While the senior officer jogged away, Alerio looked at Nodatus.

"Tell me what?" Alerio asked.

"The fort is empty. Too many smoky fires would give away just what you suspected, an estimate of the number of soldiers inside. Except, the Iberian commander knows it and we know it."

"Then why all the smoke?"

"He was trying to disguise his smoke signals," Nodatus explained.

"Their Captain used smoke to warn about an approaching enemy. I can see that," Alerio commented. "But why do you think the fort is deserted?"

"If they had enough men to hold the fort, they had enough to come down and butcher five Centuries of light infantry," the Velites officer informed him. "If they don't have sufficient forces to mix it up with us, they certainly couldn't stand against our heavy infantry."

"And the assault on the fort is to assure it's empty," Alerio guessed.

"No, Centurion Sisera. We'll know if the Iberians have fled when my scouts get back from watching the trail on the other side," Nodatus assured the young officer. "The infantry assault is training for the heavies. They get bored and unruly on a march unless they have something to occupy their minds."

Alerio stood silently and watched the smoke curl into the air above the fort. Based on the exchange with the Centurion, he was beginning to realize the direct action and blunt speech of Legionaries that created success on a fortified battle line was actually a hindrance when dealing with higher command. It was a new concept he'd have to study. As he thought, a line of big infantry shields moved by him heading for the hill and the fort.

***

The marching camp came down at dawn. While the Legion struck their tents and pulled up the stakes of the palisade, Alerio and the vanguard moved smartly over the ramp. All of the work of digging the ditch and stacking the dirt behind the defensive line wouldn't go to waste. Three Legions followed and they would use the camp as they passed through the area.

At the ten-mile mark, Alerio ceased etching on the bark. It wasn't that he stopped creating the maps. It was the changed geography that required fewer notations. From peaks and gorges, the landscape broadened and the Velites spread out. Other than keeping distances along the river to the next town, cartography paled in comparison to the naked eye and memory. Periodically, he pulled out the bark, etched a distance, and drew a faraway feature.

Tension increased in the light infantrymen as they approached Castrofilippo. It sat at the mouth of a broad valley about twenty miles trek from Caltanissetta. Being a standard day's march from the last camp wasn't anything special. What was special about Castrofilippo, it rested only nine miles from Agrigento. The coastal city where the Qart Hadasht Empire housed their mercenary army.

Act 4

Chapter 14 – Food for Thought

Shortly after the silhouettes of the riders entered the valley, the Legion's early warning system snapped into action. The heavy infantrymen of the forward Century untangled from their blankets. They moved in response to the calls from their sentries whom, in turn, reacted to a spot of torch light visible at the west end of the valley.

"I better see your cōleī on the line," their NCOs shouted. "You can relieve yourselves later. Now people, get on the line."

In the haze that lay over the gray farmland, the Legionaries staggered into their two-rank deep screen. From the lines, they peered over their shields attempting to separate shapes from the land. It was next to impossible in the weak light provided by a setting moon and yet to rise sun.

"This is going to be bad," an infantryman offered in a cracking, sleepy voice.

"Why do you say that?" his squad mate asked.

"Because no one with good intentions comes calling before dawn," the Legionary replied.

A scout drove his mount into the forward position and yanked the horse to a stop.

"Fourteen riders, sir," the cavalryman reported to the Century's officer. Backlit by a campfire, the comb on the Centurion's helmet seemed to dance in the flames as the infantry officer nodded his understanding. The rider slid off his horse, saluted, and added. "We're watching the road but, so far, there are no infantry or mounted units following them."

"Get back to your command," the Legion officer ordered. He pivoted and looked at a firepit. Speaking to a Legionary squatting beside the fire, he instructed. "Only fourteen riders. Send it."

"Yes, sir," the Legionary replied. He pulled a long stick from the pit. Holding it across his chest, the signalman raised the burning end over his head, once. Then he brought the glowing ember down and repeated the up and down motion thirteen times. After duplicating the gestures and getting a return signal from the Legion camp, the signalman put the stick back in the fire and faced the officer. "Message delivered and received, Centurion."

"Very good. Optio. Stand down half the Century," the infantry officer instructed. "The men can cook breakfast but, we have riders coming our way. I want the Century dressed, awake, and ready."

"Yes, sir."

***

The duty signalman at the far east end of the valley waved back an acknowledgement to the forward element. Then he placed the torch in the brazier and moved to a ladder. Climbing only part way down from the observation platform, he jumped the last few feet, hit the ground, and sprinted through the tents of sleeping Legionaries.

In the center of the marching camp, the Legionary on platform watch reached the main road and headed for a group of large tents.

"Signal from the forward Century," he yelled to the sentries guarding the Legion's headquarters.

"Duty officer. A signalman is coming in," one of the sentries announced.

The guards from First Century stepped out of his way and the signalman ran by the sentries, across the short approach, and into the command tent of Megellus Legion East.

**

Alerio picked up an apple, studied the fruit, then placed it back in the bowl. During the march across Sicilia, he had been assigned the early morning watch. On the first few days, he'd consumed the bowls of apples and grapes left by the servants. Now, the novelty of having food on hand and being nominally in charge of a Legion no longer overcame the lack of sleep. As with any new member of a Century, he drew the lonely, last watch before dawn. Rather than the duty being exciting as a staff officer, it was just as solitary and boring as any Legion guard post.

"Duty officer. A signalman is coming in."

Facing the entrance, Centurion Sisera watched the signalman rush breathlessly into the tent.

"Sir, fourteen riders have entered the west end of the valley," the messenger informed him.

"Any mention of infantry or cavalry?"

"No, sir. The signal was basic. Just the fourteen riders."

"Message acknowledged. Return to your post," Alerio said. He walked to a corner of the tent and nudged two sleeping forms with the toe of his boot. Not knowing which one was which, he rapid fired directions to both runners. "Call up the duty Century and have them report to the main gate. And wake Senior Centurion Lembus and ask him to join me here."

The messengers jumped to their feet and rushed from the tent. Alone for a moment, Alerio strolled to the fruit bowl. Taking an apple, he polished it on the sleeve of the tunic under his armor and took a bite. There was one thing different from being a Legionary on watch along the perimeter. As a staff officer, he could change his mind and eat whenever he wanted.

***

The long morning shadows revealed the front seven riders but cloaked the second seven in shadows.

"Senior Centurion. Is there a danger from their rear rank?" Alerio inquired.

Lembus replied out of the corner of his mouth, "If there were more of them, I might worry. But considering the age of the ones out front, I believe the second rank are their acolytes."

"Yes, sir," Alerio replied.

Lembus allowed a smile to cross his face. It seemed Sisera had learned to hold his thoughts in check.

"Centurion. Get the shields up and the men upright," the Senior Centurion ordered.

An infantry officer passed on the commands. Responding, a unit of heavy infantrymen in formation at the foot of the ramp lifted their shields and braced. Behind them and in the center of the planks leading into the camp, the Century's officer, duty Centurion Sisera, Senior Centurion Lembus, and Tribune Numitor formed a line across the planks. Behind them, Colonel Gaius Claudius sat on his mount flanked by junior Tribunes and signalmen. Pompeius was not among the greeting party. The Senior Tribune and cavalry Centurion Ephoebias were staged with mounted Legionaries deeper in the camp.

Battle Commander Claudius's gold trimmed armor caught the sun's rays. A bright flash of light reflected from Claudius' breast plate and momentarily, the fourteen riders were blinded. While they flinched, the Legion staff officers on the ramp wheeled to each side creating a pathway. Gaius nudged his mount forward into the space between the officers.

"I am Colonel Gaius Claudius, Battle Commander of Megellus Legion East. Commanding by authority of Consul Postumius Megellus and the Senate. And a citizen in good standing of the Republic," the Colonel stated as he reined in his horse. "Why have you come to my camp?"

Before any of the seven old men had an opportunity to reply, two columns of Legion cavalry appeared from between tents. They reached the main road and wheeled in the direction of the ramp. As the mounted Legionaries approached, Gaius Claudius sat calmly on his horse, the Tribunes and signalmen nudged their mounts to the side, and the seven old men and the young ones behind them clustered together.

Senior Tribune Pompeius saluted Colonel Claudius from the head of one column. Then two hundred cavalrymen thundered down the ramp and rode away from the marching camp. Gaius cocked his head to the side as if two and a half Centuries of mounted men hadn't interrupted the introductions.

"You were saying?" Gaius suggested to the fourteen visitors.

"Celebrant Dosis, at your service, Colonel Gaius Claudius. I am the Assistant Administrator for the Temple of Asclepius," the old man in the center of the riders announced. He bowed his head as if humble but, his rigid posture displayed more pride than humility. Raising both arms, he splayed his hands, and offered. "My brethren to the left and right of me are priests from the other sanctuaries at Agrigento."

The ecclesiastics jerked the reigns to reform their line and reestablish their place and their dignity.

"What can I do for clerics from the Valley of Temples?" Gaius inquired.

"It's not what you can do for us," Dosis stated. "It's what we can do for you."

"An interesting proposition. I certainly don't need infantrymen or cavalrymen as you can see," Gaius exclaimed. "But your proposal intrigues me. Allow me to offer you breakfast."

***

The envoys from the seven temples sat around a table in the command tent. Behind them, their acolytes stood ready to attend to the needs of the priests. In an attempt to maintain the balance of pairings, a young nobleman was situated behind Senior Tribune Pompeius, and another hovered behind Colonel Claudius. Tribune Numitor, head of the Legion's Planning and Strategies Section, occupied the third Republic position with Alerio stationed behind him.

"In short, my honored guests," Gaius Claudius informed the Celebrants. "I will drive the Qart Hadasht General and his army from Agrigento. Then we will trade with the citizens and open the city for business."

"With our standing, by virtue of the Valley of the Temples, we can negotiate a peace settlement between the Empire and the Republic," a priest proposed.

"Peace means a status quo," Gaius pointed out. "Having any Empire forces on Sicilia is unacceptable."

"If your heart is set on war, what do you plan for us?"

"I don't understand," Claudius pleaded.

"What my neighbor is asking, what do you plan for the Temple of Asclepius, Temple of Juno, Temple of Heracles?" Dosis explained while dipping his head at the appropriate envoy. "The Temple of Zeus, Temple of Castor and Pollux, Temple of Vulcan, and the Temple of Concordia. How will our shrines be affected by your victory?"

"Thank you for assuring my success," Gaius Claudius stated. When the mouths of all seven fell open, he smiled and questioned. "Is that a reading from the Gods and Goddesses of your Temples? Or are you stroking my mentula?"

"I beg your pardon. We came here to..." Dosis began.

"You came here for self-preservation," Gaius exploded. He shot to his feet and glared at the seven old men. "After the Republic's victory. And make no mistake about it, the Legions will prevail. We will decide which Temples worked with us and which ones aided the Empire. Is that clear enough for you?"

"We understand," Dosis said while bobbing his head in a practiced stoic manner. The other six priests imitated his stately gesture. "We of course will provide the Republic with as much support as possible."

"And while I wouldn't give you assurances of safety at this time, I will provide you with morning sustenance," Gaius said. Speaking out of the side of his mouth, he instructed. "Bring out the food. If you'll forgive me priests, I must go and review my heavy infantry."

Colonel Claudius pushed back from the table and crossed to the exit.

"Centurion Sisera, on me," he directed before pushing through the tent flaps.

Alerio stepped away from Tribune Numitor and marched after the Battle Commander. From the side entrances, servants appeared carrying bread, meat, cheese, fruit, and pitchers of vino. The envoys filled plates of food while ignoring the fact their host, the camp's commanding officer, was absent.

***

"The last time we moved across a Legion camp together, sir, we were fighting off soldiers. And I was your bodyguard," Alerio reminded the Colonel. "Should I find a shield?"

"No, Centurion Sisera. That duty falls to the First Century. I wanted to remind you that not all stories should or need to be re-counted," Colonel Claudius said.

He was referring to their escape from Echetla and the climb and fall into the city's manure piles. Blessed of Sterculius, they made their way to the marching camp where many buckets of water and lumps of soap were required to clean the merda from their bodies and gear.

"Sir, I have no idea what you're referring to."

"Excellent, Centurion Sisera. Now, let's go inspect the supply wagons."

"But you told the priests that you were going to inspect the infantry."

While Alerio walked beside the Colonel, a squad from First Century moved in a loose circle around the staff officers.

"Here's a lesson about being in command," Gaius offered. "Legionaries will do anything you ask of them, except for one thing. They will fight, sacrifice their lives, hold a shield wall against superior numbers, run twenty miles and then engage the enemy for the rest of the day. Sleep in the mud and stand watch in the rain. Almost anything their officers demand of them, our Legionaries will do."

"What's the one thing they won't do, sir?"

"They will not starve for you," Gaius answered. "Our infantrymen are fine. We need to inspect the supply wagons. This entire campaign depends on procuring enough grain to feed the men. No Legion has ever dealt with a supply trail stretching back over five hundred miles to the Capital. No sacks of grain, no campaign. It's as simple as that."

"I'm honored you thought to teach me about the supply issue, sir," Alerio remarked.

"You needed to know but that's not why I called you out of that senseless meeting," Gaius informed the junior Centurion. Seeing the puzzled look on Sisera's face, he said. "You noticed the show of strength by our cavalry, my curt words, and my confident mannerisms."

"Yes, sir. It did seem odd using arrogance and might to push away potential allies," Alerio suggested. "You could have placated them with promises and maybe earned their favor."

"Priests like those from the Valley of Temples are only loyal to their gods and goddesses," Gaius assured him. "For hundreds of years, their survival has depended on bending to the reigning political force. Right now, that's the Empire."

"You think they're working with the Qart Hadasht commander?"

"I don't know but, I would bet good coins that they'll sidle up to the winner of this war. I just don't know the depth of their loyalty to the Empire," the Colonel stated. "It's the reason I asked you to join me."

"Sir, I'm not a seer. I haven't the foggiest idea what the priests are thinking."

"I need a resourceful man of courage who can get close to Agrigento and report back on the state of the mercenary army," Colonel Claudius advised. "You can't simply walk through our camp, cross the valley, stroll unnoticed to the Valley of Temples and up to the walls of Agrigento."

"Unless I was among a group of acolytes traveling with seven priests," Alerio offered.

"They could turn you over to the city militia when you reach the valley," Gaius warned.

"Yes, sir. But it will cost them their position in the temple," Alerio described. "and qualify them for a visit from my personal Goddess."

Chills ran down Gaius Claudius' spine. He knew Sisera's deity was the Goddess Nenia and that made Alerio's meaning clear. Prayers to her were offered when someone was near death and needed help freeing their soul from a dying body.

"Besides grain, tents and equipment there should be blue robes in the supplies," Gaius stated. "Let's go transform you into an acolyte."

***

Before the sun was directly overhead, fifteen riders nudged their mounts into motion and headed to the marching camp's gate. As they passed Centuries of light and heavy infantrymen waiting to go out on patrol, Centurion Nodatus looked up. He recognized one of the faces under the hood of the riders. What Centurion Sisera was doing disguised as a junior cleric, he had no idea.

"Form up people. We have miles to march before we rest," the infantry officer shouted once the priests crossed the ramp. "Patrol, standby."

Four hundred boots rose before slamming into the dirt of the main street.

"Standing by, Centurion," the infantrymen yelled.

"Patrol, forward march."

To Alerio, the commands and responses were comforting. In the heavy infantry, the enemy was on the other side of your shield. On a mission for Planning and Strategies, he was never sure of the direction or the type of enemy he faced.

The seven priests kicked their horses and the group galloped into the valley. They passed the forward Century and didn't let up until they were almost to the western end.

Dosis tossed back his hood and glanced at the location of the sun.

"Is there a ritual that needs to be performed?" Alerio inquired.

"No. The celebrant enjoys knowing the stages of the sun," an acolyte replied.

"Knowing how long until dark would be important for a follower of Asclepius," Alerio suggested. "It would help in scheduling treatment."

"Something like that," the temple student admitted.

Dosis glanced back and inquired, "Where is the patrol headed?"

"That's no secret, sir," Alerio replied. "Had we left a little later, you'd have seen them marching to the northwest."

"Your Legions are impressive," the Assistant Administrator said.

"That they are, sir," Alerio agreed.

They rode through the small village of Favara, out of the valley, up a rise, and down into the rolling hills around Agrigento.

"Legionary Sisera, come ride beside me," Dosis instructed.

Alerio kneed his horse forward.

"Take off the hood and inhale," the priest instructed. "You can smell the sea air from here."

Alerio could see the water in the distance but not the shoreline. He threw back the hood, lifted his chin, and took a deep breath.

The pain on the back of his head was sharp, blinding, and mercifully short.

Centurion Sisera rolled forward and tumbled off his horse. Landing in a heap, he lay motionless in the dirt.

"Tie him to the horse and cover him with a blanket," Dosis ordered the students. "Hurry. I don't want him to be seen and us to be caught out in the open."

Chapter 15 – Grain, Fruit, and Witlessness

Two miles northwest of the Legion camp at Castrofilippo, Centurion Nodatus guided his horse down the embankment, urged the animal across the stream and up the far side. Behind the infantry officer, two Centuries of Velites splashed across, followed by three Centuries of heavy infantrymen.

When the last squad splashed across, a junior Tribune galloped up from the rear.

"All units have safely crossed, Centurion," the young nobleman reported.

"Thank you, Hypati," patrol commander Nodatus said complimenting the Tribune.

He raised his right arm and jerked his hand, indicating the right side. One of the skirmisher Centuries jogged out to provide flank security. The patrol commander then signaled to the left and the second light infantry Century broke away and went to cover the left side. Remaining on the center path, the heavy infantrymen, with their large shields and heftier armor, marched in the wagon tracks on the dirt road.

Once the patrol had spread out in a moving defensive formation, the Centurion glanced back. His other young Tribune rode with the infantry officer from the Thirty-third Century.

"Tribune Hypati. Please ride back and tell Tribune Rotensus that his job is to keep the flanking units in touch with me," Nodatus advised. "I know what's going on with the Thirty-third. I can see them, which makes his report from there redundant."

"Right away, Centurion," the Tribune responded.

He drew back on the reigns, kneed his horse about, and trotted back to speak with the other staff officer.

***

The gates at Agrigento swung open and Major Sucro appeared. Behind the mounted Iberian officer, columns of heavy infantrymen followed.

Celebrant Dosis saw the gates move and, in response, kicked his horse in the ribs. The animal leaped forward, forcing the Assistant Administrator to clamp his arms around his mount's neck. He wasn't alone in the display of poor horsemanship. The other six priests also held on tightly. Fear drove them. Fear they would be caught on the wrong side of the long columns of Iberian infantrymen.

The fifteen horses of the priests and students crossed the road leading to the city just ahead of the mounted Iberian officer. Once on the Street of the Gods at the Valley of Temples, they separated. Each celebrant and his follower trotted to their temple. Dosis and his student pulled up at the entrance to the Temple of Asclepius.

"After the mercenaries pass, take the Legionary to General Gisco," the priest instructed. "Assure him we are part of the Empire. And the gift of this intelligence agent is a sign of good faith from the Valley of Temples."

On the main road, the eight hundred strong Iberian force had passed through the city gates. Behind them, two hundred Northern Celt irregulars marched in loose formations. When the last Celt reached the gates, Major Sucro gently angled the columns off the road, taking a northeasterly heading. He was in no rush. His eight Companies of infantrymen only had to cover five and one quarter miles to reach the abandoned farming community.

***

Up on a rise to the left, one of the Veles squads began jumping up and down and waving their arms. Seeing the commotion, Centurion Nodatus turned to his Tribunes.

"I'm going to see what they're excited about," the infantry officer instructed. "You two ride to either side and watch for an ambush."

"Centurion. If the squad sighted an enemy formation, I don't think they'd be dancing on the top of a hill," Rotensus suggested.

"Tribune Rotensus, I don't care if there are dancing girls on the other side of that hill," Nodatus scolded. "Here's a truth for the ages. If you find something entertaining in the countryside, it's a trap. And you'll pay either with your coin purse or your life. Now spread out and mind your lines of approach."

While Rotensus and Hypati rode to either side, Nodatus kicked his mount and the horse raced up the hill. He reined back near a rock formation at the top. Seeing the patrol leader approach, the exuberant squad settled but each Legionary had a smile on his face.

"Have you been over sampling your rations of vino?" the Centurion demanded as he approached the eight amused light infantrymen. "Can you explain your…I don't even know what to call your actions?"

"Centurion. From what we've seen, the Qart Hadasht rounded up the farmers and took them into the city," the squad leader replied. "All of the fields we've passed have been harvested and the orchards picked clean."

"True. They obviously didn't want to leave anything for us," Nodatus acknowledged. "What does that have to do with the antics of your squad?"

"Because, sir, they forgot one," the Lance Corporal beamed. "From the top of the rocks, you can see fields of wheat, fat citrus dangling from limbs, and almond and walnut trees with their branches bending under the load. In short, sir, we can feed the Legion for weeks with what's down there."

Nodatus raised an arm and circled it above his head. The squad leaders, NCOs, and Centurion Tremulum from the Eighth Velites began converging on the hilltop. While he waited for them to arrive, the infantry officer allowed a smile to touch his lips and a twinkle to gleam in his eyes.

The infantry officer from the Thirty-third Century was dispatched to ride back to the Legion camp and fetch wagons. Besides searching for enemy forts or camps, the secondary purpose of the patrol was to discover and secure grain. Amazingly, they had just located a variety of foods, literally available by simply plucking them from trees and harvesting the grain from the field. Once the Centurion rode off, Nodatus waved the patrol into motion. They flowed down the hill heading for the stocked and ripe farming community.

***

Widely dispersed squads occupied strategic areas. From these spots, they could react to any threat. While those Legionaries remained armed, the rest of the infantrymen stripped down, stacked their shields, javelins, helmets, and armor, and began cutting wheat, shaking nuts from trees, and picking fruit. Soon the abundance exceeded the gathering and Nodatus was forced to draft more of the security force into hauling and sorting the bounty.

"We only have three horses," the Centurion remarked to Tribunes Hypati and Rotensus. "Divide and ride the perimeter, if you see anything suspicious, give the alarm."

The young noblemen split apart and began to circle the farming community from opposite directions. Nodatus halved the distance and guided his horse into the grain field. He would check the edge at the back then return to continue directing the harvesting operations. By then the Tribunes would pass each other in the same place, assuring the boundary was secure.

Forcing his horse into the field, Nodatus felt tall stalks, heavy with kernels, slap against his legs. He imagined the ripe husks cracking and the grains splattering to the ground as if fat rain drops. For a moment, something tickled his mind but, it passed when he reached the center of the golden field.

One hundred and ten of the First Light and Thirty-third Century moved in a line through the wheat field. A few looked up and acknowledged the Centurion before returning to singing and cutting. The cutters tossed handfuls of stalks back and another twenty-five Legionaries scooped up the stalks and deposited the wheat plants in wagons. Unfortunately, the farmers had left no draft animals, so another ten of his men were occupied with pulling the collection wagons. In the distance, he observed twenty Legionaries at the thrashing and bagging station. A thin unit of fifteen infantrymen stood guard near the Centuries' stacks of shields, armor, and weapons.

Again, something poked at his mind. Thinking it was the unsettling fact they might run out of daylight before harvesting all of the food, the infantry officer nudged his horse forward. He didn't want to spend the night in the open guarding wagons of provisions. In the best situation, the Centuries would finish picking, the wagons would arrive, and they would get the grain back to the Legion. In the bad, they would be stuck in the open overnight, set up around the odd shape of parked transports and draft horses. The elusive idea fluttered away as Nodatus crossed the field.

***

While Centurion Nodatus walked his mount through the tall stalks, Tribune Rotensus began circling his half of the community. At the end of an orchard, he reached up and plucked a yellow orange. Although bitter, the tart citrus puckered his mouth and he smiled. It was so good, he picked another.

In order to savor the second orange, he dismounted and took off his helmet. An infantryman pulling a cart filled to overflowing with oranges called to him.

"It's a good day, sir."

"That it is," Rotensus agreed.

He took a nibble and let the juice run down his chin. To wash away the bitter, he lifted a wineskin off his shoulder and took a drink. Looking around at the trees, he realized how much he missed the orchards at his father's estate. After tying his horse to a tree trunk, the junior Tribune strolled into the grove enjoying the smells and daydreaming of home.

***

Twenty Celt irregulars raced from a distant hill, hit the flat, and sprinted to the main column of Iberian infantry. Major Sucro signaled for the Companies to halt.

"Major. There are about four hundred Legionaries at the farm," one of the Northern barbarians announced. "Most are unarmored and harvesting the crops."

"Excellent. We'll kill them all and take the grain and fruit back to the city," Sucro replied. Pointing at a young officer, he instructed. "Captain Júcar. Two of your Companies have the honor of drawing first blood."

"I am blessed to be the first to spill the blood of my enemy," Júcar declared.

"Find my advance unit a way onto the farming community," Major Sucro ordered the Celtic scouts. "I want us in their midst before our blades taste their blood."

134

"We've identified the best approach," the irregular soldier promised. "We'll file into the wheat field from the corner of the orange grove."

Chapter 16 – Blood on the Golden Stalks

Centurion Nodatus gazed at the adjacent field. Behind him, the golden stalks rustled in the afternoon breeze. To his front, the stubs left after the farmers harvested the grain didn't move. Only a little dust stirred in the light gust crossing the barren field. On the far side of the cultivated acreage, hills rose, and he saw no movement other than a few birds in flight. They didn't seem agitated which was a good sign. Turning his horse, the infantry officer walked the animal through the brush separating the fields. With the unharvested field stretching out before him, he stopped and took a moment to study the operation.

The tops of Legionaries' bare heads bobbed into view along the line of wheat cutters. As if a puppet show, one appeared above the tall stalks than vanished as another further away popped into view. The men had only managed to cut half the field but, they were making progress. Further back, the squads working the thrashing racks and bagging the grain were miniaturized by distance. Pleased with the harvesting, Nodatus nudged his horse forward into the wheat stalks.

At the corner of the field, dark shapes moved among the stalks as if fish below the surface of a pond. Unattended farms always left openings for wild animals. Absent farmers, birds feasted on the grain and fruit without molestation from rock slinging workers. Wild pigs dug up roots ruining unguarded garden plots. Herds of nebrodi deer nourished on everything if left unchecked. So far, Centurion Nodatus hadn't seen many animals other than birds. It's why the movement in the corner of the wheat field near the orange grove didn't alarm him. Assuming a few boars were wandering below the stalks, he decided to frighten them off. One of his Legionaries could be gouged by tusks if the sounder of swine came into contact with the line of cutters. Not likely but, to be safe, he guided the horse towards the orange orchard intending to run off the wild pigs.

From shadows seemly moving below the husks, the closer the infantry officer rode to the edge of the field, the more he realized the shapes weren't low to the ground under the stalks. Nebrodi, he reasoned as he approached. Had he known the invading animals were deer, he would have ignored them.

Then the idea that had evaded him earlier crept to the edge of his mind...

Thrown by the Iberian infantryman from his knees, the spear impacted a couple of fingers distance below the neck of the Centurion's breast plate. Had the steel head struck from a level throw or even from a descending arch, the armor would have dented and stopped the tip. But the low angle and power behind the launch allowed the steel point to crease a groove in the armor before rising to meet flesh. The spear tip entered Nodatus' neck, cut the tendons, sliced the muscles, and finally, pierced the infantry officer's brain.

Centurion Nodatus never grasped the elusive thought.

Tribune Hypati allowed his horse to nibble the grass growing on the edge of the nut grove. Below the trees, Legionaries from the Twenty-second Century and the Eighth Velites spread out goatskin sheets. Once positioned, they used sticks to shake the branches. Laughing like children caught in a summer downpour, the infantrymen stood in the storm of falling almonds. When the last almond fell, they gathered the edges of the sheet, carried it to a cart, and dumped the harvested nuts. Then they walked to the next tree.

"It's a good day, Tribune," one of the Legionaries offered.

He was covered in dust, pollen, leaves, and almond shells. But he grinned from ear to ear.

"Better than dancing girls?" Hypati teased.

"It's a close second, sir."

The Private looked as happy as if he and his mates were attending a performance of beautiful dancing girls. Imagine, dancing girls in the countryside, Hypati pondered. Then he jerked his horse's head away from the grass, straightened and stretched his back while looking around.

Centurion Nodatus' warning echoed through his mind, "Here's a truth for the ages. If you find something entertaining in the countryside, it's a trap. And you'll pay either with your coin purse or your life."

"How many carts of almonds have you collected?" Hypati demanded.

"Five, Tribune," a Lance Corporal answered.

"That's enough. Find your Centurions, arm up, and rally at the thrashing racks."

"But, sir. There are fifty more trees we can shake," a Legionary protested.

"Here's a truth for the ages. I don't care if there is a beckoning dryad behind every tree trunk and the almonds are made of gold," the Tribune shouted. "Collect your gear and move to the racks."

The Legionaries dropped the sheet and began walking towards their equipment.

"What's with the Tribune?" one asked.

"Something spooked him," another offered. "Or he doesn't like almonds."

"What do you think Nodatus will have to say about the staff puke interrupting the harvest?"

"I don't know. Does the Centurion like almonds?"

"You have to admit the Tribune has the makings of an infantry officer," the Lance Corporal suggested.

"How do you figure?"

"Beckoning Dryads, golden nuts, and truth for the ages," the squad leader replied while reaching for his armor. "He seems to have the language down, if not the tactics."

While the Centuries assigned to the almond grove geared up, Hypati kicked his horse and sent it charging in the most direct route to the wheat field. Cutting through the next grove, the junior Tribune slowed.

"Gear up. Rally at the thrashing racks," he shouted while momentarily reining in his mount. Then it was heels to flanks and he cried as he dashed off. "Rally up."

The Legionaries picking ripe walnuts off the ground looked at the staff officer. They hadn't witnessed the Tribune go from mellow to manic. Assuming he was passing on orders, they ran for their armor and weapons.

"You heard the order. Strap it on and move it out," Centurion Sirpeum advised.

By then, Hypati was through the walnut trees and galloping around a brick building heading for the racks and grain bagging station. As he rode, his thoughts spun, and he tried to calm his nerves. He needed to be precise when explaining to Centurion Nodatus why he was sounding the alarm without any evidence.

***

Hypati rounded the building, straightened the path of his mare, and followed a low stonewall towards the thrashing racks. While the wall was constructed to keep animals away from the grain storage building, it was also used as a wagon and cart yard. In this case, a young infantry officer sitting on the wall spoke with an Optio. The Tribune spotted them and jerked the reigns.

"Where's Centurion Nodatus," Hypati shouted while dragging the horse's head around, forcing the animal to tightly cut the corner.

Both men looked up into the flushed faced of the staff officer.

"The last time I saw him, he was riding the field," Centurions Tremulum from the Eighth Velites answered.

Both Legionaries pointed at the line of cutters as if the staff officer didn't know the direction to the wheat field. Hypati scanned the waving grain searching for Nodatus. It took a few moments to locate the senior officer's horse.

It stood nibbling on wheat with no sign of the senior Centurion.

"I see his ride but not Nodatus," Hypati remarked.

The Legion NCO hopped up on the wall and peered around the Tribune's mount. Before anyone could question anything, four armed squads of skirmishers raced into view.

"Orders, Optio?" a Tesserarius inquired.

"Where did you come from," their Sergeant responded. "And why are you here?"

"The walnut grove," the NCO replied. "Where's the fight?"

"I don't know of..."

Hypati interrupted the Optio and instructed, "Form a screen in front of the thrasher racks."

"Sir?" the Corporal requested of his officer.

"Form up as directed. We'll get this sorted out later," the infantry officer said. "Now look here Hypati..."

Then the Centurion laughed at the positioning of the Tribune and the Optio. By standing on the wall, the NCO resembled a short brother who needed a ladder to reprimand a taller sibling. Then four squads of heavy infantrymen jogged from the other side of the building.

"What are you doing here?" Tremulum asked after stifling the laughter.

"Tribune Hypati ordered us to stop harvesting almonds and report here," a Tesserarius answered. "Where do you want us, sir?"

The officer from the light infantry grinned at Hypati and begged, "Where do you suggest I place the squads, Tribune?"

140

"Join up with the Velites at the thrasher racks," Hypati said while twisting to point at the thirty-two light infantrymen just setting their line.

From the elevated height of horseback and from standing on the wall, the Legion staff officer and NCO had a clear view of the sea of wheat over the thrashing racks and bagging station. The golden stalks rippled in the breeze, then the rows parted and men carrying big shields and short steel swords rose up and stood momentarily among the grain.

No roar of battle rage or angry cries accompanied the strange soldiers. They raced silently through the field, heading on an angle to intercept the unarmored and unaware wheat cutters.

"Push the screen out, Centurion," Hypati ordered in a deep commanding voice that surprised the young Tribune. "Out passed the stacked weapons. Give the cutters a safe refuge."

To his surprise, the infantry officer was off the wall, yelling for the squads to follow, and sprinting to keep up with his Legionaries. He didn't think of challenging the junior staff officer's commands.

Hypati kicked the mare into motion and gave her a heading to the racks.

"Where's the patrol's signalman?" he asked while using the horse to wade into the crowd gathered around the grain separation screens. "I need you to sound the assembly."

"But Tribune, the trumpet is behind the wall where it's safe," the Private complained. "Do you want me to go and get it?"

The separating and bagging area rested on low ground. None of the Legionaries working the stations were able to see what was developing out in the field.

"Where is an Optio?" Hypati demanded.

All of the Legionaries at the racks and bagging station were caked in dust from separating the grains from the shafts. He couldn't tell old from young let alone Private from Sergeant.

"Optio Dionigi. Thirty-third Century, sir. What can I do for you?"

"Get the trumpeter on the wall and have him sound the alarm," Hypati instructed by pointing at the brick building. "Take these Legionaries with you and create a fallback position at the wall."

"Will you be in command there, Tribune?"

"No. I'm going to see about saving some of our wheat cutters."

***

Captain Júcar was of two minds about the situation. There was no doubt the Latian officer had to die. He caught the Iberian advance element sneaking through the wheat. It was just that Júcar hated things to be out of his control. And with one spear throw, his plan of attack collapsed. On the other hand, the infantry soldier had performed a near silent kill with the spear. There was nobility to be found in such an accomplishment.

Still on his hands and knees, the Captain slapped the shoulder of each man who crawled by.

"Go. Go," he urged the next infantryman.

"That horse is sticking out like a tall sheep in a herd of short goats," warned the commander of one of the Captain's Companies. "It can only be ignored for so long."

"What do you suggest?"

"Stand up and fight, Captain," the Lieutenant urged. "before they realize we're here and start organizing."

"Then we will fight," Júcar professed. "Pass the word Lieutenant. We go on the attack at the count of one hundred. Ninety-nine, ninety-eight…"

The Lieutenant rolled away and grabbed two NCOs.

"Ninety-seven, ninety-six," he whispered to the Sergeants. In turn, one crawled forward still counting and the other moved to the rear with the same count on his lips. The Lieutenant from the second Company received the count and passed it along to his NCOs.

There was a rush of soldiers moving up as the Iberians positioned themselves for the attack. At the count of two, one hundred Iberian soldiers stood up, scanned, and located the enemy troops cutting stalks. At the count of one, they began jogging towards the unarmored Legionaries.

***

Tribune Hypati rode out of the thrashing area, topped the rise, and his stomach revolted. Bent low, the Qart Hadasht mercenaries moved as swiftly as wolves with the intensity and focus of a hungry pack. He raced by the still organizing Legion defensive formation and began shouting while nearing the wheat cutters.

"Retreat, retreat. Enemy sighted," he screamed.

There had been no trumpet alert, or calls from the NCOs, to abandon the wheat harvest. Curiosity at the actions of the junior staff officer more than fear caused several Legionaries to look up from the cutting.

The Iberians angled in from the side. Leaning down, the Legionary on the end of the row of cutters was unaware of the danger until he bounced off a shield. Stumbling to his right, he collided with the next man. Both died as two Iberians came on-line, stabbed them with their short swords, and charged over the bodies. Drops slung from the falling and rising blades speckled the golden wheat with red blood.

A third Iberian caught up and he slammed into the third Legionary from the end. As with his squad mates, the Latian was sliced and stomped by the growing line of soldiers.

Resembling a wave breaking along the shoreline, Captain Júcar's first Company began forming into a seemly unstoppable wall of shields and swords. Two more Legionaries were thrown down by the Iberians. They also died in the dirt under the husks of grain. By then, a few Legion infantrymen noticed the growing row of enemy shields. They shouted warnings and raced for their equipment. But not enough Legionaries understood the danger, they continued to sing and cut stalks.

The junior Tribune intended to ride behind the cutters warning them as he passed. But the speed of the enemy's advance threatened to cut off the Legion infantrymen from their war gear. Without their armor and shields, they were at the mercy of the Iberians. Hypati drew his gladius and jerked the mare's head to the front. After she was head-on to the side of the Iberian shields, he kicked her hard in the ribs. The mount and the Legion staff officer surged forward, driving towards the heavy infantrymen.

***

Centurion Labrum, the second most senior infantry officer in the patrol, strolled from the lemon grove to the orange orchard. The first thing he noticed was the Tribune's mount tied to a tree. The second thing to catch his eye was a glimpse of soldiers moving beyond the citrus trees.

"Optio Tagacis. Gather the Century and gear up," he advised. "We have company."

His second in command didn't reply. Rather, the Sergeant ran and grabbed the shoulders of his Tesserarius and a Decanus. After a few words of instructions, the Corporal and squad leader ran to spread the warning order. Only then did the Optio reply to his officer.

"Rally location, sir?"

"The thrashing racks," Labrum ordered. "We'll see what Nodatus has in mind. Send someone to find the squads from the Eighth and get them moving."

"Yes, sir."

The two squads that stood sentry formed a sixteen-man wall to protect the rest of the squads. Once all of the heavy infantrymen of the Twelfth Century were ready, Centurion Labrum led them away from the orchards. Optio Tagacis took a position in the center and the Tesserarius brought up the rear to be sure all of the Legionaries remained with the Century. Nobody noticed the pair of eyes watching from high up in an orange tree.

Labrum picked up his pace when the trumpet blared the assembly call. Then he was around the brick building and saw the signalman standing on the stonewall. Beyond him and out in the wheat field, the infantry officer took in the double line of enemy shields. One file sprinted behind the Legion cutters, closing off the rear and preventing the Legionaries from reaching the defensive screen of thirty-two. Unbalanced and not close enough to engage the enemy, the wall was formed by a mixture of light and heavy infantrymen.

It appeared hopeless and the veteran line officer debated whether to join the infantrymen on the wall or take his Century and reinforce the sixty-four Legionaries standing out in the open.

Then, young Hypati charged in from the other side of the field. His sword swiped downward but glanced off a shield. It wasn't that the Iberian was an expert with the shield. The cause of the weak strike was the junior Tribune guiding and fighting the mare. While the mount wanted to veer away from the armed men, Hypati held her head tight and drove her into the row of enemy infantrymen.

The staff officer swung again but his blade was deflected by an enemy sword. Another Iberian sliced vertically under Hypati's armor. He rolled back with the reins wrapped around his hand. The motion caused the mare to rear back as well. Between her rider's erratic behavior and the men shouting and slashing at her, the normally even-tempered animal became a war horse. She kicked, charged, bit, and slammed her chest forward. Her disruption halted the Iberian advance. Hypati and the mare went down but not before creating an opening in the overlapping Iberian lines.

Veteran infantry officer Labrum judged the distance and the situation. He snapped his head around and shouted at Tagacis.

"I'm taking five squads up," he informed the Optio. "Take the other five and secure that wall. Make sure I have somewhere to go when we come back."

"Yes, sir. You'll have a home," Tagacis assured him. Then to the Century the Optio ordered. "First five squads on the Centurion. The rest of you follow me."

Taking advantage of the momentary gap in the Iberian lines created by Hypati's sacrifice, twenty cutters raced through. They sprinted by the Legion defensive screen and stopped at their gear. With hands shaking from anger, they strapped on their armor swearing vengeance the entire time. Then a commotion rose from behind the twenty partially armed Legionaries.

Forty veteran infantrymen and an experienced officer ran by and linked up with the original sixty-four. The twenty men who escaped the Iberian trap ran up and joined the screen. Many of them were still settling helmets on their heads and shields on their arms.

"Standby to move up and engage," Labrum bellowed.

He didn't have the luxury of letting the newly arrived Legionaries finish dressing. There were eighty-six men trapped in the wheat field on the far side of the mercenaries' lines. And the Iberians were breaking off units to hunt the unarmored Legionaries.

"Standing by, Centurion," the one hundred and twenty-five Legionaries responded.

In an instant, the defensive screen changed. No longer a stationary defensive formation, it transformed into a Legion battle line.

Chapter 17 – Battle at the Farming Community

"Draw," Labrum commanded. Gladii scrapped as the blades came free from sheaths. Then he directed. "Pivot right."

Repeating the infantry officer's order, the Legionaries swung their formation until they faced the nearest line of Iberians.

"Forward. Keep your shields tight," the infantry officer warned. "Velites. Pull back and guard our flanks. Do not let them turn our corners."

Locked in beside each other, the Legion heavy infantrymen stomped the ground as they closed with the enemy. The wheat cutters, who made it to their weapons, shields, and armor, screamed for mercenary blood. When the Legionaries clashed with the first Iberian Company, they had numerical superiority.

"Advance, advance," Labrum shouted to be heard over the war cries of the combatants.

The big Legion shields shot forward, slammed into the opposing shields rocking Captain Júcar's men. Then before they recovered, the shields withdrew and the steel tips of seventy-two gladii struck. Because the Iberians were trained to keep their shields tight, only three fell from stab wounds. On the next advance, two more crumbled from the lightening quick Legion thrusts.

Watching the efficiency of the Latians and the growing number of his injured, the Lieutenant compressed his line, doubling up and hardening the center of his fighting rows. His Captain also saw the men fall, and he made a decision.

"Lieutenant. Get your infantrymen into that fight," Júcar directed the commander of the second Company.

The Iberian infantrymen swung off their line of advancement and sprinted to join their comrades in the battle. While the movement ended the Legionaries' numerical superiority, it opened a path for the trapped Legion wheat cutters. The eighty-six ran directly for their shields and armor. None even considered escaping for the safety of the wall.

Now all Centurion Labrum had to do was extract his Legionaries from a shield against shield confrontation.

"Step back," the infantry officer commanded. "Step back, back."

***

Optio Tagacis stood on the waist high stonewall. Although tempted, he resisted the urge to watch the fight in the wheat field. Instead, the veteran NCO directed the removal of wagons, carts, and stored items from the area surrounded by the stonewall. Legionaries pushed all but one wagon out of the yard. The last one was flipped on its side, the axle and wheels removed, and the bed shoved into the opening, replacing the flimsy gate.

The wall occupied three sides and provided an obstacle for an attacking force. The brick building protected their rear. To keep it secured, he assigned a squad of skirmishers to watch for anyone demolishing the walls and attempting to attack through the storage structure.

Tagacis didn't expect to be in the wagon yard too long. Once Centurion Labrum arrived, he expected the patrol to go on the offense. The purpose for clearing the space was to create a medical treatment area. It was a good plan until squads from the Eighth Century of light infantry came from the direction of the nut groves. They were carrying seven wounded. Shortly after, the backs of the Twenty-second Century shuffled into view. Stepping to the rear, the heavy infantrymen maintained a line of shields holding back Iberian infantry while protecting Legionaries supporting their injured.

The Optio turned and looked across the distance studying the battle in the wheat field. He had at first thought those Iberians were the extent of the enemy forces. Obviously, he was wrong.

"Signalman. Sound the retreat," he instructed the trumpeter. Then to his Corporal, he ordered. "Take five squads out. Bring Centurion Labrum and our men home."

"I'm on it," the veteran Tesserarius assured him.

The Corporal jogged to where the five squad leaders from the Twelfth Century stood talking. While he passed on the orders, Optio Tagacis jumped down and began placing Legionaries around the stonewall. What had been an emergency treatment area for the wounded was now the patrol's main defensive position. Or it would be, once all the Legionaries reached it.

***

Tagacis vaulted the stone barrier and raced for Centurion Sirpeum. Behind him, the wall was defended by a mixture of heavy and light infantry shields.

"Sir, Nodatus is missing. Labrum and Tremulum are managing the fight on the open ground," the Optio reported. "Orders, sir?"

"Tagacis, you're a veteran of more battles than I've been alive for," the infantry officer said. "You want an order? Get my wounded to safety so the Twenty-second can concentrate on killing those cūlī. I trust you've organized the defense?"

"It's secure, sir," the NCO informed the officer. Waving at the fortification, the Optio directed a dozen men to come out and carry the wounded away. Once they were clear, Tagacis leaned in so only the infantry officer could hear him. "It'll take half your men to hold this line if they were behind the fence, Centurion. And that would free up the other half to keep a lane open for Centurion Labrum's units."

Sirpeum laughed and nodded his head in amusement. The veteran NCO had managed to correct the infantry officer's thinking and get what he wanted, without overstepping his rank.

"Excellent idea. I'll take five squads…" the officer began.

Optio Tagacis stepped in front of the officer and shouted for Sirpeum's Sergeant.

"Laurentius. Give me your Tesserarius and five squads at the front," Tagacis bellowed. "Centurion Sirpeum is assuming command of the Legion fortification."

The second line of the Twenty-second Century peeled away and raced to the corner of the partition. They formed a line and positioned their shields effectively extending that wing of the stonework far beyond the structure. Men from the Eighth skirmishers jumped the stones and ran to create a second rank.

"Get behind the barrier, sir," Laurentius directed as he moved in behind the shields.

"But I want to stay with the men, Optio," Sirpeum protested.

"I understand. But trust me, sir," his Sergeant promised, "We will be there shortly."

To walk away from a fight seemed cowardly. He about faced and began marching to the wall. Centurion Sirpeum felt as if all the eyes of the men inside the waist high structure were judging him. Then from behind, he heard his Optio order three advances.

The tightly packed Iberian soldiers in front of the single line of Legionaries made the advances ineffective. At the stone structure, Sirpeum paused to look back at his squads. They hammered their shields forward but there was no gap to gather momentum. A useless maneuvering of shields as was the jabbing with the gladii. The steel tips did no more than poke the solid row of Iberian shields. One curious thing, while the Legionaries were doing the drills, Optio Laurentius ran down the line leaning over each Legionary's shoulder before moving onto the next man.

After the third advances produced no changed. The shields remained locked in a face-to-face shoving match.

Then Laurentius centered himself behind the line, cupped his hands around his mouth, and shouted.

"Knee," the Optio screamed.

The forty infantrymen of the Twenty-second Century did nothing for a count of five. Then all of the Legionaries took a half step back and dropped down onto one knee.

Centurion Sirpeum's jaw dropped. With the awkward position of their feet and legs, his men were in danger of being trampled. A cry of warning and frustration boiled up from his gut, but it never reached his throat.

***

The advances worked as Optio Laurentius had hoped. While there was little room for movement, the changing pressure of the Legion shields and the love taps with the gladii caused the Iberians to stiffen their line and lean forward. Pushed from behind, when his Legionaries dropped to their knees, the first rank and a few from the second row of mercenaries fell forward.

Individually, the Legionaries tipped their shields back, catching, and throwing the soldiers behind them.

"Throw one and go," each infantryman screamed as he rolled to the rear and tumbled over the dazed Iberians.

Coming up on their feet, the forty men of the Twenty-second Century raced for the barrier. Behind them, the second and a few from the third row of Iberians faltered. Trying not to step on or get tangled up with their own men, the careful footwork delayed their pursuit of the Legionaries.

Centurion Sirpeum suddenly realized he stood in a bad location. Forty Legionaries and an Optio bore down on him. Misjudging the speed and intensity of his infantrymen, the infantry officer put a foot up on the wall and started to climb.

The first Legionary slammed into the officer and the infantryman holding the shield powered himself and his Centurion over the partition. Sailing above the stones in twos and threes, the forty infantrymen soared through the air, crashed to the ground, and lay there taking a survey to see if they made it off the battle line alive.

"Get it up," cried Optio Laurentius as he came unsteadily to his feet. "This isn't over yet my fleet footed warriors. Get your flying mentulas up and on the stone fence."

By the time the Iberians sorted themselves out, shields extended the height of the waist high fortification and it bristled with javelin shafts. Heavy infantry now manned the Legion's defensive position. If the Iberians wanted Legion lives, they would have to come in and take them. But it wouldn't be easy.

***

Centurion Labrum grabbed Tremulum and pulled the light infantry officer to his side.

"We are going to break off," he informed Tremulum. "What I want is a leapfrog maneuver. Take six squads, fall back, and set up the first hop."

"Is that enough to hold a line?" the skirmisher officer asked.

It was a valid question. Forty-eight men wouldn't create a very large backup position.

"It'll have to be," Labrum replied. "Our Legionaries are exhausted. That's all I can spare off this line. But if we don't move now, we never will."

Tremulum jogged to his Optio.

"Synodus. Count out six squads," the infantry officer informed him. "On my command, sprint them back. We're disengaging."

"About time, sir," Synodus stated.

The NCO went to different areas of the fighting line and selected squads. The object was to remove men from the battle without weakening any one area.

Tremulum held up five fingers. He curled one back, "One." When his hand formed a fist, the Velites officer called, 'Five'. Then he turned and ran. Twenty paces later, he spun and held his arms out level with his shoulders. Standing in that pose, he watched as men pulled back, turned, and ran at him. He counted forty-eight away before the first one reached him.

"Form up on me. On me."

Once the squads arrived, Tremulum looked from side to side. Stretching to his right and left was a third of the available Legionaries. Still on the original battle line, were the other hundred infantrymen.

Disengaging from a battle line fight was difficult. Turning your back to the enemy meant death. Stepping back repeatedly resulted in heavy casualties due to missteps and exhaustion. That left only shove and run. Hopefully, the men arrived at a safe zone before the enemy fell on them from behind. In essence, it was a planned, organized rout.

Tremulum couldn't hear the command, but he witnessed the shove as the one hundred and five Legionaries pushed the Iberian's back. Then, the infantrymen ran.

"Brace," the skirmisher officer commanded the men on either side of him. "Stay strong and give them a moment to catch their breath."

If you have time, Tremulum thought. Once the Iberians realized the Legionaries were attempting to break off, they ran after the infantrymen. Three slow Latians fell to sword strokes from faster enemy soldiers. But the rest sprinted to the new battle line.

One by one, they reached the row of Legionaries, reversed course, and stepped into the combat line.

"We lost three," Tremulum reported to Labrum. "They were good men."

"Maybe so," the heavy infantry officer replied. "But they had one problem."

"What's that?"

"They were slow. Ready to do it again?"

"You should lead this hop," Tremulum offered. He glanced back to judge the distance then turned to the front. "Or not."

"Thinking better of it, are you?" Labrum inquired. He thought the light infantry officer wanted out of the shield wall fight. "I don't blame you."

"Either one or none of us can go," Tremulum stated. "The hop line is already set. But they do appear cynical."

Labrum glanced back to see his Tesserarius and Legionaries from five of his squads leaning on their shields looking bored. All his embattled men needed to do was reach that line and forty fresh gladii would join the fight.

"They do seem jaded," Labrum suggested. "Let's give them something to do. Break off nine squads and take them twenty paces behind my Corporal's line."

***

Eight hops later, Labrum, Tremulum and their Legionaries passed through squads from the Twenty-second and the Eighth Centuries. Once the isolated units were within the Legion lines, the defending Centuries pulled back. At the barrier, they hopped over, and other Legionaries pushed their shields up, closing off access.

The wagon storage yard absorbed all the living Legionaries. As formidable as the position was and as much as they were thankful to the Goddess Minerva for providing the walls, the officers had one regret. Too many of their men and fellow officers were lying dead in the dirt outside the stone fortification.

"Set up a rotation," Labrum ordered. "I want every man fed and rested for when the Iberians try to breach our defensives."

"Do you think they'll try?" Sirpeum inquired.

"Centurion. As sure as the Goddess Nenia has had a busy afternoon," the senior officer assured him. "From the looks of the dirt under your armor and in your helmet, the Goddess of death wasn't the only one who had a busy afternoon. Go get something to eat and sit for a spell."

Sirpeum wanted to tell Labrum about being launched over the stone partition. But it was a good story and better shared over mugs of vino with a group of officers. The Centurion went to check on the wounded and on the Legionaries from his Century. Once that was accomplished, he planned to eat and rest. Hopefully, the

Iberians would hold off long enough for him to finish the tasks.

Chapter 18 - Bleed for the Wall

There were many situations hated by military men. Among them were tangling with a wasp's nest in a bivouac after a long day in the field, digging snakes out of a pile of rocks when an NCO ordered a structure built and, having to navigate an obstruction before finally getting to fight an enemy.

The stone abutment and shields equaled a difficult enough obstacle. Add to that, behind every shield stood a Legionary more deadly than a venomous snake. And, there was the abundance of small iron tips flying and poking the air. If the iron javelin head penetrated a shield, it bent, and the shaft became weighed down and awkward to hold. The lucky Iberians fled to the rear to break the shafts free from their shields. The unlucky ones were carried to the rear where the medics pulled the javelins free of their flesh.

On the other side of the stone wall, the Centurions rotated their Legionaries to keep fresh arms and legs at the forefront of the fight.

"I've been watching their injury rate," Sirpeum offered.

"Are you a medical officer now?" Labrum questioned.

"No. But if the Iberian surgeon charges for each stitch, he's fast becoming rich," explained the infantry officer. "I think they need an excuse to withdraw and head home."

"It's your idea. Do you want to deliver the message?"

"The Twenty-second Century will go over the fence," Sirpeum advised. "I'll let the Eighth do the chucking."

"Tagacis. Gather enough javelins for six rounds and stack them at the barricade wall," the senior infantry officer instructed his Optio.

"One hundred and sixty javelins will leave the other walls short, sir," the NCO advised.

"It will. But, if we don't do something, the Iberians will come over the barriers. It'll be belly to belly gladius work anyway," Labrum replied.

***

The Iberian commander and his two Captains sat on their horses. Not far away, their infantrymen surrounded and assaulted the Legionaries from three sides.

"We have a superior number of infantry and a tactical advantage," Sucro said in frustration. "Why won't they come out from behind those ramparts and do battle?"

"I believe, sir, the answer rests in your question," Captain Júcar suggested. "Unfortunately, the cowardly Latians are bleeding us mightily from behind the bulwarks. Pardon my brash observations, Major."

"Speak freely, Captain. There seems to be something on your mind."

"The Iberian infantry fears no enemy in an open field confrontation," Júcar proclaimed. "What is beneath our reputation is digging Latians out of their hole."

"And you propose, Captain?"

"We return to Agrigento and prepare for the next engagement with the Legion," Júcar stated. "If that meets your approval, Major?"

"An interesting plan," Sucro admitted. "However, there is a reason I am in command of this expedition. Right, Kese?"

Like Júcar, Captain Kese also commanded four Companies of Iberian infantrymen. But he was junior to Júcar and from a less wealthy family. His station required him to avoid making suggestions to the senior officer and simply wait to agree with the Major. That being as it was, Kese's Companies were taking excessive casualties while pressing the attack along the west wall. In his mind, he concurred with Júcar. Returning to Agrigento was an excellent idea.

"Without a doubt, Major," the junior Captain acknowledged.

"I've been helping Kese on the west barrier. I had the Companies wait until we massed before having a go at the wall," Sucro bragged. "We've pummeled the Legionaries into near submission. Now, Captain Júcar, is not the time to abandon the assault. Rather, it's time to press our advantage. Precisely there, at the west partition."

In response to the Major's announcement, a facial muscle twitched in the junior Captain's cheek. Lifting a hand to his face, Kese concealed the nervous tick.

***

Behind the west barrier, the surviving members of the Veles Century stood to the rear of the battling Twenty-second. While the heavy infantry defended the abutment, the skirmishers waited for commands.

"Eighth Velites, standby," Tremulum called the light infantrymen to order.

160

The infantry officer's familiar voice cut through the sounds of grunting and clashing from the battle. In case it didn't, Optio Synodus and the Century's Tesserarius repeated the cry.

"Centurion, standing by," the fifty remaining skirmishers answered.

Thirty-five of them grasped a javelin in each hand. Interspersed between them, fifteen others, plus the NCOs, held five more of the Legion stabbing and throwing weapons.

Standing in front of the Velites was a rank of heavy infantrymen.

"Twenty-second Century, back them off," Sirpeum ordered.

At the words from their officer, the sixty remaining heavy infantrymen of the Century raised their shields. When the top of the wall reached the bottom quarter of the shields, the Legionaries smacked the Iberians. As if they used a mallet, the Legionaries hammered their shields into the tops of the helmets and the shields of the mercenaries.

The Iberians across the barrier staggered from the unexpected thrashing. Then the sixty Legionaries from the Twenty-second stepped back, separated, and drew their gladii.

The thirty-five light infantrymen stepped forward into the gap between the heavies and jumped up on the stone structure. From the heights, they chucked javelins down into the massed Iberians. When both were thrown, they reached back, grabbed another, and flung that one.

After launching one hundred and five javelins, they crouched. Then the thirty-five skirmishers uncoiled, stretched for the sky, and leaped backward off the wall.

Ducking under the soaring Velites, the heavy infantrymen used a three-step approach before hurdling the stone barrier. Bleeding, confused, and trying to remove their dead and wounded, the front two ranks of the Iberians were in no shape to deal with sixty charging Legionaries.

Shields hit and drove back the unprepared soldiers, creating an opening in front of the stone fortification.

"Brace," Sirpeum screamed.

The sixty heavy infantrymen locked their shields and paused. For two heartbeats, while the infantry officer hopped the west barrier, the battle halted. Men crying out in pain, whimpering, or calling for their mothers rose above the clash of shields and weapons from other sectors of the fighting.

"Advance," Sirpeum ordered as his feet hit the ground. "Advance. Advance."

The lull, in front of the west divider, ended with the grunts of sixty Legionaries powering their shields forward. Pulling back the shields, sixty coordinated gladii tips shot forward and found Iberian flesh. As devastating as the first, the second advance dropped more soldiers to the ground. Where the injured fell, they were stomped during the third advance.

Enhancing the Legionaries ground attack, the Eighth Velites remounted the stone partition and resumed raining javelins down on the mass of soldiers.

"Fall back," Sirpeum instructed.

This time he ran and vaulted the stone unassisted. When the heavy infantrymen reached the wall, the skirmishers jumped away, clearing the top. While the Legionaries withdrew by hurdling the barrier, the senior Centurion grabbed Sirpeum and pulled him off to the side where Tremulum waited.

"Message sent," Labrum commented to the two Centurions. "Think it was received in the spirit it was sent?"

The three infantry officers couldn't hear the screaming from the other side of the stone fortification and far behind the Iberian ranks. If they could have listened in, they'd know the reaction to their brutal memorandum.

***

"Captain Kese. Your infantry has failed me," Major Sucro yelled. "You will discipline your Lieutenants when we get back to Agrigento."

"Major. There is only one of my Lieutenants still alive," Kese began to explain. "The other three fell…"

"Yes, yes, take that into consideration when devising the punishment," Sucro blustered. Then the Major declared. "We've beaten the Latians. In an orderly manner, begin the withdrawal. Captain Júcar. Your Companies will cover our rear."

"It'll be my honor, Major," Júcar professed.

Kese kneed his mount towards his men at the west wall. After reining in, he ordered his NCOs to pull the soldiers back. His remaining Lieutenant was closer to the barrier helping to organize the defense while the wounded were removed.

"It was an ugly fight," a veteran Sergeant stated to his Captain. "If we hadn't delayed, we could have breached that tiny partition."

"But we did pause, and we didn't," Kese replied. "Back us out of this quagmire. I want shields up while we move. I'll not lose another man to those javelins."

"And if the Legionaries come out after us?"

"They will be the responsibility of Captain Júcar's Companies," Kese responded. "Our fight for today is over."

**

"Well, Centurion Sirpeum, I believe the Iberians have had enough of your Twenty-second Century," Labrum complimented the heavy infantry officer. "You call it. Do we let them go? Or climb the barrier and drop a few more Iberians?"

Sirpeum glanced around the perimeter of the stone wall. Everywhere his eyes fell he saw wounded and dead Legionaries.

"This soil has been blessed in blood enough for one afternoon," he replied. "I think we'll let them go."

The Centurions allowed the Iberians to retreat without interference. In the calm following the battle, the injured groaned and the severely wounded bled through their bandages. Other Legionaries gave in to the Goddess Nenia and allowed their souls to slip from their ruined bodies.

Centurion Labrum walked among the Centuries offering compliments or comfort, whichever was required. On his second pass, a figure came from around the building. The infantry officer stopped and watched.

"Report, Centurion," Tribune Rotensus demanded.

"Where have you been, Tribune?" the veteran Centurion questioned.

"I was cut off and couldn't make it to the defensive position," the staff officer replied.

"I can see that," Labrum acknowledged. He reached out and picked a twig with two leaves from an orange tree off the Tribune's head. The infantry officer tossed the twig aside and added. "I'm sure you had it rough, Tribune."

Act 5

Chapter 19 – Point of Impact

"What have you got there?" a rough voice inquired.

A section of the horse blanket lifted, and sunlight touched Alerio's cheek. As he had done since the devotee led his horse from the Valley of Temples, the Legionary maintained the façade of being unconscious. Just as the corner of the material fell, Centurion Sisera partially opened an eye and caught a glimpse of a busy portal.

Merchants, craftsmen, and tradesmen passed through the gate, some leaving and others arriving. Figuring he was at the entrance to Agrigento, Alerio relaxed and focused on keeping his breathing slow and steady. Held in his hands were the ends of the rope Dosis' people had used to bind his wrists.

"This, my good man, is a Republic spy. Assistant Administrator Dosis at the Temple of Asclepius captured him," the temple's student announced. "Being a good citizen, my Master sent me to deliver the spy to General Hannibal Gisco."

"A spy, is he?" the rough voice growled. "Maybe I should kill him and post his head on the gate. It'll serve as a warning to others trying to infiltrate Agrigento."

The sound of a blade sliding out of a sheath caused Alerio to perk up. He had come this far; it would be a shame to have to run away or even die before gathering information about the city and the enemy forces.

"Sergeant. I am sure the General will allow you to behead the agent. And support your plan to post his head above your gateway as a cautionary sign," the apprentice priest advised. "Both are fine ideas and, no doubt, come from your blessed heart. However, you might want to think of the intelligence General Gisco can extract from the Latian. You have to admit, it's difficult to question a dead man."

"When you put it like that, how can I argue," the guard admitted. "What temple are you from?"

"The God Asclepius watches over all men while they are negotiating to keep them in good health," the devotee said. "A healthy body makes for an astute mind."

"So, you and me were, I mean, I was negotiating with a priest of Asclepius?" the militia man gushed.

"When you put it that way, how can I argue," the acolyte said. "You have a knack for deliberating. Perhaps you might consider becoming a diplomat, Sergeant of the Guard."

"Who me? Oh, no, no. I'm a simple soldier," the NCO chuckled. "Get on with you mission priest. Yo, Corporal, the priest thinks I should be a diplomat."

"Does he know how quickly you draw your sword when you get frustrated?" a voice farther away questioned.

"The display of strength is also a bargaining maneuver," the student priest uttered while jerking the horses into motion.

Under the blanket, Alerio relaxed and allowed the apprentice from the Valley of Temples to guide the Legion spy into Agrigento. Behind them, he heard the rough voice speak then fade into the noise of the street.

"See there Corporal. A blade is a diplomatic tool," the Sergeant commented. "Don't laugh. The God Asclepius, himself, recognizes the tactic. I told you not to…"

***

People closed in on either side of the horses. Due to the swell of people coming in from the countryside, the student priest was forced to shout for people to stand aside. The second time he did, Alerio dropped the ropes and slid off the horse.

"Make way. I am on business for the God Asclepius," the apprentice priest advised. "The God appreciates…"

Something pressed against his sandaled foot. Looking down, for a heartbeat, he couldn't place the acolyte in the blue robe walking beside his horse. Then it dawned on him, and his eyes shifted to the horse behind him. The blanket rested across the horse's back with no protuberance or bumps outlining an unconscious Republic spy.

"It's too crowded, brother," Alerio said while gathering a fist full of the novice's robe. "We should walk like humble folks."

A jerk pulled the apprentice off his mount and into Alerio's arms. Freeing up one arm, the Legion staff officer balled up a fist and pounded the student in his side. On the first punch, the pain of a broken rib took the novice's breath away and doubled him over. The second punch connected with his jaw and the future priest collapsed over Alerio's arm.

"Excuse me, where can I find an inn?" Alerio inquired. He looked at several faces of the people passing by. "My fellow apprentice requires a place to rest."

"Two streets down and on the left," a man replied.

"See how nice people are when you ask kindly," Alerio said to the comatose apprentice. "You don't have to go around clubbing people in the head. And when you do, you'd best be sure the knots you tie them up with are tight."

Alerio took his time walking the apprentice through the crowd. He watched ahead for just the correct item. When he spotted it, he shoved the novice out front supporting the barely conscious man by sticking both arms under the student's arms.

"Donations for the temple," Alerio said while hiding his head in the back of the student priest's neck. His arms emerging from under the armpits appeared to belong to the disciple.

It should have been apparent and would have been on a deserted street or in an empty room. But on the crowded thoroughfare, with people jostling the parties involved, it wasn't obvious.

Alerio leaned the novice forward, extended his reach from under the armpit, and snatched a gold neck chain from around the throat of a man dressed in a robe of rich fabric. Then the Legionary ducked into the crowd and moved, bent over so his head was below the level of the people on the street. Tossing the novice over his shoulder, Centurion Sisera broke into a jog.

Fortunately for the assaulted party, the man in the blue robe pushed people aside as he fled, allowing the man to give chase while shouting for the city militia. The thief, dressed as a student from the Valley of Temples, ran into the alleyway beside an inn. By then, two militia men joined the victim. They broke free of the crowd and sprinted down the lane in pursuit.

"There he is," the wealthy man bellowed. "and there's my chain."

The three stopped and stared down at the thief. Stretched out half over a low fence behind the inn, it appeared the robber had tripped and knocked himself silly. Proof of his crime was the gold neck chain clutched in his fist.

"We know how to handle impostors in this city," one of the city guards boasted.

"And we know how to protect the temples," the other added. "We'll strip him of that robe and toss him naked into a dark holding cell."

A block away, Alerio pulled the blue robe off and shoved it into a rain barrel. After a moment to soak and sink the fabric, the Legion spy rolled down the sleeves of his woolen trousers and shirt. Then he reached down to the inside of his left leg and unwound a piece of black silk. Once free, he pulled the Ally of the Golden Valley dagger from the leg. As he walked away, the Centurion reached under the shirt and wrapped the silk around his waist.

***

The masses of people on the streets didn't thin as Alerio dodged and snuck through gaps between groups. They ambled while he rushed. It wasn't that he was being chased or hunted. The reason for haste was his need for information. While he knew where to get it, he did not have an exact location. The tight crush of human bodies continued and even worsened in the middle of the city. Until he reached the center of Agrigento, the flow of carts and pedestrians was in the direction he walked. Then movement changed into a gentle whirlpool as people circled and looked for places to settle. On the back side of the swirling multitudes, he bobbed and weaved, heading against the flow of traffic.

Elbows and forearms came into play the closer he got to the warehouse district. Forcing a path through the farmers and tradesmen newly arrived from surrounding towns and villages, Alerio moved upstream. Then Fortūna smiled on him. Or maybe it wasn't his good fortune but Nemesis sending an arrogant thief to the Legion officer for punishment.

It was only a light touch. In a crowd as packed together as the one on the street, a victim shouldn't have noticed the brush of a hand against fabric. But the woolen workman's cloth had been washed repeatedly in ocean water. The soft material flexed, and Centurion Sisera felt the fingers move around his waist seeking his coin purse.

Alerio seized the offending wrist and jerked the thief around, so they were face to face. A second hand gripped the front of the thief's shirt to keep him from fleeing. Beside watching the shifty eyes set in the narrow face, Alerio judged the tension in the man's body.

"Don't. Just don't," Alerio warned when the pickpocket flexed and reached for a knife strapped to his side.

Without releasing the shirt front, Alerio snapped his elbow up and knocked the thief in the jaw.

"Don't do that again."

Ignoring the advice, the street thug reached for the hilt. Using leverage on the captured wrist, Alerio yanked the man's shoulder and shirt, throwing him to the side. In full swing, the thief collided with and collapsed around Alerio's knee. But he didn't go to the ground.

"You keep that up and you'll get hurt," Alerio scolded. Rolling his fist, he gathered more material of the street thug's shirt and pulled the man in close.

"Let me go, Latian. I haven't done anything."

A distant memory in the form of words from the veteran Centurion and Optio who trained Alerio came to mind.

'In a screen, keep the enemy to the front. As long as you can feel the Legionaries on either side of you, you're fine. But in an urban environment, when you face an enemy, be aware of the one behind you. He is moving in with the goal of sticking a blade between your ribs.'

"Now see here," the thief offered in a friendly manner. "Maybe we can work something out?"

The pickpocket's tone was cordial, and his body relaxed. For anyone taking note, the two men appeared to be friends who stopped to chat. An inconvenient place but there was nothing unusual about the distance between them considering the crowded street.

Then the thief's eyes shifted to peer briefly over Alerio's right shoulder. A fleeting glance, not much more than a flicker but, it was enough to alert the Legionary.

"This should have been bloodless," Alerio complained. "One, two, three…"

"What are you counting?" the man demanded.

"Four, five," the Legion officer stated. Then the thief's eyes shifted again. Only this time, they were raised as if looking at something or somebody close by. Alerio shook the man so hard his head rocked back and forth on his neck. "Six."

Dizzy from the violent shaking, the thief barely registered the Latian's hand reaching for the knife at his side. Or the twirl that spun the robber around and into the path of his accomplice. He was bent backwards then pulled upright. The only sensation to break through the swirling confusion was a warm, wet dampness on the back of his neck.

Alerio had wrenched the man hard, jerked the knife free of its sheath, and rotated the cutpurse around. The second thug was just bending forward. He was into the last step before sinking the blade into Alerio's back. Leaning forward, the Legion weapons instructor shot an upper cut at the underside of the second thug's jaw.

It would have been a powerful punch worthy of any boxer participating in Apollo's sport. But the addition of the knife blade emerging from Alerio's fist, turned the upper cut from a punch into a point of impact kill. Blood spewed on the back of the pickpocket's neck before his cohort fell to the street.

"This should have been easy," Alerio grumbled while dragging the thief through the crowd and away from the body. "All I wanted was some information. And now this."

They reached the side of the road and Alerio pulled the man into a space between buildings.

"The brickwork in Agrigento isn't as good as we have in the Capital," Alerio commented. He cleaned the thief's knife with big strokes on the front of the man's shirt. The motion and exaggerated gestures brought the blade up and close to the thief's eyes. He quivered and went limp. That's when the Legion officer asked. "How do you want it?"

"Kill me quickly," the pickpocket replied while squeezing his eyes closed. "Goddess Algea spare me."

"Causing you pain wasn't what I had in mind," Alerio explained. "I was speaking of the coins I'm going to pay you."

"You're going to pay me?"

"Yes. A silver coin or, if that's too difficult for you to exchange, I'll make it several copper coins," Alerio stated. "Answer one question. Then forget you ever saw me. However, before you answer, know that the next time I see you, you will die begging for the Goddess Nenia to free you from Algea's blessing."

The thief eyes popped open, and he stared into Alerio's face.

"I've never seen you before," he announced. "What's the question?"

***

Two blocks before the northwest gate, Alerio stood at the corner of an intersection and watched the city's militia. They inspected all the carts, wagons, and bundles entering Agrigento. At first, he thought they were looking for weapons. But the motive became clear after a few moments of observation. From every exposed stash of food, the soldiers extracted a portion. No doubt calling it a tax, the confiscated bread, dried meat, grain, and fresh fruit ended up in carts. Once one was full, militiamen rolled the cart away.

Alerio took the side street and spotted his destination at the end of the block. As with most, the compound sat away from the surrounding commercial structures with a wall that would make any Villa owner proud. Amazingly enough, despite the chaos caused by the influx of people into the city, the gates stood propped open. As he approached, the Legion staff officer could see into the courtyard. Parked in the center of the yard were two half-filled wagons and in the shade of the main building, two teams of horses stood waiting.

"You could wait until we are gone before moving in," a man slight of build said.

Alerio reached back and pulled the Golden Valley dagger from under the black silk wrap.

"I'm not moving in," Alerio proclaimed while extending his hand and the dagger. "You could call this a friendly visit."

"Ah, I see," the man acknowledged. He took the dagger and ran his hands over the hilt. "Welcome to Agrigento, Corporal Sisera. Unfortunately, we can only offer information and treatment to an Ally of the Golden Valley. Sanctuary is beyond our means at the moment."

A closer look at the wagon beds revealed they were filled with personal belongings and not trade goods.

"Are you going somewhere?"

"I am Asphodel, the manager of this Golden Valley trading house," the man offered. He turned and waved a hand in the direction of the roof before strolling towards a doorway. "Come inside and I'll explain."

Two sections of roof tiles lifted and Alerio caught a glimpse of a pair of loaded crossbows. The Golden Valley assassins might be leaving but, they hadn't allowed their guard to drop.

***

There were few items on the shelves in the office or on Asphodel's desk.

"You might want to update the markings on the hilt. I've been promoted to Centurion," Alerio corrected. "And I won't be needing a place to stay. A little information is all I require."

The trading house manager directed Alerio to a chair. Then he pulled a small throwing knife from a fold in his robe.

"Congratulations on the promotion, Centurion Sisera," he said as he plucked at the hilt of Alerio's dagger with the tip of the knife. "What can the Golden Valley do for you?"

"Let's start with why you're packing," Alerio suggested while indicating the empty office. "Then tell me the troop strength of the mercenaries in Agrigento and I'll be on my way."

Asphodel placed the dagger on the desk and spun the weapon. While it twirled, he folded his arms. Both hands vanished under the sleeves of his robe. Anticipating a test of skills, Alerio adjusted to the edge of the seat and braced.

Throwing knifes appeared from inside the robe and Asphodel flicked both wrists. From a full spin, Alerio's dagger stopped. Blades on either side of the hilt held it still. But while the dagger was motionless, Alerio wasn't.

The Legion officer dove from the chair, somersaulted across the floor, and came up with his hands in an unarmed defensive position. His back firmly against a

176

wall and his right shoulder guarded by the sideboard of a stack of shelves. Without a gladius or the dagger, it was the best defense he could offer.

"Very good. Most people would have gone for the weapon," Asphodel reported. In his hands were two more knives. "Or made an attempt to reach the door."

"You have me at a disadvantage," Alerio admitted. "The dagger is the only blade I have until I get to the Valley of Temples. I wasn't about to leave it."

"Stand down," Asphodel called out. A sliding trapdoor above the entrance opened and a young man dropped from the ceiling.

"He is backed into a corner and defenseless," the apprentice assassin boasted. "I could easily kill the Legionary."

A smile crossed Asphodel's face before it faded.

"Centurion Sisera. Please finish your move and show us your hand," the manager of the Golden Valley trading house requested.

Nodding his understanding, Alerio lifted a leg, snapped kicked around the sideboard and unseated the bottom piece of shelving. The hardwood flipped into the air and Alerio caught it before stepping back against the wall. Then he lifted his left hand. A sharp piece of iron from a broken coat hook protruded from between his fingers. The rest of the hook remained nailed to the sideboard of a shelf.

"Your easy prey has a shield and a weapon," Asphodel lectured his student. "I showed him a threat and he reacted. It was your decision to guard the exit. At this point you should have withdrawn and formulated a new attack plan. Now, get back to loading the wagons while Centurion Sisera and I talk."

As much as the apprentice assassin attempted to hide it, his disappointment at being surprised by an Ally of the Golden Valley hurt his pride. Alerio tossed a salute at him before retaking his seat.

"The young think they know it all," Asphodel continued. "General Hannibal Gisco is normally in charge of Agrigento. I say that because the General's history is battles against tribes in open field confrontations. All my reports tell me he has never defended a city under siege."

"The Legions aren't planning on a siege," Alerio assured him. "The mercenaries will meet us, and we'll annihilate them."

"If they come out and fight," the representative of the Golden Valley remarked. "The General has ordered every civilian from the surrounding towns and farms to come into the city walls. As they enter, he has the militia collecting and stockpiling food."

"The storehouses must be almost full."

"They are. Except Gisco has thirteen thousand Iberian heavy infantry, eight thousand Celt irregulars, and five thousand militiamen to feed," Asphodel explained while listing the Qart Hadasht merchantry forces. "Add to that, the farmers, craftsmen and the residents of the city, and the General has to feed well over fifty thousand people. Less three."

"Less three?"

"My assistant, my apprentice, and me," Asphodel described. "In a few weeks, there won't be any honest trade or commerce in Agrigento. I'm closing the trading house until either the Republic claims victory, or the Empire solidifies its hold on the region."

"Do you have a preference?" Alerio inquired.

"Not really. The Golden Valley does not involve itself in politics."

"I have a final question," Alerio stated. "Could you use another assistant? Just as far as the Valley of Temples."

Chapter 20 – Teacher

Consul/General Postumius Megellus rode into the marching camp at the head of his Northern Legion. Waiting at the gate, Gaius Claudius, Battle Commander for the General's Eastern Legion, saluted from the back of his horse.

"Gaius. What's the situation?" the General asked.

"Sir. The head of Planning and Strategies has prepared maps and a briefing for you and your staff," Colonel Claudius replied.

"Excellent," Megellus declared. "I'll get with you and Zenonis later. We'll go over our tactics."

The General, his staff of Tribunes, and elements of the Eastern Legion's First Century trotted across the ramp and into the camp. While most of those accompanying the General left, a horseman followed by two squads of veteran Legionaries hesitated. He turned his mount and walked to the Battle Commander.

"Colonel Claudius. I don't need a map or a Tribune to tell me something is bothering you," the man in the gold trimmed armor pointed out.

"Colonel Zenonis. Don't you want to attend the official briefing?" Gaius Claudius asked the Battle Commander for the other Legion.

"I don't need a bunch of stuffy, self-important Tribunes to give me a puppet show," Zenonis replied. "Tell me why the long face?"

"The only activity from the Qart Hadasht commander in Agrigento was a trap," Claudius reported. "It hurt us but didn't diminish the Legion's fighting ability."

"I've arrived and now we're two Legions strong," Zenonis stated. "What am I missing?"

"The twenty thousand infantrymen and artillery men from Syracuse," Claudius reported. "And the promised fifteen thousand light infantry from our Sicilia allies haven't reached us."

"Are you afraid we'll be defeated before Consul Vitulus' Legions and our allies arrive?"

"No. I don't fear defeat," Gaius Claudius exclaimed. "I'm worried the Qart Hadasht commander, and his mercenaries will dig in behind the city walls and turn this campaign into a long siege."

"Even if it does, they can't hold out forever," Zenonis commented.

"Holding out works both ways," Claudius described. "Look around. The land has been stripped. We're five hundred miles from the Capital, one hundred thirty from Republic soil, and the Empire controls the sea."

Battle Commander Zenonis from Megellus Legion North peered around at the cleared landscape beyond the camp's picket stakes. Then he swallowed and dropped his chin letting his eyes settle on Gaius.

"Colonel Claudius. I think our supply Centurions had best put their heads together and begin stockpiling food," Zenonis suggested. "No doubt, the commander in Agrigento has already started."

***

At sunrise, three separate entities moved. A reinforced vanguard left the Legion marching camp at Castrofilippo, a segment of the Iberian and Celt mercenaries began a march, and Asphodel snapped the reins setting his small caravan into motion.

Alerio didn't know about the Legions' advance unit. They were far to the southeast beyond the city walls and across a wide valley. In Agrigento, on the opposite side of the city, the two wagons rolled from the Golden Valley Trading House. A few blocks later as Asphodel guided the wagons to the main artery, Centurion Sisera became aware of the movement of the Iberians and Celts.

"Master Asphodel. Sorry to hold you up," a city guardsman announced while stepping in front of the horses. "There's troop movement as you can see. We're ordered to keep traffic out of their way."

Glancing over the head of the militiaman, Alerio saw Iberians marching on the thoroughfare. Spears, swords, armor, shields, and helmets filed by. After a long while, the rows changed, and the light infantry Celts replaced the heavy infantrymen.

"Shouldn't be long now," the guardsman advised.

Asphodel nodded at the assertion then shifted and stared at Alerio.

Feeling the assassin's eyes boring into him, the Legionary asked, "What?"

"Don't you find their direction of march interesting?" Asphodel questioned. "And where are their supply wagons?"

Before Alerio could respond, the militiaman stepped to the side, and the manager for the trading house snapped the reins. The wagons rolled onto the main road, turned, and followed the soldiers through the north gate.

***

The reinforced vanguard located a creek with a spring, moved downstream from the fresh water source, and began driving stakes into the soil. Across a flat area, skirting the edge of the Valley of Temples and up a rising road, the southern gate of Agrigento stood vigil over the Legion engineers.

"So that's Agrigento," a Tesserarius commented to his Optio. "We've seen it. Can we go home now?"

Together, the Century NCOs paced along a section between engineering sticks.

"Very funny," the Sergeant offered. He gazed up at the heights. "I'd guess it's about three and a half miles away?"

"It'll seem closer if the gates open and begin spewing Iberian soldiers," the Corporal remarked.

"We'll handle that if it comes to it. Until we have to fight, we get to dig," the Optio proclaimed. "Call the Century over. Stage two squads as sentries and get the rest digging."

Almost as a lure for the Qart Hadasht commander, the Legion engineers traveled with five Centuries of heavy infantry and two skirmisher Centuries for protection. Five hundred and sixty Legionaries discouraged a lightly armed response.

However, the isolated Legion detachment was vulnerable, almost inviting a major response from the mercenaries. The size of the vanguard, by designed, begged the Iberians and Celts to come out from behind their walls.

The Centuries assigned to the engineers dug the first line of the defensive ditch and watched for an attack. A mile away and out of sight at the town of Favara, four hundred and fifty cavalrymen waited. General Megellus staged the mounted Legionaries there not to battle with a force coming from Agrigento. They were positioned at the edge of the valley to act as a screen to secure the engineering detachment's retreat. In the hills west of Favara were sixteen hundred Legionaries, the real responders. The twenty Centuries of heavy infantrymen lounged in the woods eating cold rations, complaining, and waiting to counter the Empire's mercenaries. The rest of the four thousand heavy infantrymen of the two Legions were armored and standing by in the marching camp.

Unfortunately, the gates never opened, and no soldiers came out to defend their territory. That meant, all day the bait Centuries sweated, chopped roots, and shoveled dirt to the inside of the ditch.

"Sir. I thought the Qart Hadasht forces would come out and throw us off their land," the Optio suggested.

"Truthfully, Sergeant, so did the Tribunes from Planning and Strategies," the Centurion admitted. "We'll dig until midafternoon. Then we'll march back to camp. There is one benefit."

"What's that, sir?"

"Our Centuries will be excused from work details for a few days."

"That's a benefit, sir," the Option assured the infantry officer. "I'll pass the word. It'll help motivate our squads."

***

"You do realize, Centurion Sisera, the temples have their own security," Asphodel warned.

"I've encountered temple bullyboys before," Alerio commented.

"This, my friend, is the Valley of Temples," the manager of the Golden Valley trading house added. "A place visited by the ultra-wealthy, the very poor, from Kings to paupers and all social classes in between."

The wagons bounced on the road bricks as the caravan descended from the city. On both sides were commercial buildings, conveniently situated to service visiting worshipers.

"I'm aware of the economics of temples," Alerio said. Then he thought about the times he donated to the Goddess Nenia at her Temple. The sums were but the shrine was in Rome under the protection of the city's militia. Here, on the coats of Sicilia, the shrines existed outside the city and rested only a mile from the shoreline. Each temple was a prime target for pirates or rogue fleets. After reassessing, Alerio asked. "How proficient are the temple guards?"

"An excellent question," Asphodel complimented. "At each temple, Hoplites patrol throughout the day and night. A pair at each temple with the remaining sixty-eight in their barracks available as a quick reaction force."

"You're saying, I can't just walk into the Temple of Asclepius and demand my gladii and Legion knife back," Alerio informed the assassin. "What do you suggest?"

"The Dulce Pugno prefer night maneuvers," Asphodel informed the Legionary. "Myself, I've found that just before dawn presents an excellent opportunity to complete a contract."

"If it's good enough for the Sweet Fist, it works for me," Alerio professed. "Any ideas where I should spend the day?"

"We will camp on the shoreline while waiting for transport," Asphodel offered. "You are welcome to join us, if you'll work with my apprentice."

"I promise not to hurt him."

There was a crinkling of the goatskin cover as someone walked over the wagon's load. In three steps, the student stood behind Alerio and Asphodel.

"What can a common soldier teach me?" he bragged.

"Sisera?" Asphodel commented.

"Definitely, and I won't hurt him," Alerio said.

Neither man gave the apprentice the satisfaction of looking back. Asphodel kept his eyes on the horses and the road while pointing at the Iberians. Alerio watched as the columns of mercenaries turn north on a coastal road. The Legion officer couldn't understand Asphodel's emphasis on the direction of march by the Qart Hadasht forces. They appeared to be leaving Agrigento.

***

The assistant from the trading house went to speak with captains from the merchant ships that dared beach at Agrigento. With war looming, the transports were few, desperate for any trade, and anxious. The first priority, find a vessel going to Syracuse. Then, locate one that wouldn't sink during the voyage.

While the assistant trader sought transportation, Alerio, Asphodel and the apprentice, Orestes, erected a tall, open sided tent.

"What's the best approach to the Temple of Asclepius," Alerio asked.

"You'll work for your answers," Asphodel responded. "Show my apprentice what it means to face a Legionary."

"I don't need any help from an infantryman," Orestes blurted out. "We were taught that soldiers fighting in a screens meant they had suffered too many blows to the head."

"He is opinionated, isn't he," Alerio commented.

"I am standing right here, Latian," challenged Orestes. "Pull your blade. I'll silence my teacher and install some respect for a Dulce Pugno."

"Young one, I have enormous respect for the Sweet Fist," Alerio said while drawing the Golden Valley dagger. With the hilt in his hand, he rubbed the crescent shaped scar on the top of his head. "You'll notice this knife wound. It was installed by a pair of brash, baby assassins. They marked me, I killed them."

Orestes pulled his knife and sneered, "I am no baby. I will cut you badly."

"Hold," Asphodel commanded. He sat at the edge of the tent and looked up at the Legionary. "Sisera, this is taking a serious tone. Are you alright with this sort of confrontation?"

186

Alerio walked over to the assassin and held out the ally of the Golden Valley dagger.

"If you'll indulge me," he said while offering the dagger. "Swap this for a standard blade."

From under his robe, Asphodel produced two different knives. He held them on the palms of his hands. Alerio selected one and replaced it with his dagger.

The Golden Valley manager and the apprentice expected Alerio to assume a guard stance. Instead, the Legionary flipped the knife, caught it by the blade, and threw it at the apprentice's feet.

"Pick it up," Alerio ordered.

"I have my own," Orestes insisted while holding up his blade. Reaching down, he snatched the knife from the ground and held it up. "I don't need another one."

"But you do," Alerio said softly. "As a matter of…"

Orestes turned his head slightly, attempting to hear the Latian's words. Alerio leaped across the space, used the sides of his hands to part the apprentice's arms. Taking advantage of the opening, Alerio head butted the young man. Staggering back, Orestes ducked to the side to avoid a punch. But no fist or elbow came at him.

Alerio shuffled forward and leaned in as the young man straightened. The Legionary's hands found and settled lightly against Orestes' wrists.

The apprentice assassin smiled at the close contact. Rotating his fists, he brought one blade high and stabbed low with the other. But the Legionary's hands moved, mirroring the motions, and redirecting the knives. In frustration, Orestes set one foot and kicked out with the other. Before the leg straightened and connected, Alerio's leg snapped across and drove into the side of Orestes' knee. The youth flinched at the pain and began to withdraw the leg.

Alerio lowered his knee by stepping forward and hooking Orestes' stabilizing leg. Both hands drove the knife wrists outward while the Legion weapons instructor again snapped his forehead into Orestes' face. There was a wet crunch, and the dazed apprentice sank to the ground.

"He has promise," Alerio remarked while snatching the knives from Orestes' hands. "But he has an exasperation issue."

"You mean his attitude is vexing?" Asphodel guessed.

"No. He is aggressive, well trained, and calm under stress," Alerio responded. "But there is something he is trying to prove. Or a goal he is rushing towards."

"His destiny is to be a Dulce Pugno, a defender of the Golden Valley," Asphodel stated.

As an ally of the sect, Alerio was familiar with the deadly services provided by the valley's trading houses. It was the reputation of the assassins known as Sweet Fists that caused fear and kept their enemies from acting against the valley and the individual trading compounds.

"I don't know all the workings of your society," Alerio explained. "But I know when a Legionary is looking too far into the future. Your young Sweet Fist has his eyes on a distant prize."

"Orestes. Is this true?" Asphodel inquired.

The youth crawled to his knees with his head lowered. Raising his chin, he displayed bruised cheeks and a red nose. Dried blood streaked his face.

"I will be a Dulce Pugno first, Master," Orestes proclaimed.

"First? What comes second?"

"I have an ambition for the future," Orestes informed his mentor. While he spoke to Asphodel, his eyes stared at the Legion officer. "The Dáskalos is correct."

"Dáskalos?" Alerio asked. He walked to Asphodel and dropped both knives at the man's feet. "I'll have my dagger back."

"It means teacher or instructor," Asphodel informed the Centurion. He extended the Ally of the Golden Valley dagger. "Your talent is etched prominently on the blade."

"Every time I visit a trading house, the manager tests me and uses the results to lecture their apprentice," Alerio exclaimed. "I assumed all allies were treated the same."

"Few visitors meet the apprentices. Even less see them," Asphodel said. "You, Centurion Sisera, are different."

"Dáskalos. Thank you for sparing my life," Orestes grunted while climbing to his feet. "And for the lesson. What fighting style did you employ?"

"It's called sticky hands," Alerio replied. "The trip and head butt are simply street brawling."

"It's very effective, Master," the apprentice said using an honorific and bestowing a high status on the Legion officer.

"The training session is complete," Asphodel declared. "Orestes, explain this future you envision?"

"As ordered, I trained by covertly observing the workings of the temples," the youth informed his teacher. "At all of them, I scrutinized their handling of donations, their hierarchy, dietary intake, and manner of worship. During the clandestine practice, I became enamored by the healing practices at the Temple of Asclepius."

"You want to become a celebrant of Asclepius?" Asphodel asked in disgust.

"No, Master. I want to study the healing arts for the good of the Golden Valley," Orestes corrected. "I find the snakes in the temple unsettling."

"Have you observed Assistant Administrator Dosis?" Alerio questioned.

"I have. Are you acquainted with the cleric?"

"He took my gladii, my rig, and my Legion knife," Alerio offered. "I plan to get them back and express my displeasure while doing so. Do you have a problem with that?"

"No, Master Sisera," Orestes assured the Centurion. "But you'll need me to guide you to the priest's quarters. The compound of Asclepius is difficult to navigate, and the novices move between healing houses throughout the night."

Alerio and Orestes turned and waited for Asphodel to express his opinion.

"Future surgeon Orestes still has to complete his training as a Sweet Fist," the master assassin informed them. "And, it is important to practice the skill of infiltration at every opportunity. Let tonight be one of them."

***

Alerio leaped, hooked his hands on the wall, and pulled up until his eyes cleared the top. While the Legionary used caution in his approach, the apprentice

190

assassin ran to the structure, planted a foot at waist height, and ran up the wall. When his chest cleared the barrier, he twisted in the air, dropped, and landed face down on the top course of stone.

"We start wall climbing when we are very little," Orestes whispered. "The guards neglect the rear wall because the only structures back here are snake buildings and gardens."

Swinging his legs back and forth, Alerio caught the top stone with a heel. Scooting, he moved until his body rested on the top and ended up facing Orestes. Even laying head-to-head with the apprentice, he could barely make out the other man in the dark.

"When I was little, we picked rocks from the soil and built walls," the Legionary uttered. "Which way is Dosis' room?"

"On the other…"

The sound of boots on gravel rose to them from the bottom of the hill. They had climbed it to reach the base of the wall and knew the distance. Cascading waves told the tale of hundreds of boots trudging along the base of the hill.

"It has to be the large Qart Hadasht detachment we saw earlier," Alerio suggested. "I guess they're patrolling the shoreline."

"It's a bad tactic," Orestes offered. "Why parade thousands of men up and down the coast when a few patrols would be more efficient. And why keep them a mile from the water if they are watching the beach?"

"And in the dark," Alerio said then stopped. "Unless, they're maneuvering into an attack position."

191

"Against what foe?"

"There is only one close by," Alerio remarked. "Megellus Legion East."

The staff officer dropped off the wall, landing outside the temple compound.

"You are not going to retrieve your blades and seek your vengeance?"

"No Orestes. I'm going to warn the Legion," Alerio informed the apprentice. "Duty takes priority over my personal wishes."

"And there you go, Dáskalos, instructing right up to our parting," Orestes stated. "Follow this wall. At the end of the temple compound, you can continue straight ahead. Once you are beyond the Valley of Temples, you will be in open country. Or you can cut across the valley, skirt Agrigento, and head directly to where your Legion is camped."

Alerio started to thank him. But the Legion staff officer realized he stood on the hill alone. The apprentice assassin had already faded into the night.

Act 5

Chapter 21 – Beware Sacrificial Gifts

It being closer to dawn than the middle of the night, Alerio jogged to the eastern corner the Temple of Asclepius'. Peering around the wall, the Centurion witnessed the majesty of two other temples.

The Temple of Castor and Pollux glowed on the high ground across a broad paved boulevard. Blazing in the night, the temple dedicated to the adventuring brothers, Castor and Pollux, shown so brightly that men aboard a ship at sea could recognize the structure. A fitting tribute to brothers who rode the white sea foam of waves. Most often, they were depicted in statues, paintings, and tile inlays as standing with white horses. As an infantryman and not a sailor, or a sophisticated nobleman with money for equestrian pursuits, Alerio held little adoration for the Gods of sailors and horsemanship.

But, as a Legionary, he could respect the competition represented by the temple adjacent to Asclepius'. Not as well-lit as the tall building across the valley, the Temple of Olympian Zeus displayed small flames of evenly spaced braziers along the top step. In the morning, the compound would fill with athletes starting their day with lusty voices raised to the God of sky and thunder. Competitiveness fit with the ethos of the Legion heavy infantry; Win at all costs. A code, Centurion Sisera embraced fully.

Throwing a salute in the direction of Zeus' Shrine, Alerio braced and prepared to rush to the start of the new compound. Then he paused as the clanging of shields and spears alerted him to soldiers climbing the hill. His plan to sneak the mile and a quarter to the end of the Valley of Temples faded. The large group of Iberians and Celts at the bottom of the slope had sent up flank security. This told him a few troubling things about the mercenaries.

They weren't simply patrolling the coastline. By sending out flank security, they signaled the columns were moving fast. Fast enough that their commanders worried about being caught unaware by an attack from out of the dark. Considering night maneuvers were reserved for emergency withdrawals or moving stealthily to ambush an enemy, Alerio assumed the Qart Hadasht forces were positioning for a battle.

Unless the Syracuse fleet had landed and deposited the promised twenty thousand allied troops, the other available target for the Empire's surprise attack was the Legion marching camp. Alerio turned his back on the slope, faced between the complexes, and slinked down into the Valley of Temples.

***

Walkways, gardens, and spaces with benches for quiet reflection were separated by low walls. While lengths of shrubs allowed for bent over sneaking to avoid detection, the short parapets at the ends required Alerio to crawl. Stooped, the Legionary walked slowly through the green sections then sprinted across open zones to the next hedge row. When the final line of shrubs ended, the Legionary dropped to his belly and crept forward to the edge of the boulevard.

From his knees behind the stone barrier, Alerio glanced to his left. Up the rise, he could see the front of the

194

Temple of Asclepius. Shifting to the hill on the other side, his eyes traced a paved road up to the Temple of Vulcan. The brightly lit Temple of Castor and Pollux sat up the hill to his right front and directly to his right was the structure dedicated to Olympian Zeus.

To reach the opposite side of the boulevard would take a hard sprint. But, Legionaries ran, jumped, and sprinted. It wasn't the exertion required to cross the open avenue that worried him. Being detected by the temple guards and having them sound an alarm was his biggest worry. He rose off his knees and placed both hands on the stone wall. Then, he sank back to his knees with only his eyes and forehead showing above the stonework.

A cavalry patrol trotted into view from beyond Zeus' temple. As they neared, Alerio recognized the riders in the flickering light from the sanctuary of Castor and Pollux as northern Celts. The Legion officer judged them not to be Etruscans or Insubri but irregulars from another tribe of barbarians. With the riders on the boulevard, there was no way for him to cross over and escape unnoticed.

Slings have a limited effective range. Usually viewed as a nuisance weapon unless directly on top of an enemy, the stones served more to harass than disable. And part of the unnerving came from the whirling sound of the leather strings. Several slingers twirling their weapons created a noticeable buzzing. Almost as if a swarm of angry bees were attacking the enemy. Although the rocks hurt more than bee stings, human nature caused the whistle of slingers to send chills up the spines of soldiers.

Horses didn't confuse slings with bees. Yet, three of the cavalry mounts reared up. The beasts threw their riders over their haunches and onto the pavers of the boulevard. Before the riders could collect themselves, ten Greek Hoplites armed with long spears charged from the sides of the avenue and surrounded them. Three more of the heavily armored men carried their big round shields strapped to their backs. It was necessary as their hands were busy folding slings and stuffing them into pouches. Horses don't confuse slings with bees, but they did react violently to rocks launched by expert slingers.

"This is the Valley of Temples," a Hoplite officer announced. "By what right do you ride so boldly on the Street of the Gods?"

"By instructions from General Hannibal Gisco, commander of the Empire forces," a barbarian challenged. "Under his orders, we ride where were want when we want."

"Show them," the officer for the temple guards instructed.

Thirteen spears swiped the air knocking the six mounted Celts to the ground. Unhorsed but uninjured, they joined their fellow cavalrymen in peering over steel spearheads, up shafts, and into the facial openings of Hoplite helmets.

"This is the Street of the Gods," the officer reiterated. "Uninvited loiterers are asked to leave on their own. Or..."

There was a pause. While the cavalrymen squirmed in embarrassment and discomfort, the Greek solders stood as still and steady as the statues in the temples.

"Or what?" the patrol leader demanded.

"We pile your dead bodies in a cart and haul your disrespectful cūlī to a hole beyond the valley," the officer replied. "My men are a little on edge tonight. What with you mercenaries running about and the Republic's army gathering. I wouldn't deny them a sacrificial gift. Go ahead, draw your swords, and resist."

The patrol leader looked briefly at the flames reflecting off the deadly spear tip aimed at his throat. He raised his arms away from his sword and the short spear lying next to him.

"We will ride out," he promised.

"You'll walk," the Hoplite officer responded. Then he raised his arm and twirled his fist in the air.

Ten archers stood from the sides of the boulevard and leaped the wall. All had an arrow notched and their bow half drawn. One of the bowmen came from ten feet off to Alerio's right. Had the Legionary attempted to race across; he would have been dead before reaching the halfway point.

Then as if a God had purposely divided the Hoplites, the temple guards parted. Half walked the cavalry patrol towards the east while the other half marched off to the west. With streaks of pink threatening sunrise, Alerio had no option. He stood, jumped the wall, and sprinted onto the Street of the Gods.

***

The slope rose gently from the valley to the top of the ridge. Beyond the rear of the temple compounds, Alerio broke east figuring to get beyond the business district. Located between the walls of Agrigento, the Temple of Heracles, and the Temple of Concordia, the commercial enterprises complimented the business district on the west end of the Valley of Temples.

Closer to the city than the other shrines, the Temple of Concordia occupied a hilltop of its own. Alerio stayed away from the base of the temple's hill and slipped up to the backside of a row of businesses. Locating an alleyway, he glided into the darkness, and moved to the front of the stores and the street. At the end, his mouth dropped open and he sank against a wall.

Squatting at the mouth of the alley, Centurion Sisera's eyes glazed over and the veins in his neck throbbed. Teams of Hoplites marching in pairs passed guard teams stationed in the center of the street. With lantern light illuminating the pavers, the road between the commercial buildings was as bright as a cloudy day. For some reason, the temple guards felt it was necessary to man sentry positions along the road between the Temples of Heracles and Concordia. If they feared for the safety of the priests, standard military tactics would have them splitting up and defending each temple individually. These tactics created a defensive line as if guarding the entire Valley of Temples against a gathering horde.

As infuriating as being blocked by the Hoplites, the orange ball of the sun began to appear over the buildings across the street. Alerio's heart raced at the thought of not warning the Legion about the Iberians sneaking up from the south. He just couldn't think of any way to slip by the Hoplites. Then a revelation came to him. The temple guards were all facing in the same direction.

Thinking back to the cavalry patrol being escorted off the Street of the Gods, Centurion Sisera stood, reached to his waist, and untied the rope holding his trousers up. The black silk got wrapped around his thigh to hold the Ally of the Golden Valley dagger. Then nude, except for the piece of silk and his boots, Alerio stepped onto the road and called out.

"Greetings Greeks. Guardians of the Gods. I bid you a good morning."

The pair of Hoplites watching the east alley spun around at hearing the voice. It took a lot of self-control to keep from laughing at the smiling, naked man. Their Lochias would have them on extra duty for a week if he caught them being anything other than serious while on duty.

"Where are you going, veteran?" one of the Hoplites inquired.

His observation that the obviously disturbed man was a combat veteran came from the battle scars. The insane individual had a crescent scar on his head and indentions on his side and thigh from arrow wounds plus numerous other scars.

"Into the sun," Alerio announced as if it was self-explanatory. He held out his arms, displaying more scars, and lifted his chin as if to allow the sun's rays to bathe his face. "The God Sol Indiges calls to me. Come with me brothers. The sun beckons."

"Sorry. We're on duty," the other Hoplite said. "But you go right ahead."

Alerio staggered a little for effect. Then he pulled himself upright, marched across the road, passed the guards, and strolled into the opposite alleyway.

"I can't figure it out. Is it love from Tyche that allowed him to survive all those injuries?" the other Hoplite offered. "Or does Furor have him in an embrace?"

"I'd say he's both lucky and crazy," the first guard suggested. "Did you see the wounds on his back?"

None of the observations reached Alerio and they wouldn't have bothered him if he heard. His goal of escaping the valley accomplished, the Legion officer rushed down the alleyway ignoring the Hoplites. Then he slid to a stop and sank into a squat. Ranks of Iberians and Celts stretched out to either side in an open field. Now he understood why the Hoplites crewed a defensive line and faced eastward. They were stationed there to prevent any deserters from reaching the Valley of the Temples.

Alerio waited between the buildings for the weak morning sunlight to get the lay of the land. Far to the front of the massed Empire forces, a Legion maneuvered into maniples preparing to engage the Qart Hadasht army.

A couple of soldiers happened to glance back. Noticing the nude man with the silk on his thigh, they alerted their neighbors. Soon an entire section of the back row of soldiers were laughing at the smiling, crazy, naked man. Alerio stood, nodded, and waved to each of the infantrymen as if greeting old friends. All the while, he looked over their heads and speculated on how to reach and warn the Legion.

***

Horns blared and drums beat a rhythm. In response, the Iberians stepped off and, in an orderly manner, marched down the hill. The naked man followed them. By shouting nonsense words and gesturing as if directing troops in combat, he confirmed his lack of good sense. Strutting back and forth in the open area between the supply wagons and the rear of the infantry, Alerio maintained the charade for the benefit of the Empire support personnel.

The mad man spun with his arms out as if gathering arm loads of air. Alerio only faced Agrigento briefly. It was just enough to estimate that the Qart Hadasht mercenaries had traveled a little over two miles from the city's walls. Facing to the front, he guessed the distance between the Centuries' maniples and the Legion supply wagons was the same. By then, the distance separating the front ranks of the opposing forces had narrowed to several hundred feet. While the combatants were almost upon each other, Centurion Sisera felt no closer to delivering his warning.

It would take a blessing from Mendacius for the Centurion to filter through the Iberian infantry, pass among the Celt irregulars, and reach the Legion skirmishers. Cunning and deception were easier to perform in the night and less likely to work under the morning sun. While looking at the field of Iberian spears, Alerio recalled one of the training drills his early instructors inflicted on him.

***

Every weapon had a weakness. Performance suffered or even ended if the physical structure became corrupted or parts broke. Sometimes maintenance solved the issue. Sharpening and oiling a rusty steel gladius would recover the blade and render it serviceable. Installing new hair and sinew strings allowed bows and bolt throwers to resume launching arrows and rods. But a misshapen spear shaft ended its usefulness. Due to improper storage, a flaw in the wood, or excessive moisture, some shafts bent. When they warped beyond any hope of straightening, the armorers knocked off the spearheads and tossed the curved poles to the side of the wagon bed. Alerio continued his manic actions until he located the armorer's wagon carrying the extra spears and abandoned poles.

"Get away from my wagon," the Iberian armor growled. "A veteran touched by Lyssa or not, I will beat you. Take your insanity somewhere else."

"Pole. I just want to touch a pole," Alerio pleaded as he scooted close to the side of the wagon.

"I said get away from me and my wagon," the armorer shouted.

A Lieutenant called and signaled for the supply wagons to move forward with the infantry. The armorer turned away and Alerio reacted. He rushed to the wagon and leaned over the side. Selecting two spear shafts with extreme curvatures, the Legionary snatched the pole from the wagon and ran.

"Come back for more and you'll get a taste of steel," threatened the armorer.

After checking, the armorer realized the stolen poles were the most damaged from the stack. Deciding it wasn't worth pursuing the thief, he snapped the reins and walked beside the mules. The team and wagon reached the bottom of the hill and walked onto the flat where the battle lines were forming.

Alerio raced to the rear rank of the Iberian infantry. A few steps from the soldiers, he tossed the poles lightly into the air, extended his arms, and caught the bottoms of the bent spear shafts in his palms.

"Lookout," he shouted when the poles leaned to one side.

Alerio sprinted to his right in order to keep the poles balanced on his hands. When they began to fall forward, he called out, and jogged to keep them on his palms. Soldiers laughed, stepped aside to allow the insane, naked man to continue chasing the balance of the curved poles.

The shafts wobbled to the side, then ahead, then to the other side and afterward, forward. Alerio balanced the spear shafts and moved deeper into the ranks of infantrymen. His acrobatic act worked in two ways. It let him move towards the front of the formation and allowed Alerio to look around and count the Qart Hadasht forces.

"Yo, Celts. Look at this fool," an infantryman on the front row called out.

The Empire skirmishers glanced back and chuckled. Stumbling from the ranks of the heavy infantry, the juggler jerked then raced into the Celt's loose formation while trying to keep his palms under the swaying poles.

"Is the Latian touched?" one of the irregulars asked.

"Look at him. What do you think?"

"Shouldn't someone tell him, he's in the middle of a battlefield?"

"I don't think he would understand."

The mad man almost lost control of the poles. In his struggle to keep the balance, he reached the front row of the Qart Hadasht skirmishers.

Across the field, Velites fingered javelins and nervously pointed. Anticipating contact with the Celts, they indicated specific light infantrymen. Alerio hoped a few of the Legion skirmishers recognized him. An iron javelin through the chest as he made his break for the Republic's line, was not in his plan.

***

Battle Commander Gaius Claudius nudged his horse closer to the third maniple of his heavy infantry.

"Remember your training. Listen to your Centurions. Permitte Divis Cetera," he yelled.

In response, a roar erupted from the rows of Legionaries. The Colonel's phrases were repeated for the men on either end of the lines. Receiving the loudest response were his words, "Leave all else to the gods."

"Colonel, the Empire's mercenaries are moving," Senior Tribune Pompeius announced. "But there's a disturbance in their ranks."

Everyone associated with the command staff knew of Gaius Claudius' blessing from Theia. In a show of defiance, he refused to watch the Iberian infantry march through the gates of Agrigento. Using the superb vision from the Goddess, he could easily get lost in the details, and appear to be worried. Avoiding the appearance to his Legion of being apprehensive, the Colonel relied on his staff to report on the enemy.

"What kind of disturbance?" the Battle Commander questioned.

"Sir, it looks to be a nude juggler entertaining the infantrymen," Pompeius offered. "Is that normal for the Iberians?"

"Senior Tribune, I haven't the foggiest notion," the Colonel admitted. "What's the movement?"

"They're coming off the slope and spreading out on the plain," Pompeius reported. He paused before adding. "The nude acrobatic has moved beyond the front rank and is preforming among their irregulars."

"You really want me to look, don't you, Senior Tribune?" Gaius Claudius asked.

"It is the oddest military tradition I've ever witnessed," Pompeius said. Turning to the Senior Centurion, he inquired. "Have you ever seen anything like that?"

"Can't say that I have," Fratris Lembus replied. "It would be a distraction in the ranks. I would never allow it."

The senior advisers to the Battle Commander didn't notice when Claudius finally raised his head and peered over the heads of his infantrymen.

"You there. Get to the supply wagons," the Colonel ordered a junior Tribune. "Draw a tunic, gladius, sheath belt, armor, armored skirt, and a Centurion's helmet. Come to think of it, requisition a shield while you're at it."

"Is there a problem?" Pompeius questioned.

"Not for us," the Colonel said dismissing the Senior Tribune's comment. Twisting his head until he located the Senior Velites Centurion, Gaius Claudius advised. "Qualis. Before long, a naked man will be sprinting from the Qart Hadasht's line. Be sure he reaches our lines and is escorted directly to me."

"Yes sir," the skirmisher officer acknowledged as he kicked his horse into motion.

While Tapeti Qualis galloped his mount between the heavy infantrymen, Gaius Claudius motioned to the Legion's First Centurion.

"What do you need, sir?" Bruno Sanavi asked as he marched to the Battle Commander.

"Our front rank is about to have a visitor," the Colonel stated. He glanced up to check on the location of the nude man. "I don't want him to catch a Celt spear between his shoulder blades when he crosses no man's land. Send a squad to defend him but don't make it too obvious."

"Not obvious, sir?"

"That's correct. I don't want the Empire's skirmishers to see our preparations," Gaius Claudius directed. "His run will come as a surprise, and I need his defenders to be a surprise as well."

The First Centurion jogged to his Twelfth Squad and began speaking with the veteran Decanus.

"I don't understand, Colonel," Senior Tribune Pompeius protested. "What details did you see that a man with average sight can't?"

"I recognized the naked man. Legionaries who were at Messina refer to him as Death Caller. In the past, I called him a war demon as he defended me," Gaius Claudius informed his staff. "You know him as staff officer Sisera."

"The juggler is Centurion Alerio Sisera?" Lembus asked.

"He is, Senior Centurion, and I assume he has information for me."

Colonel Gaius Claudius had no idea of the real value of Alerio's intelligence. If he did, he might have ordered a larger response and started the battle sooner. But that would have been a mistake.

Chapter 22 – A Difficult Maneuver

Alerio tossed one pole into the air. It flipped and traveled a body's length away. Rushing to get under it, Centurion Sisera barely arrived in place to catch the misshapen shaft. One landed in his palm, and he shot the second pole towards the sky. Racing at full speed, he stopped, dropped to a knee, and caught the shaft.

A few Celt skirmishers banged on their shields in appreciation. Almost as if embarrassed by the signs of approval, the crazy, harmless juggler tripped over his own feet. The shafts began to topple. Trying to stabilize the falling poles, the mad man ran a short distance. Then he stopped and the poles became rigid on his palms. Bending at the knees while lowering his arms, he let the back of his hands almost touch the ground. Posed with the poles sticking up beside his ears, he listened to more soldiers bang on their shields. It never occurred to any of the Qart Hadasht mercenaries, the dual control of the shafts could also represent skills with spears.

From the squatting position, Alerio vaulted upward. Launching both shafts from ankle height, the warped poles soared high into the sky. All of the Celts craned their necks to keep them in sight. A few allowed gasps to escape their lips in astonishment at the elevation reached by the flying sticks. While their eyes peered upward at the spinning shafts, the insane, naked man didn't watch. He was occupied sprinting across no man's land, heading for the Legion's skirmishers.

***

Several Velites shuffled out from the lines of Legionaries. For a couple of heartbeats, Alerio assumed they were reacting to him. But the javelins positioned at their shoulders never launched. Rather, the Legion skirmishers trotted forward in a wedge formation. He ignored the Legionaries as sweat stung his eyes. Where the distance between the two battle lines didn't appear to be far, during the actual run he realized they were. Exhausted from his earlier theatrics and the mad dash, his legs screamed for relief.

Alerio panted and gasped. It was a combination of the exertion and nerves. Any step could be his last. All it would take was a Celt with a strong arm and Centurion Sisera would find himself face down and pinned to the ground by a spear.

Just as the thought passed through his mind, three spear shafts impacted to his left and right. Then several arrows whizzed by his ears. Ducking or diving to the ground was the natural inclination. Either move spelled death. Alerio cleared his mind, reached down into his gut for courage, and powered forward.

No spears reached him, letting Alerio know he had outpaced the Celt irregulars. Then four arrows peppered the ground to either side. Out running archers was harder. To help his cause, he burned the last of his energy running a zigzag pattern.

The lack of sleep, the juggling, thirst, the run, and being a target, caught up to Alerio. He stumbled and

208

broke his stride. Partially blinded by the sweat in his eyes and the blood thundering through his veins, Centurion Sisera slowed.

In an act of defiance, he smacked his naked butt. And although the Qart Hadasht archers had no way of hearing over the distance, he screamed, "Hit this, you perfututum cūlī."

Then his feet got tangled up, he tripped forward, and fell.

***

The arm was solid as an oak branch. And the body attacked to it, strong and muscular. Altogether, the big Veles easily managed the weight.

"No time to lay down on the job, sir," he advised while lifting Alerio to his feet.

Remembering the archers and fearing for the skirmisher, the naked Centurion choked out.

"Enemy archers and incoming arrows. Mind your shield and back away," Alerio whispered, knowing light infantryman carried smaller shields. "Leave me."

"Sorry, sir, I can't do that," the skirmisher remarked. "They wouldn't like it."

Alerio's eyes stung but he was beginning to recover his senses. Shaking off the supporting arm, he inhaled and wiped away the moisture from his eyes. With clearer vision, he felt something was different.

Centurion Sisera realized that he stood in shadows. Glancing up, he noticed the backside of a wall constructed of big Legion shields supported by ten heavy infantrymen. The barrier protected him and the five Velites hovering over him.

"Your choice, Centurion," a veteran Lance Corporal suggested from the defensive screen.

"Choice, Decanus?" Alerio queried.

"Yes, sir," the squad leader answered. "From here we can attack the Qart Hadasht and get a little revenge. Or we can fall back to our formation."

"I usually like armor and weapons before going into combat," Alerio replied. "And right now, it's more important for me to see the Colonel than to earn a chest full of medals."

"Standby for a rapid retreat," the Lance Corporal called out.

The heavies and the light infantrymen shouted back, "Standing by, Decanus."

"Move. Watch your sides and tops," the Lance Corporal instructed. "Velites. Do you have the Centurion?"

"The staff officer is secure."

Alerio felt a hand on his shoulder and two skirmishers move in beside him. With five armored bodies pressing in, he felt smothered.

"Can you give me a little space?"

"All the space you need, sir," the big skirmisher replied. "in about fifty feet."

"Let me guess," Alerio said. "It's about fifty feet to the Legion lines."

The units shuffled back under the protection of the interlocked shields.

"For a staff officer, he's pretty sharp," another Legionary offered. "But he is out of uniform."

"Out of uniform," another of Alerio's escorts ventured. "Hades, the Centurion is naked."

"Yes, sir. All the space you want," the huge skirmisher said trying to deflect and cover the disrespectful remarks. "You'll be free in about thirty-five paces from here."

***

The lines of the infantry maniples parted to allow the sixteen men to pass through the Legion lines. Most ignored the units that had been out front although a few chuckled when the naked guy was guided by.

It wasn't until they approached Colonel Gaius Claudius that Alerio realized the defensive screen had been held by a squad from First Century. When the Decanus offered to attack the Qart Hadasht, he had only been half teasing. On his word, the veteran squad probably would have assaulted the mercenaries and happily drawn some revenge blood.

"Centurion Qualis. May I present the wayward Centurion," the large skirmisher announced. "We didn't have time to dress him."

"Very good, Optio. Get back to your Century," the Senior Velites officer instructed. Then he turned to the Battle Commander. "Sir?"

Distracted by the advancing Qart Hadasht forces, Gaius Claudius ignored Qualis and Sisera.

"Lembus. Call the Legion to order," the Colonel announced to the Senior Centurion. Then to Pompeius, he warned. "Standby the Tribunes to carry orders. Signalmen, to my side."

The command staff came alert, and the Legion took a breath, flexed, and prepared to go into action.

"Colonel. I need to speak with you," Alerio insisted. "Your rear and the baggage train are in jeopardy."

"Sisera. I've seen you covered in blood and up to your eyebrows in merda," Gaius Claudius replied. "In both cases, I was glad you were there. But I will not hold a conference with a naked staff officer."

"This is important, sir."

"Get dressed, then talk to me," the Battle Commander informed Alerio. He was splitting his attention between the bare officer and the converging battle lines.

A young Tribune rode up, reined in his horse, and looked down at Alerio.

"I assume these are for you, Centurion," the nobleman offered.

He tossed an officer's helmet and a short-sleeved tunic to Alerio. After letting a skirmisher's shield, gladius belt, chest piece, and an armored skirt fall to the ground, he kneed the mount and went to his position with the other junior Tribunes.

While he dressed, Alerio studied the wagons, support personnel, and guard detail. They were over a mile to the rear of the Legion. Then, shifting his eyes, he perused the hills to the southwest. Beyond the rolling land, the blue waters of the ocean were calm. But the staff officer knew what the mounds hid and that made him anything except calm.

Once armored and armed, Alerio marched to Gaius Claudius. Lifting his chin to lock eyes with the mounted Battle Commander, he pointed to the high mounds.

"Last night I saw units of Celts and Iberians move into those hills," Alerio reported.

212

"How many?" Gaius inquired.

"I don't know. But the Qart Hadasht command consists of thirteen thousand Iberians and eight thousand Celts," Alerio reported, using the numbers he got from Asphodel. "Plus a few thousand city militia."

Gaius Claudius turned and stared at the approaching mercenaries. As if having decided on a plan of action, he twisted back to Alerio.

"We have six thousand Iberians and six Celts coming at us," he remarked. "From what you say, I could have another seven thousand heavy infantrymen coming up my cūlus at any moment."

"Yes, sir," Alerio commented.

"Senior Tribune Pompeius, I hope you are ready," the Colonel called to the group of Tribunes.

"Ready for what?" Pompeius asked while guiding his horse to the Battle Commander.

"For your own command. Send two messengers to the marching camp and alert General Postumius Megellus and Colonel Zenonis that Megellus Legion East is surrounded and outnumbered."

"How do you know that?" the Senior Tribune questioned. "I don't see any units surrounding us. Are you taking the word of this junior staff officer to change your entire battle plan?"

"Do you not want the command, Senior Tribune?"

"Of course, I do," Pompeius assured him.

"It's going to be a short assignment if you don't get those messengers moving," Gaius Claudius warned.

"What do you mean, Colonel?"

"I mean you will be dead and so will your Legionaries if Colonel Zenonis arrives any later," Gaius replied. "Senior Centurion Lembus. We have a change of Century assignments."

Pompeius trotted off to write the messages and Lembus rode from the rear of the maniples. In the moment before the Senior Centurion arrived, Gaius Claudius looked down and studied Alerio.

"You are a Legion officer, Centurion Sisera."

"Yes, sir, thank you," Alerio replied to what he thought was a compliment.

"I was going to add, an officer doesn't walk around with a Veles shield strapped to his back," Gaius Claudius pointed out.

"Sir, I will gladly put down this shield at the end of today's fighting," Alerio responded. "Until than Colonel, I think I'll carry it."

"It looks silly on a staff officer. But I ordered it for you based on your prior performances," Gaius Claudius said with a chuckle. "By the way, I'm assigning you to Senior Tribune Pompeius' staff."

"Wherever you need me, sir," Alerio assured the Battle Commander.

"It's not where I need you," Gaius stated. "It's Myrias Pompeius who needs you. He's never been in combat before. Keep him alive, Centurion Sisera."

"Yes, sir."

***

The Legion skirmishers launched one volley. Their purpose was to break the unity of the enemy's front row. In this case, it didn't work. The Celt irregulars absorbed

214

the javelins and tossed spears in reply. The Legion light infantry readied another throw.

"Velites to the rear," Lembus ordered.

The words from the Legion's Senior Centurion shocked the Legion as the order to withdraw shot through the ranks. At the front, the Centurions and NCOs of the skirmisher Centuries felt cheated and dishonored by the retreat. They had yet to close with their Qart Hadasht counterparts.

"Step back," the Centurions directed in spite of their feelings.

Without the Velites as a buffer, the Qart Hadasht skirmishers rushed ahead of the Iberian infantry. Their spears fell among the lines of Legionaries, taking a few heavy infantrymen to the ground. The wounded were picked up by the light infantrymen as they filtered through the Legion maniples.

"Qualis. What in the Goddess Pietas' name is going on?" the gathered Centurions complained. "How can we do our duty from behind the lines?"

"You aren't out of this fight," Qualis assured his ten light infantry officers. "The Colonel is expecting a second Empire force. He wants five Centuries back at the wagons. Believe me, this is going to be an ugly day with plenty of fight to go around."

The Velites split with five Centuries running to the rear. One hundred and fifty Legion horsemen joined them in the race to protect the wagons and supplies. Falling in as a fourth line behind the heavy infantry, the remaining five Centuries of skirmishers waited for their opportunity to fight. While Qualis and Senior Cavalry Officer

Ephoebias managed the division of their Centuries in a neat and orderly manner, First Centurion Lembus didn't have the same luxury.

***

From the first throw to the first brace, the likelihood of smoothly peeling off Centuries became impossible. The Iberian heavy infantry slammed into the Legion's heavy infantry and the two sides began a deadly dance. On the periphery, warriors fought and died, giving ground, or capturing a few bloody lengths on the flanks.

But, the heart and life of the battle was the center of the combat line. The dark, throbbing, and terrifying place between enemy shields where death prowled, waiting for sharp blades to carve out an advantage. It was from this bloody cauldron that Senior Centurion Lembus needed to extricate half of his Centuries.

"Senior Tribune, pass the word. I went every other Century of the Third and Second Maniples off the line and rallying behind the command staff," Lembus directed.

While the messengers received their orders, Senior Centurion Lembus scratched his face and looked along the line of his battling First Maniple.

"What about them?" Pompeius questioned once the junior Tribunes rode to deliver the message.

"If I pull any of the First, the Iberians will pour in like a spring flood over a broken dam," Lembus replied.

Raising his arms, he signaled for the Centuries, still on the lines, to shift. The shift drill automatically instructed the remaining Centuries to fill in the gaps. By the time the junior Tribunes raced back to the command area, the

216

Second Maniple was once again a solid row of Legionaries.

"The Colonel wants half the Legion at the baggage area," Pompeius reminded him.

"Send your lads out again," Lembus directed. "At each end, three Centuries of the First will come out and one and a half of the Second Maniple will move up. It'll collapse our battle front but it's all I can do with half a Legion."

The Senior Tribune issued the orders and the horse messengers galloped away.

"Tribune Seplasium will assume my duties," Pompeius informed the Senior Centurion. "I'm taking half of the Tribunes to the rear. For nothing, if no mercenaries show."

"If they don't, enjoy your day," Lembus offered. "I'll see you later."

Senior Tribune Pompeius saluted the Senior Centurion, reined his mount around, and trotted off to assume his first command. Lembus watched the Senior Tribune ride off in the direction of the ranks formed by the relieved Legionaries.

With a pained look on his face, the Senior Centurion elevated his arms out from his sides.

"Standby," he shouted before bringing his hands together above his head. As his hands clapped, he ordered. "Step back. Step back."

It was going to be a grind, fighting off a superior number of Iberian infantrymen. Adding to the pain, every Legionary under his command would do it walking backward for over a mile. Senior Centurion Lembus acknowledged the pace, numbers, and distance together made for a miserably long afternoon. He also knew there was nothing he could do about it. "Step back. Step back."

Chapter 23 – A Bevy of Infantry Officers

While the four hundred light infantrymen jogged for the wagons, the heavies came off the line and gathered around Alerio, two signalmen, and a handful of junior Tribunes.

A rider, so slender and petite he could have been a child, raced up.

"Centurion Sisera?" the young nobleman inquired.

"Here, Tribune," Alerio replied. He raised an arm and waved the youth over. "What can I do for you?"

"Colonel Claudius said that it would be a grand idea if the Legion's four bolt throwers were on station," the Tribune informed Alerio. Sliding off the horse, he added. "And in case Senior Tribune Pompeius disagrees, you should take this horse and request forgiveness later."

The lad handed the reins over then sprinted off to rejoin the Battle Commander's reduced staff. Alerio glanced to the rear rank of the fighting Legionaries to see the Senior Tribune speaking with the Senior Centurion. As Alerio leaped onto the animal's back, Pompeius exchanged salutes with Lembus and guided his horse away from the battle lines.

Senior Tribunes carried a lot of authority and never so much as when assigned a combat detachment. If anything happened to Gaius Claudius, Pompeius might consider Alerio's actions to be disrespectful or even subversive. The staff officer should wait and argue the need for artillery with Pompeius. However, based on the Senior Tribune's earlier remarks about wanting proof of the mysterious second Qart Hadasht force, Alerio would lose the debate. Knowing the political ramifications, Alerio put heels to the horse's flanks and sent the beast racing for the supply wagons.

He flew by the five Centuries of Light Infantrymen reaching the supply wagons while the first Veles was still a quarter of a mile away.

"Senior engineer, break out the bolt throwers and set them up," Alerio instructed as he reined in the horse.

"No problem, Centurion," the artilleryman responded. He stood in the bed of the wagon, rotated his face, and twirled an arm in the air. "Just one thing. Which way is the enemy? My war machines can't reach the fighting from here."

"Before the morning is through engineer, you'll have Iberian targets as thick as the stubble on your face," Alerio assured him. "Pull your people in and position the ballistae facing generally southwest."

The problem with Centurion Sisera's instructions, they required the forty men assigned to the weapons to stop digging the marching camp's ditch. As if it wasn't enough disrupting that segment of the trench construction, Alerio rode to the Centurion of the rear-guard Century.

"Pull your people out of the dirt and dress them for war," he ordered.

"On who's authority?" demanded the infantry officer.

"Colonel Gaius Claudius," Alerio reported. Although far beyond the Battle Commander's suggestion, he felt it was justified. "Give us an expanding security ring in a decagon shape."

"You sound as if you don't know where the enemy is coming from," the Centurion remarked.

The infantry officer pointed and silently questioned the battle raging a mile away. Rather than following his arm, Alerio eyed the hills to the southwest. No advance units of Qart Hadasht mercenaries marched through the saddles between peaks. Without proof, he had to confess that he didn't know.

"We're not sure," Alerio commented. "So have your squads maintain visual contact."

"I hope the Colonel knows what he's doing," the infantry officer stated. "The General is expecting us to have half the defensive ditch finished. If we leave it like this, he'll be in a 'non capimus' mood when he and Megellus Legion North arrives."

"I'll stand his ire, if it comes to his taking no prisoners," Alerio promised. "You get your Legionaries out of the trench and into the field."

"Optio. Tesserarius. Get them out and dressed," the infantry officer ordered his NCOs. He waved his arms indicating directions from the proposed marching camp. "We're going with a ten-sided patrol area. Decani keep an eye on the adjacent squads."

While the heavy infantrymen dressed, Alerio looked towards the weapon transports. The four wagons were positioned tails on to the hills. From each, men pulled thick timbers. While teams pounded in pegs to hold the wooden beams together, other team members threaded rods through holes to reinforce the measured and finely shaped timbers. Each torsion artillery piece grew in height and heft. During the assembly, the senior engineer walked to Alerio.

"The ballistae are usually constructed for fixed fortified defenses or sieges on main gates," he remarked. "I'm not sure what good you expect us to do against a line of dirt hills?"

"Can you lower those things?" Alerio questioned.

"Centurion, they are tall apparatus as you can see," the artilleryman replied. Then in confusion, he proposed. "We could dig holes and set them in the bottom, I guess."

"No. I meant can you tilt them and shoot into ranks of attacking soldiers?"

"Well sure. But we'll need to stake them in place after elevating the tail," the engineer offered. "Once that's done, we can't shift the aim much."

"Lift the tails but wait until we see the enemy before pegging them down," Alerio ordered. "I'm going to organize the Velites."

The four hundred light infantrymen reached the partially dug trench. Having no orders, they stopped and began milling around.

"Just like the Legion," a Private complained. "Run here, run there, and then stand around waiting."

"That should be the Legion slogan," another replied. "Hurry up and wait."

"Dumbest thing you've ever said," the first commented. "No one would ever say such a thing."

They hushed up when a staff officer rode up.

"What are we doing?" one of the officers questioned Alerio.

"Separate out one hundred and fifty of your best archers. Have them draw bows from the supply wagon," Alerio instructed. "The rest will need extra javelins."

"You sound serious," another infantry officer remarked. "I thought we were preparing a fallback position for the Legion?"

"Let me make this simple. There are thirteen thousand Iberians in Agrigento," Alerio replied. He indicated the battle still a mile away. "Over there are six thousand of their heavy infantrymen."

The four officers glanced around at one another and at their Velites.

"Where are the rest of the Iberians?" one of the Centurions inquired.

"I don't know," Alerio admitted. "But along with the missing seven thousand Iberians will be two thousand Celt irregulars. Is that serious enough for you?"

The infantry officers turned away from Staff Centurion Sisera and faced their Centuries.

"Who passed archery in basic?" they demanded. "Raise your arm. Optios confirm their qualifications and get the best of them to the armory wagons."

While the light infantrymen prepared to defend against a superior force, Alerio peered northward. He studied the demeanor of Senior Tribune Pompeius, the set of his shoulders and stiffness in his posture. After a moment of reflection on his decisions, Centurion Sisera kneed his horse around. Facing the approaching Tribune, Alerio prepared to defend his actions against a superior officer.

***

"Sisera, you may be Gaius Claudius' pet Cane Corso," Pompeius accused as he rode up.

Trailing behind the Senior Tribune were five junior Tribunes and two signalmen. The young noblemen grinned at the inference that the Staff Centurion was a housebroken Mastiff. Wisely, the signalmen maintained neutral expressions on their faces.

"Yes, sir. And I bite," Alerio confirmed.

"What did you say to me?" Pompeius demanded.

"I was agreeing with you, Senior Tribune," Alerio informed him. "I have served as a 'canem de bello' for Colonel Claudius. And as his dog of war, I have killed. Not sure about actually biting, I may have been wrong about that. But, if you count gladius strikes, my steel did bite into flesh and bone…"

"What in Hades name are you babbling on about?" Pompeius challenged.

"Dogs, sir," Alerio stated. "You asked about dogs of war, didn't you?"

Alerio had no idea what he was talking about. He only knew that he had to keep Pompeius too busy to stop the assembly of the ballistae and the collection of extra weapons by the Velites. If he could signal the officers of the eighteen Centuries of heavy infantry that marched in behind the Senior Tribune, he would send those Legionaries to the armory wagons as well.

"I meant to remind you of your place, Centurion Sisera," Pompeius scolded. "Until we sight an enemy, we will continue digging the defensive ditch for the marching camp."

"Yes, sir," Alerio said before suggesting. "Let's walk the stakes to be sure they are correctly placed."

"We have competent engineers for that," the Senior Tribune answered. Then his eyes landed on the four bolt throwers, and he puffed up his cheeks. "I did not order the unpacking of the ballistae. Or the disruption of the engineer's duties. We have a trench to dig."

"Sir, Colonel Claudius believes…"

"Centurion Sisera, and I use the title loosely," Pompeius sneered. "for some unfortunate reason, the Battle Commander decided to split his Legion. Regrettably, he remained in the fight while sending me here to construct a fallback position. Despite him burdening me with a political hack like you, I intend to finish the basic marching camp."

"With your permission, I'll ride the perimeter," Alerio requested.

"No, you've done enough damage," Pompeius advised. "You will stay with me and my command staff. I have a bevy of experienced infantry officers who will follow orders without overstepping their bounds."

"Yes, sir," Alerio responded. "Where do you want to start?"

"I'll begin by having the bolt throwers secured from aiming at the ocean."

Alerio and the staff followed the Senior Tribune towards the center of the proposed camp. They had crossed the boundary for the outer perimeter and Pompeius had just raised an arm to get the senior engineer's attention.

"Brace, brace, brace!"

Although far to the south and out of sight down a slope, the individual voices of three desperate squad leaders carried to the command staff. Only one thing would cause three Decani to instruct their widely dispersed squads to set their feet and put their shoulders into their shields.

"What is that?" Pompeius asked.

"Sir, orders?" Alerio requested.

"I. What is that?"

Many NCOs and officers represented themselves well in a garrison environment. They excelled while living in a world of controlled schedules, routine orders, and tight discipline. But eventually, the superb barrack's commando came face to face with destiny. And in that instance, they failed.

Yelling to rally his patrolling Legionaries, a Centurion appeared at the top of the slope on the southern edge of the proposed marching camp. Also responding, his Optio, Tesserarius, and five squads ran into view and moved to converge on the Century's officer. The Centurion turned and with pleading in his eyes, he looked across the baggage wagons at Senior Tribune Pompeius. The commander of the detachment stared back with a blank expression on his face.

"That's contact with the enemy," Alerio shouted. He grabbed a junior Tribune by an arm and almost pulled the young nobleman off his mount. "Get to the armory wagons. Order the archers to take up positions in front of the bolt throwers. And order the light infantry to attack to the south."

"But Centurion, the Senior Tribune hasn't instructed…" he started to protect.

A hard squeeze of his arm made the young man flinch under the pain.

Then Alerio prompted him with these words, "Remember, I bite."

As the junior Tribune raced off to deliver the messages, Alerio looked at the eighteen Centuries. Kicking his mount, he galloped his horse back to the newly arrived units.

"Do you need me to hold your hand?" Alerio growled. "We have three squads in contact with the enemy. Legionaries of the heavy infantry, stand by."

"Standing by, Centurion," fourteen hundred and forty voices roared back as they stomped the ground.

"Non capimus!" Alerio bellowed the order to spare no one and take no prisoners.

The veteran Centuries left the ranks first and ran towards the south. As they moved over the ground, they broke formation, spread out, and by the time they neared the far edge of the camp, they were in a Maniple line. Close behind, the experienced infantrymen, trailed by the newest Legionaries, also spread out into their Maniples.

When two hundred and fifty Velites sprinted from the wagons and cut in front of the line of heavy infantrymen, Centurion Sisera had a frightening realization. The half Legion was going into battle without a Battle Commander. After a glance at Pompeius, who mumbled something about needing to analyze the situation, Alerio kneed his mount and waved for the junior Tribunes to follow him. Together, they galloped to the south to face the enemy.

Act 6

Chapter 24 – First Centurion

They were cocky and seemingly fearless. And, being two thousand strong, they should have overwhelmed the Legionaries. Except their courage came not from discipline but, from tribal bravado. In the first few moments of contact, the cutoff squads formed three islands bristling with sharp javelin tips. After suffering casualties, the Celt irregulars flowed around the circles of Legion heavy infantrymen, intending to move onto softer targets. They would never reach the lightly defended wagons, support personnel, and pack animals. Instead, the Empire skirmishers were fated to collide with a Legion battle line.

Centurion Sisera clamped his knees to the flanks of his mount and motioned frantically with both hands for the Maniples to widen. Four of the veteran Centurions noticed his nonverbal commands and, to Alerio's astonishment, they passed on the instructions.

During the maneuvering, the third rank dissolved so the double line of heavy infantrymen could stretch almost two thousand feet wide. But every man was assigned with none in reserve. Unlike most Legion operations, there would be no rotation back for a rest. The Centuries were all committed at the point of attack.

"Brace and hold," Alerio shouted.

Surprising him again, the orders were passed up and down the Maniples. When the first wave of northern barbarians threw themselves at the line of big infantry shields, they were stopped in midstride. Then they were crushed against the faces of the shields as others attempted to force their way through. More Celts came from behind and slammed into the mass of their fellow mercenaries. Soon, several rows were stuck and stacked in front of the veteran Legionaries. Despite the pressure, the Legion's journeymen warriors held their shields and bodies rigid and unmoving.

Alerio watched the Celts until the ones coming from the rear slowed, saw the log jam, and began looking for a way around the battle line. Only then did he release the Republic's military might.

"Step back," he bellowed the first direction. Then he added the attacks. "Advance, advance, advance."

Heartbeats passed from when Centurion Sisera issued the commands to when the orders were on the lips of every Legionary. In three additional pumps of the heart, the double line of fourteen hundred and forty infantrymen took a pace to the rear.

The shields backed away, the front pressure vanished, and the Celts fell over each other. Resembling a tumbling stack of firewood, they toppled to the ground. Then, the Maniples advanced.

The front rank of Legionaries bashed down with their shields, pulled them back to their chests, and stepped forward. Slashing at the Celts on the ground, they made one cut with their gladii, stomped once, and stepped onto the piles of Qart Hadasht mercenaries for the next advance. Following them, the second Maniple stabbed with javelins, stomped multiple times to be sure the enemy remained down before moving forward with the veteran Maniple.

On the third advance, the Celt chiefs called back the men who were not entangled near the combat line. Seeing the number of Qart Hadasht irregulars drop when most went to rally around their leaders, the three squads of trapped Legionaries broke their circular formations and sprinted for the Legion lines.

A cheer went up from the Maniples as the thirty infantrymen raced from among the Celts. Slamming aside any standing in their way, the squads bore down on three separate sections of the Legion lines. The ranks parted to allow the running Legionaries to safely pass through.

In front of Alerio, the first escaping infantryman reached the hole and sprinted between cheering Legionaries. Then the second one in the file stopped to kick a Celt. When two more of the squad paused to dish out punishment, Alerio screamed.

"Come through, come through, in the name of Janus, come through," he yelled.

But the angry, and probably still frightened, infantrymen didn't heed the prayer to the God of gates and doorways. Five more stacked up, ignoring their Decanus as the squad leader pushed to get them moving. It wasn't only Alerio and the Centurions in the vicinity watching the delay. An astute Celt chief noticed the opening. Shouting for the tribesmen around him to follow, the Qart Hadasht Lieutenant raced towards the breach.

"Lock shields," Alerio ordered.

This time, the infantrymen delayed in responding in hopes of saving their comrades. In frustration, Centurion Sisera changed tactics and warned.

"Brace and prepare to defend your position."

Realizing an enemy force was coming at them, the infantrymen began to close the hole. But the squad Legionaries, seeing the fissure narrow, forced their way through, keeping the shields back and the opening clear.

The squad leader caught a spear in the back of his neck and was flung to the ground. What two thousand Qart Hadasht skirmishers couldn't do, a breakdown in discipline by his own men did. The Decanus bled out under stampeding feet. The next squad member caught a foot in the back and, on the way to the ground, the tip of a blade. Then the Celts were at the gap.

Interlocking shields held by trained Legionaries were almost unmovable. But an edge without support could be shoved away. The Celt officer slammed a shield aside and dove behind the Legion lines. Close on his tail came a horde of his light infantrymen.

There were no reserves or a third rank to close the opening. Seeing his formation about to fail, Alerio leaped from his mount. As his feet hit the ground, the staff officer flung the light infantry scutum off his back. While running forward, he settled the shield on his forearm and drew his gladius. Then with a roar, Centurion Sisera attacked the breach.

***

As the Legion staff officer charged, the Celt officer stopped. On either side of him, Celts with their backs to their leader fought with Legionaries who had swung back to open the hole. With the addition of Alerio, the narrow rift hosted three distinct battles. Two on either side, struggling for control of the breach, and one in the center caused by the Centurion with the small shield. The Qart

Hadasht officer puffed out his chest, positioned his shield, and raised his sword.

Alerio sized up the northern tribesman. He was taller and heavier than the Legion officer and carried a larger shield and longer sword. In a stand-up fight, the Celt leader had the physical advantage. The situation prevented the Legion weapons instructor from offering an honest duel.

When the large blade began a horizontal cut, Alerio still at top speed, dropped onto his side. Using momentum, he slid forward supported on the light infantry shield and his left leg. The right leg he cocked. Once he neared the war chief, the Legion officer kicked the Lieutenant's knee. Big man or not, a fractured kneecap doesn't support weight. While the Celt leader crumpled, Alerio tucked his left leg, dug the edge of his boot into the soil, and while sliding, popped to his feet.

Rotating his upper body, the Legion officer simultaneously smashed in the mercenary officer's helmet with his scutum while blocking a spear thrust with his gladius. Stepping around the comatose Celt, Alerio pivoted and trapped the shaft under his shield. Then he brought his blade under the shield and stabbed the tribesman between the legs.

A bleeding groin doesn't immediately kill or put the enemy out of action. What the injury does is cause panic and worry about one's testes. In a reflex action, the Qart Hadasht light infantryman reached down with his shield hand to investigate if his family jewels were still intact. Alerio used the laps in concentration to whip the gladius from a low attack, around his back, and over his shoulder, before burying the blade in the Celt's neck. In the end, it didn't matter if his genitalia was attached, dead men don't father children.

Alerio's peripheral vision told the real tale of the breach. While he could slow the tide, as long as the gap remained, Empire mercenaries would continue to crash through the Legion battle line.

On his left and right, six Celt skirmishers fought three of the Republic's heavy infantrymen for control of the opening. The soldiers pressing them backward while the Legionaries struggled to pivot forward and seal the break.

It was a losing position. No matter how talented he was, Alerio couldn't prevent the mercenaries from pouring through the gap. Once enough passed the line, the outnumbered Legionaries would be forced to fight melee style. The result was death and the ruination of the supply wagon and the remainder of Megellus Legion East.

A solution occurred to the Legion officer, and he whispered her name in payer and added a request.

"Goddess Nenia. If it's to be, come quickly for me."

Then Alerio flung the length of his body into the legs of four Celts. Their legs folded and they fell back over the Legion officer. With room to use the big shields, the infantrymen on that side pressed forward, hacking the mercenaries on the ground and those in the breach.

Every man who claims the title of Legionary has earned it. One brutal tactic taught by the instructors in training was the Legion stomp. More than a way to stay together in rhythm or move together in formation, the stomp was a weapon as deadly as their shields, javelins, and gladii. Unfortunately for Alerio, he hugged the ground, lying under the Celts and positioned to receive the Legionaries' stomps.

Gladii hacked and stabbed as the Legionaries slaughtered mercenaries and began closing the gap. And, as if hooves from great oxen, hobnailed boots trampled arms, necks, torsos, and legs. Alerio attempted to crawl away from the pounding boots, but the bodies blocked his escape route.

***

Crippled or dead? The idea flashed through Alerio's mind as he rolled a leg off his neck and scooted under the bottom edge of a Legion shield. While avoiding a bashing, his move placed him in the direct path of a Legionary's big foot. The infantryman didn't look down, how could he? He was busy positioning his scutum to block spears and swords. He and two others shoved the Celts back while attempting to seal the opening. Alerio gawked at the foot as it lifted into the air, shifted forward, and began to descend.

"Don't hurt our only staff officer," a Centurion shouted. He shoulder-blocked the Legionary, reached down, clamped a fist on Alerio's armor, and plucked him out from under the bodies. Then as he examined Alerio's arms and legs for injuries, he scolded. "Centurion Sisera, that was the most foolish thing I've seen in a long while."

"I couldn't think of any other way to give our men an advantage," Alerio offered.

The infantry officer wasn't tall or broad across the shoulders. But his eyes flashed with intensity and the scars on the flesh of his arms told a veteran's tale.

"Tribune. Bring the staff officer's horse over here," he bellowed to the cluster of noblemen. "Come on lads, their light infantry isn't going to hurt you."

Alerio and the Centurion backed away as the Legionaries gave one last push and sealed the breach. Mercenaries on the other side of the battle line, who charged the sector where the gap existed, spread out their attack. Suddenly, being on either side of the combat line was the safest place to be in the open field. The Legion's heavy infantry shields protected the holders and absorbed the strikes. And as long as the Legionaries remain stationary, the Celt mercenaries could dodge the gladii and javelins. Neither side gained ground nor seriously injured the other.

A Tribune nudged his mount towards the two officers while guiding a second horse.

"What's your name, sir?" Alerio inquired.

"Capiti Rapacis of the Sixth Century," the Centurion replied. "And officers don't sir each other. Well, unless one is a nobleman and can give you a job when the General disbands the Legion. And for your information, I don't have a job for you."

Rapacis took the reins of the second horse from the young Tribune and handed them to Alerio.

"Now get on your horse, Sisera, sort out your command staff, and give me a feel for the distribution of the enemy forces."

Then the veteran infantry officer reached up and gently pulled the Tribune off his horse.

"You can have your mount back when this is over, lad," Rapacis explained as he jumped onto the horse's back. "Right now, the Legion needs him more than we need another mounted Tribune."

Indignant at the manhandling, no matter how mild, the young nobleman scuffed his feet on the way back to join the other Tribunes. As angry as he was, he was smart enough not to challenge Centurion Rapacis' authority.

"You'll be assuming command?" Alerio questioned.

"In the name of the Goddess Minerva no. I will not," Capiti Rapacis said referencing the Goddess of wisdom. "You're in command, Sisera."

"But you said what I did was unwise. The most foolish thing you've seen in a while," Alerio reminded the Centurion. "Now you're putting me in command of a half Legion?"

"It was foolish. But, one of the bravest actions I've ever witnessed. Sisera, any man who is willing to sacrifice himself to save a Legion should be in command of a Legion," Rapacis responded. "I'm going to act as your Senior Centurion."

"I'm barely a staff officer," Alerio admitted. "What am I supposed to do?"

"Hades, Sisera. If you're smart enough to ask that, you're far ahead of every other staff officer I know," Rapacis stated. "My job is to work the mechanics of the Legionaries. While I'm dealing with the Centuries, I can't watch the enemy. That's your job. They move, you report it, and the Legion counters."

"Like if I said, slap the Celts to the ground and get us back to the ballistae and archers," Alerio suggested.

He wasn't looking at the Centurion. Rather his eyes were peering over the Maniples at the trees on the far side of the field.

"Those are exactly the type of instructions I need," the infantry officer acknowledged. "From those, I'll issue orders to control the withdrawal and we'll…"

"No, really, Rapacis. I mean get us moving," Alerio informed the infantry officer while lifting an arm.

Capiti Rapacis twisted around to look in the direction indicated by Centurion Sisera. To his shock and horror, column after column of Iberian infantrymen marched from the tree line.

Alerio smiled despite the situation. At least now, he could report to Pompeius that the missing seven thousand Iberians have been located. Unfortunately for the Senior Tribune and the Legion, they were about to get a very close look at the Empire's heavy infantry.

Chapter 25 – Javelin Issue

"We'll need to stick them before we can disengage," Rapacis declared. "Throw two, rotate, and step back."

Alerio sent the Tribunes along the lines where they passed on the instructions to the Centurions. Then, first time Battle Commander Sisera pointed at the two signalmen to hold their attention while he locked eyes with Rapacis.

"The Qart Hadasht heavies aren't moving away from us," the infantry officer warned. Seeing Alerio nod his understanding, Rapacis added. "The Legion is yours, Centurion Sisera."

When the last two junior Tribunes galloped away from the Centuries of Velites on the ends, Alerio lifted both arms to shoulder level.

"Signalmen, sound the attack," he ordered while shooting both arms above his head.

Rolling over the Maniples, the blasts from the trumpets set the Legionaries into motion. Nothing changed with the front line except they lowered their shields by placing the bottom edges in the dirt. Behind them, the second rank flexed their right arms and launched javelins.

There was no arch during the short flight or weakening of force. Eight hundred and forty shafts thrown from close range broke Qart Hadasht shields, bones, and their will. Turning, the survivors attempted to retreat. But another flight of javelins impacted their lower backs and legs. Each hitting with the force of a kick, knocking the hapless Celts to the ground.

The carnage started with trumpets and ended with Legion officers and NCOs directing the second rank to step forward. Coming off the attack line, the relieved Legionaries sheathed their gladii, scooped up the remaining javelins, and trotted away.

"It's a clean separation, Centurion Sisera," Rapacis announced. "Move your command staff to the next rally point."

Alerio saluted the acting Senior Centurion, brought his horse around, and led the signalmen and Tribunes towards the northern end of the field. Jogging Legionaries passed the mounted riders, some carrying wounded or helping injured. Although new to command, Centurion

Sisera knew to display confidence and not to rush. But nerves overrode common sense for one of the Tribunes. He nudged his horse ahead of the others.

"You will fall back and await Centurion Rapacis' pleasure," Alerio scolded the young nobleman. "Or I will unseat you, give you a shield, and put you in a Maniple until you learn courage."

With his head hanging low, the junior Tribune turned around and walked his horse back to the original battle line.

**

Once at the top of the rise, the supply wagons and the four ballistae came into view. Alerio noticed double ranks of archers on either side of the bolt throwers. The total number of bowmen exceeded the one hundred and fifty skirmishers he sent to the armory wagon.

"Where did the extra archers come from?" he wondered out loud.

"Those are the Legionaries from the cavalry detachment, sir," one of the signalmen responded. "I guess they figured being mounted during a fixed battle wasn't a good idea."

"I don't care about their reasoning," Alerio admitted. "What's important is the additional offense."

The retreating infantrymen stopped at the top of the slope. Except for those carrying wounded to the incomplete marching camp, the rest turned and set their shields. From horseback, Alerio shifted his attention from the camp to the line of Legionaries moving to the bottom of the hill. Centurion Rapacis and the junior Tribune lagged behind waving their arms encouraging the men.

Although they didn't need much urging as halfway across the field, the leading edge of the Iberian infantry jogged after them.

"Orders, Centurion?" a Tribune inquired.

"You and your horseless companion get to the camp and inform the ballista engineer he needs to breakout his razor," Alerio directed.

"Razor, sir?"

"Just tell him a herd of Iberians are coming," he replied. "You can stay there and help coordinate the artillery and archers."

The one on the ground grabbed the tail of the other's mount and used it to help him keep up while they trotted away. Glancing beyond the Tribunes, Alerio studied the formations of the bowmen. Both were parade ground square with straight ranks. Turning away from the rear, Alerio watched the Legionaries and infantry officers chugging up the hill. From the slope, Centurion Rapacis made a throwing motion then indicated the area behind him by jerking a thumb over his shoulder.

"Tribunes. Alert the Centuries. Prepare two. Throw on my command," Alerio ordered.

The noblemen raced to deliver the message and Alerio let his eyes fall on the Legionaries standing in front of him.

Each infantryman started with three javelins. A single rank of the half Legion had used two to uncouple from the Celts. His new order to launch two more left the ranks with no reserves. Each infantryman, depending on the number of wounded and equipment failures, would have only one for the retreat.

Looking over his shoulder, Alerio studied the ground between the hilltop and the bolt throwers. Hard rocky ground stretched to a creek and on the far side, pastureland churned up by Legion boots ran flat to the artillery pieces. He didn't remember how far it was when they charged out to save the trapped squads.

"This is the final volley, until we reach the supply wagons," Alerio mumbled.

Neither signalman replied. They were accustomed to commanders talking out loud. And both understood the Legionaries needed their last javelin to keep the Qart Hadasht infantry off their shields. No extra javelins meant no throws to keep the Iberians away while they crossed the open ground.

***

"It doesn't seem fair," Alerio said to himself while pointing with both arms to alert the signalmen. "A man can run forward and attack. But make him walk backwards, and all he can manage is defense."

"What's that you're saying?" Centurion Rapacis inquired as his horse topped the rise.

"Nothing. Just thinking," Alerio responded. He surveyed both sides of the line. His Centuries stood suspended with javelins hoisted while Rapacis' line passed through the ranks. Clapping his hands over his head, Centurion Sisera shouted. "Launch one javelin."

Alerio had controlled infantry in combat before. Although the units were composed of oarsmen and pirates. This occasion was different. The troops were Legionaries. And there was something empowering and heady about commanding the Republic's heavy and light

241

infantry. His chest swelled when the trumpets blared in response to his order.

Eight hundred and forty javelins arched into the air, nosed over at the top of the arc, and fell among the mercenaries. As if slapped down by invisible fists, the front rank of the Iberian infantry was driven off their feet and pinned to the ground.

The lucky ones caught the iron tips in their shields. Softer than steel, the javelin heads bent and weighted down the arms holding the shields. Out of necessity, the stricken stopped to work the javelin heads out of their gear. For the unlucky who didn't get their shields up, the iron tips mangled flesh. Between the dead, the wounded, and the disabled shields, the front rank of the Qart Hadasht infantry stumbled to a halt.

Shouting, kicking, and threats by Lieutenants drove the next rank through the casualties and up the slope. Seeing the dramatic results of a rain of javelins, most held their shields over their heads. To support and stabilize the weight, they balanced it with the hand holding the spear. This put both arms and their primary weapon over their heads.

"You are a cold-blooded piece of work, Centurion Sisera," Rapacis complimented. He looked down at the enemy and marveled at how close Alerio allowed them to get. "I'll take my Maniple to a halfway point and wait."

"Don't do that. If you pause, it'll lock us into a battle of attrition. Remember the Qart Hadasht General is bringing seven thousand heavies to the party," Alerio advised. He never took his eyes off the slope and the advancing ranks of Iberians, especially those on the front rank with shields held over their heads. "Get your line to the armory wagons so they can rearm. We can make it, but I'll need your lads to make it rain javelins."

"Are you sure you're a staff officer, Sisera?" Rapacis questioned. "Because you're acting like an infantry officer."

"Centurion, in my heart I am a Legion heavy infantryman," Alerio replied. He tipped his head and nodded at the single rank of Legionaries standing casually in front of him. "Truth? I'd rather be with them holding a scutum than sitting on a horse jawing with you."

"Welcome to command, Centurion," Rapacis offered while turning his horse. Once facing the wagons, he signaled 'go' to his Centurions. Before the Maniple of Legionaries jogged away, they dropped their last javelin. The infantry officer glanced sideways at Alerio. "Don't be late Sisera. You know how much Senior Tribune Pompeius hates it when someone throws off his schedules."

Alerio didn't reply. But he did allow a smile to grace his lips. Then he held his arms out from his sides and extended fingers towards the signalmen. Twisting his neck, the staff Centurion watched until most of the fleeing Legionaries had reached the creek.

"Standby to hurl," Alerio shouted shifting his gaze to the front and the Iberians climbing the slope. This time instead of raising his arms, he brought his hands together in front of his body. Just before they struck, Centurion Sisera ordered. "Throw one."

The clap from Alerio's hands barely escaped his palms before the shrieking of the trumpets drowned out the sound.

***

Captain Júcar fumed at his staff. Somehow his Lieutenants had allowed a small force of Latians to break contact and reach the hilltop. He glared at the line of Legionaries along the pinnacle then shifted his gaze down to the cautious maneuvering of his soldiers.

"I sneaked seventy companies behind the enemy in an historic night march. Then in some fashion I've yet to understand, you allow barely sixteen companies to stop you. And then to make their escape," the Iberian Captain bellowed. "Get up that slope and kill them. Now. Or by the Goddess Epona, I'll trample every last one of you under the hooves of my horse."

From the center of the field, the commanders raced to their companies and in frustration rained their own threats down on their junior officers and NCOs. The result was a surge that started in the rear and rolled forward until the first rank was being pushed up the hill.

Júcar knew he could blame the Celts and their rash advance. That alone gave him confidence he would survive the wrath of General Gisco and Major Sucro. But keeping his position wasn't the same as excelling at his profession. For that, he needed the Legionaries dead.

Looking back to the hilltop, he smiled at the progress of his infantrymen. Soon they would swarm over the pesky Legionaries. Even as he gloated, something confused the Captain. The Latians' reaction to their coming doom seemed odd. They stood almost casually along the crest, some even leaning against their shields.

***

Just before his hands struck, Centurion Sisera ordered. "Throw one."

As the sharp notes of the trumpets faded, Legionaries pulled javelins from behind their shields. The weapons weren't lifted to shoulder height. Most, in fact, stopped at hip level before the infantrymen pulled back their arms and launched the javelins down the slope.

In a flat trajectory that followed the incline of the earth, the shafts sailed down the hill. At the front rank of Iberians, the weapons passed under the shields being held overhead and into chest armor, naked arms, legs, and the faces of the soldiers. With one throw, Alerio's Legionaries crippled the Qart Hadasht forces more than the two previous volleys combined.

"Throw one," Alerio shouted again. Then he directed the signalmen. "Sound the retreat."

More dead and injured pitched back from the second javelin. With the soldiers bunching up, the Iberian advance stalled.

Tightly packed, the bodies fell back while the soldiers lower on the slope pushed upward. The wine press effect forced some of the wounded down, entangling them in the legs of the next rank. Another portion of the dying raised up before tumbling downhill over the helmets of their comrades.

While the cries of wounded on the ground were muffled, those on top of the Iberians screamed and flung blood as they rolled. Not being able to see the crests or knowing what kind of beast was attacking, the companies stopped and braced.

Alerio looked down the slope and into the faces of disoriented ranks of enemy soldiers. They could be at the top and on him quickly if they weren't tangled up and paused.

"Let's go," Alerio instructed as he nudged his horse into a trot. "Signalmen. Standby to sound the form ranks."

The Tribunes delayed in following. Instead, they filed by the hilltop to see the results of the javelin work. They all agreed the staff Centurion had judged the distance well. None voiced a suspicion or questioned if Sisera had allowed the Iberians to come too far up the slope. Once they had a look, the noblemen kicked their mounts into motion and raced after the retreating Maniple of Legionaries.

***

Catching spears between your shoulder blades was what the instructors in training called turning your back on an enemy. Alerio felt tension in his upper back and rotated his head to look over his shoulder. At the crest, Iberian infantry poured over the top and moved rapidly across the rocky ground.

"Get to the creek and set a defensive line on the other side," Alerio instructed the Tribunes. Then to the signalmen, he ordered. "Go. Once you're across, sound the form up."

The noblemen and mounted Legionaries raced away and soon passed the ragged line of jogging infantrymen. In the distance, they splashed across the creek, and circled around.

Alerio would take Legionaries over any other infantrymen in an equal fight and even against a larger force. But there was an army chasing his eight hundred and forty men. Those were odds not even Mercury would gamble on.

Rather than riding for the creek, Alerio guided his horse diagonally across the field and reined in behind seven men lagging behind.

"It must be a good day to die," he called to the cluster of struggling Legionaries. "I guess the Goddess Nenia has no other souls to free today."

Hearing the voice of the staff officer and his warning about the Goddess who freed souls, the Legionaries lifted their legs higher and pumped their arms harder. The trumpets blasted and Alerio glanced back.

A few Iberians raced ahead of the massed ranks and threw spears. The shafts carved paths through the air but fell short. Their next toss or the one after would reach Alerio and the slugs. He so wanted to charge ahead of the Legionaries and cross the creek. But a Legion officer had to show courage, making it a moral imperative to continue herding the slow men.

"Looking to catch a spear between your shoulder blades," he sang out. "Is this a good day to die?"

"No, Centurion," they shouted while extending their strides.

Alerio glanced up and saw Legionaries splashing into the creek. On the far side, others turned and claimed a position. As each shield fell into place, the likelihood of a spear striking a Legionary lessened. While the threat from thrown spears dissipated, the chance of death from jabs and thrusts across a battle line increased.

Between the rushing Iberians and the forming Legion defensive screen, the eight Latians struggled to reach the creek. The infantrymen ran with Centurion Sisera riding on their heels and offering a bigger target. During the flight, Alerio fully expected to catch a spear between his shoulders.

Chapter 26 – Drop blade, grovel then perish

Three of the ten infantry officers moved in on Alerio as his horse splashed across the creek. The other seven maintained positions on the line behind their Centuries.

"Dismount," one Centurion insisted.

Alerio glanced around and noted the Tribunes and signalmen were standing on the ground.

"This is a knife fight, Sisera," offered another of the officers. "You've brought us as far as you can, and we appreciate it."

"There's not much a commander can do at this point. Except catch a spear by staying up on a horse," the third Centurion pointed out. "We're down to less than two javelins in each Century."

"From here to the marching camp, it's blades and shields," the first infantry officer stated. "It's not the dominion of a staff officer."

The three Centurions couldn't decide if the laughter from Sisera was sarcastic or if the staff officer was actually happy to be relieved of the responsibility. He slipped off the animal's back and rubbed his hands together.

"Excellent. Where do you want me?" Alerio inquired while walking to a stack of equipment left by stretcher-bearers after crossing the creek. He selected a heavy infantry scutum and a plain helmet. After tossing his officer's helmet to a Tribune, he advised. "I'll need that back later."

The trio of infantry officers exchanged looks of wonder when Sisera fitted the shield to his right arm. Obviously, the staff officer had no training or idea how to mount an infantry shield.

"Stay with the Tribunes," one instructed Alerio. "We'll be stepping back fast. We can't have a staff officer on a lark fouling our Maniple."

"I agree. The left end works," Alerio announced. Three spears came over the defensive formation and impacted near the group. The points sank into the soil with the shafts sticking almost straight up. "It's time to move the Centuries. I'll see you at the marching camp."

The Tribunes, signalmen, and infantry officers watched as the staff Centurion sprinted down the rank of four hundred and twenty Legionaries. At the end of the formation, he had animated words with the Centurion, the Optio, and the Century's Tesserarius. Finally, the Century's officer turned to face in the direction of the gathering and held out his arms as if signifying he surrendered. Then the infantry officer turned his attention back to the Legionaries on the end section of the combat screen

The three Centurions watched Alerio stroll to the end of the formation. He touched the edge of his scutum with the shield of what had been the last infantryman on the Legion line.

"Maybe Sisera was arguing against the suicide position," one of the Centurions suggested.

"Sir, I don't think that was the argument," one signalman advised. "I've been beside Centurion Sisera since this operation began. And I believe he is finally getting what he wants."

"And what does he want, Private?"

"To fight, sir."

"Signal all Centuries. Begin stepping back," the Centurion ordered while waving so the Legion line could see the motions. Then his eyes fell on the staff Centurion's helmet, and he instructed the Tribune holding it. "Be sure that gets to the armory wagon when this is over. I don't think Sisera will be around to claim it."

***

Eight hundred and forty shields created a front of about two thousand feet. Wide enough to stop the Iberians' charge. But, as the old saying went, some things were a mile wide and a foot deep. The Legion formation certainly met those specifications. The infantry Centurions designed it to prevent them from being immediately enveloped by the enemy. Once the shields clashed, the Legion Maniple would begin stepping back and collapsing towards the center. While the maneuver created ranks in the middle, it put escalating pressure on the Legionaries stationed on the ends.

"Alerio Sisera," Alerio said introducing himself to the Legionary on his right. Nudging his right arm mounted scutum against the other man's shield, the Centurion

250

smiled and tilted his head at the approaching Iberians. "Nice view."

"Storax, sir," the Legionary replied. "Whose camp stew did you urinate in?"

"I could ask you the same," Alerio said. His referenced the possibility that being ordered to the most dangerous position in a battle screen was punishment for some transgression. "I'm an extra shield. What about you?"

"My Centurion described me as duplicitous," Private Storax explained.

Alerio gulped and questioned his decision to join the combat screen.

"Why? Are you treacherous, unfaithful, or dishonest?"

With enemy infantry coming at their location, both infantrymen could be killed in a short while. There was no reason to be polite.

"Sisera. I am a man of devotion," Storax reported. "Plus, I am the strongest shield in my Century."

"I don't see a contradiction between prayers and a strong left arm."

"Well, you see, when I'm not honoring the Gods, I drink a bit," he confessed. "And that side of me is guilty of all three sins."

"Two questions for you Private Storax," Alerio inquired. "Are you drunk right now?"

"No opportunity today," the Private answered. "Although looking at what's heading our way, I wish I was. What's the second question?"

"Can you sing?"

Storax spit on the ground, cleared his throat, and in a clear powerful voice, began to sing.

If men gather that mean you harm
Overwhelmingly you feel alarm
Adjust your shield and grip your hilt
And ask yourself if your luck is built
Pray to Jupiter that you have a later
Survive you will, if you are able
Question if you are laudable and honest
Could your soul be more flawless?

The Iberians marched across the rocky ground. If they had been tribal, they would be running, and the mass of charging bodies would easily break the Legion Maniple. Plus, swifter units breaking away from the main body could run around the ends. But the disciplined soldiers fell victim to their own organization and structure. None of their Lieutenants wanted to abandon their formation. As a result, columns of Iberian infantry traipsed straight at the line of Legionaries.

Do you respect the Gods and the laws?
Stand up for the citizens' cause?
Are you worthy of the Republic for which you fight?
Then beg the Sky Father to share his might
Send an enforcer to steady your arm
A winged avenger as a bolstering charm

The Legion Maniple moved back one step at a time. By necessity, they moved slower than the attackers. One side rushed to reach the defensive screen, while the other side attempted to keep the shields tight and orderly.

The strength of my body
The force of my strikes
Grace me Goddess Bia
With the vigor to fight

Don't let me faulter, fade from the battle, lose heart,
drop blade, grovel then perish

The singing spread from the left side and, as flames
devour logs, it spread to the far side. With each phrase, the
Legionaries withdrew another two steps. But the soldiers
gained four, bringing them closer together.

The will for the struggle
The zeal for my life
Bless me God Zelos
With the hunger for strife
Don't let me faulter, fade from the battle, lose heart,
drop blade, grovel then perish

The rocky ground on the far side of the creek slowed
the Iberians while the flat pastureland aided the
Legionaries. Adding to the delay in the battle, the banks of
the stream caused a wobble in the mercenaries' front. It
didn't last long.

If men gather that mean you harm
Overwhelmingly you feel alarm
Adjust your shield and grip your hilt
And ask yourself if your luck is built
Pray to Jupiter that you have a later
Survive you will, if you are able

Stress and fear mixed, causing a fire in the hearts of
some anxious men. If injury and pain awaited, they would
rather get it over with immediately. Enough Iberians
embraced the emotions that a strip of soldiers peeled away
from the formation and sprinted ahead.

Question if you are laudable and honest
Could your soul be more flawless?
Do you respect the Gods and the laws?

Stand up for the citizens' cause?

The goal of the Centurions was to keep the mercenaries off their shields as long as possible. As the ragged group of screaming soldiers approached, the infantry officers ordered one of their two javelins thrown. From a dead run, Iberians were slammed to the ground by the Legion weapons, or they had to stop and work the iron point from their shields. A self-fulfilling prophecy came to the ones who reached the Legionaries. They died. The Legion line continued to retreat unencumbered but, it cost them. They were down to one javelin.

Are you worthy of the Republic for which you fight?
Then beg the Sky Father to share his might
Send an enforcer to steady your arm
A winged avenger as a bolstering charm

Up to that point, the thin Legion line stretched far enough to match the enemy. It worked as the Iberian Lieutenants didn't separate their Companies and attempt to circle the ends. They concentrated their forces on breaking the Legion's weak center. Even with the focus on the middle, military doctrine required a containment force on the flanks of the main body.

The power of my fury
The control of my armor
Favor me God Kratos
With the means for valor
Don't let me faulter, fade from the battle, lose heart,
drop blade, grovel then perish

The squad assigned to one end of the laughably single row of Latians, jogged out of formation. Thinking bonuses and glory for breaking through the Legionaries, the ten soldiers rushed forward. Fate hurled them to the left side of the Legion and into the blade and scutum of Centurion Alerio Sisera.

The day for my victory
The triumph over my woes
Grant me Goddess Victoria
With the end of my foes
Don't let me faulter, fade from the battle, lose heart,
drop blade, grovel then perish

"How was that?" Storax inquired.

Keeping his shield against Storax's, Alerio pivoted out, reached across with his left arm, and hacked into an approaching Iberian's spear. Driving the weapon off to the side, he lifted his foot and stomped on the shaft. It splintered and bent. The soldier fell back as the Legion line moved away.

"An appropriate song. We could use the help from Jupiter's winged assistants," Alerio answered while stepping to the rear and straightening the defensive screen. "Sing it again."

***

If men gather that mean you harm
Overwhelmingly you feel alarm
Adjust your shield and grip your hilt
And ask yourself if your luck is built

Seeing their fastest man lose his primary weapon, the soldiers held back to allow their best spearman to move ahead. He would break off the end and chew up the Latian. Of that, the containment squad was sure.

Pray to Jupiter that you have a later
Survive you will, if you are able

Question if you are laudable and honest
Could your soul be more flawless?

He came in low, his spear level, and tip pointed mid shield. Alerio judged that the massive shoulders driving the shaft could easily take a man off his feet with one solid thrust. When the spear shot forward, the Legion weapon instructor tilted his shield.

Do you respect the Gods and the laws?
Stand up for the citizens' cause?
Are you worthy of the Republic for which you fight?

The Iberian took a giant step forward in order to drive the Latian off his feet. Alerio rolled his shield, deflecting the spear tip to his left. For less than a heartbeat, the shaft protruded along Alerio's side between his scutum and his left arm. Taking advantage of the off balanced spearman and his awkward foot positions, the Legionary captured the shift and gyrated violently to his left. Over committed and holding on with a strong grip, the Iberian spearman stumbled sidewise, tripped, and fell to the ground.

Then beg the Sky Father to share his might
Send an enforcer to steady your arm
A winged avenger as a bolstering charm

After a breath, the shaft came free. The Iberian found himself on his knees following his plunge off to the side. The mental process of orientation and reacquiring his target kicked in. Although out ahead of his squad, the spearman wasn't out of the fight. He brought his spear up to meet a flying Latian.

Alerio released the shaft from under his arm and used the shield to brush away the steel head of the weapon. At the completion of his spin, the Legionary planted a foot

256

and pushed off. In mid jump, the spear rose but he was already inside the arc of the shaft. Coming down, he hacked with the gladius and started to back away. But the spearman not only had heavy shoulders, but he possessed thick bones to support the muscles. Alerio's blade caught in the Iberian's spine.

The strength of my body
The force of my strikes
Grace me Goddess Bia
With the vigor to fight

Yanking at the gladius while watching two Iberians shuffle forward, Alerio almost panicked. Separated from the Legion, he was prey for the pair of Iberian infantrymen and the ones behind them.

Don't let me faulter, fade from the battle, lose heart
drop blade, grovel then perish

On the third tug, the bones and gristle separated and Alerio's gladius slid free. Plodding backward, he moved to rejoin Storax. Four steps then five, and as the two spearmen closed in on Centurion Sisera, he realized he couldn't locate the Legion line.

The will for the struggle
The zeal for my life
Bless me God Zelos
With the hunger for strife

The spears in his face prevented Alerio from looking back and locating the Legion. Resembling wolves hunting an isolated sheep, the pair of Iberians jabbed and stepped forward with confidence. Except this sheep had teeth.

Rotating his scutum ninety degrees, Alerio used the length to push both spears up while he dropped to his left knee. Before the spearmen adjusted, the Legion weapons instructor reached under the shield and slashed his blade across unguarded shines. As the Iberian spearmen collapsed to the ground, Centurion Sisera rose from his knee and hopped backwards.

Don't let me faulter, fade from the battle, lose heart
drop blade, grovel then perish

A scutum came around him and Alerio felt himself guided back and to the right. Far to the right it seemed. Then Private Storax released him and jammed his shield against Centurion Sisera's.

"You hold a line as well as you sing, sir," Storax offered. "Not worth a brass coin. Gods. I need a drink."

Alerio realized why he couldn't locate the Legion position. The Centurions had begun folding the line and building up a second rank in the center. Eventually, the formation would become a fighting square. Until then, he and Storax were on the end with a squad of angry and determined Iberians coming at them.

If men gather that mean you harm
Overwhelmingly you feel alarm
Adjust your shield and grip your hilt
And ask yourself if your luck is built

There was more than one type of defensive tactic possible while backing up. Reactive used only blocks to fend off attacks. It crossed Alerio's mind and tweaked his nerves at the same time. He wasn't the passive type.

"Storax, no matter what happens, keep your scutum high," Alerio ordered. "and your javelin working."

"But I won't be able to see where or whom I'm skewing," the Private complained.

"Don't worry, I'll send them your way," Alerio promised.

"What are you, Sisera? A staff officer, an unruly infantryman, or someone sent by the Gods to test me?"

"Probably, a little of each," Alerio responded. "But right now, I'm a Legion weapons instructor. And the Iberians are about to get a hard lesson."

Storax raised his shield and began mechanically stabbing the air with his javelin. On the fourth fruitless jab, the Legionary on his right side observed.

"You have no target, and you can't see. You aren't hitting anything."

"Don't tell me, tell Centurion Sisera…"

Before he could finish, a voice, sounding like a wet fishing net slapping on rocks and scraping scales for screaming aquamarine life, bellowed forth from Storax's left. Somewhere in the squishy, grating voice were the words to the song.

Pray to Jupiter that you have a later
Survive you will, if you are able
Question if you are laudable and honest
Could your soul be more flawless?

As a teen, Alerio had been taught when fighting multiple foes, find a way to separate them. If only momentarily, force some of them out of contact. Put them on the ground, against a wall, or smack them in the head and let their minds go dark. Anything to reduce the odds. The six Iberians in two rows rushing at him, certainly qualified as multiple foes.

Do you respect the Gods and the laws?
Stand up for the citizens' cause?

259

Are you worthy of the Republic for which you fight?

Alerio shuffle-stepped to the left and away from Storax. When all six spears shifted to follow, the Legionary jumped right and forward. He ended up beside two lengths of shafts. The shorter ones of those jutting from the rear row of the Iberian formation and longer ones from the three men in front. The spear heads jerked with some flying up, others circling, or being pulled back. All attempting to bring the steel tips in line to stab the Legionary. But every moving shaft had a fixed point. It was gripped in the hands of a spearman.

Driving with his legs, Centurion Sisera powered the first Iberian back where he collided with two of his squad mates. They tangled up putting three of them temporarily out of the fight. The third soldier in the rear caught Alerio's gladius blade on the side of his head. He dropped. With only two soldiers to battle, the Legion weapons instructor pivoted so they stood between his scutum and Storax's plunging javelin.

Then beg the Sky Father to share his might
Send an enforcer to steady your arm
A winged avenger as a bolstering charm

Alerio shoved one in front of the Private and kicked the legs out from under the other. Almost simultaneously, the two solders screamed their last breath. One on the tip of Alerio's gladius and the other on the point of Storax's javelin. Spinning, Alerio looked for the next threat.

"That was fun," Storax proclaimed.

His voice was clear enough that Alerio knew he wasn't talking from behind his shield.

"Cover," Alerio warned.

Ducking, he dodged two thrown spears. Centurion Sisera's breath caught in his throat until the sounds of the steel heads impacting a Legion scutum reached him. Then he attacked the Iberians who, having chucked their spears, were drawing their swords.

The power of my fury
The control of my armor
Favor me God Kratos
With the means for valor

The three soldiers had untangled and two thought to bring the Latian down with their spears. But once thrown, they paused for a heartbeat believing they couldn't have missed at the close distance.

Alerio disregarded the two fumbling with their swords and leaped at the last Iberian with a spear. The shaft swung in the weapons instructor's direction. Just before it steadied on Alerio's chest, he chopped into the wood. With the blade buried in a long fat splinter, he pushed the shaft towards the ground. Fighting to maintain control of his weapon, the spearman lifted against the downward pressure. Before the two struggled very long, Alerio lifted a foot and stomped down on the shaft. The entire length of the spear slammed to the ground, taking the Iberian down with it. In one step and an extension of his arm, Alerio stabbed into the back of the spearman's neck.

Don't let me faulter, fade from the battle, lose heart
drop blade, grovel then perish

The last two soldiers from the containment squad looked at their fallen comrades and backed away. Reinforcements would be coming, and they would just as

261

soon have another squad reap the glory of turning the Legion line.

"Sisera. Put away your mentula and move your cūlus," Storax yelled.

Glancing to his left, Alerio saw the line of Legion shields had moved far away. The only Legionaries in the vicinity were Private Storax and Centurion Sisera. Together they began running for the rows of Legionaries near the center of the formation.

They were four paces into their run when a cluster of Iberians angled towards them. It was turn and fight or catch a spear between his shoulder blades. Just before Alerio turned, a lightning bolt clipped his shield. The force knocked the Legion officer to the soil. Then surprisingly, Storax dove down beside him.

"What was that?" Alerio demanded. He attempted to shake feeling back into his arm and shoulder but, his right side remained numb.

"Bolt throwers," the Private replied.

A third swish passed over their heads. Finally, wailing and cries of pain reached them from the Iberians. In the midst of the agony a fourth bolt split the air, and as if an iron fist, it split soldiers in half as it punched through the ranks of Iberians before coming to rest in one poor soul's gut.

"I counted three," Storax offered.

"No, it was four bolts from the ballistae," Alerio countered while rotating his painful right shoulder. "We should go."

"You know something, sir," Storax said as they came to their feet and began running for the Legion ranks. "I think I'll give up drinking."

The day for my victory
The triumph over my woes
Grant me Goddess Victoria
With the end of my foes
Don't let me faulter, fade from the battle, lose heart
drop blade, grovel then perish

Chapter 27 – Ditch Detail

The two isolated Legionaries reached the formation, spun around, and set their shields.

"Sisera. Get out of my ranks," the Century's officer ordered. "You've done enough damage for one day."

Believing his individual battle with the Iberian squad had hurt the Legion line, Alerio ducked back through the three ranks of infantrymen.

"Go get on the proper head gear, Centurion," the infantry officer directed when Alerio stepped clear of the Legionaries. "And lose that shield."

In the center of the fighting square, the most experienced Centurion stood with his fist pressed into his sides. As was tradition, when there was no Senior Centurion present the most experienced infantry officer took charge. Alerio shook off his weariness and walked to the officer.

"Why did you collapse the line prematurely?" Alerio questioned.

As if they were fast growing vines, the Iberians wrapped around the fighting square. To the north and south, the mercenaries stacked up ten infantrymen deep, on the east and west, the bolt throwers limited them to three men in a stack. Anyone standing beyond that thickness was swept away by bolts from the ballistae.

"Tribune, return the staff Centurion's helmet," the experienced officer directed the nobleman holding Alerio's head gear. Then, once Sisera settled it over his head, the Centurion answered. "Our right side folded like a threadbare tunic. We lost a Centurion, his Optio, and half a Century before we contained the breach."

"After that failure, pulling in the left side makes sense," Alerio acknowledged. "Although, it would have been nice to have a warning."

"The Centurion called out. But his lay priest ignored the withdraw order," the infantry officer explained. "That maniac Legionary stayed out there to cover your right side."

While the infantry officer and staff Centurion talked, the ends of the fighting square compressed. On the verge of collapsing, the Legion heavy infantrymen surged forward, regained the lost ground, and straightened their lines. The Legion detachment held back the Qart Hadasht forces but, they weren't making any headway towards the marching camp.

Suddenly, individual shouts rose from deep in the Iberian ranks. In response, those battling the Legionaries pulled back from the battle screen. As the pressure lifted the Legionaries noticed it was more than a break in hostilities. The Iberian infantrymen jogged from the combat zone, collected their wounded, and marched away.

"That's interesting," the experienced Centurion observed. Turning to Alerio he inquired. "Orders, staff Centurion?"

"Signalmen, sound the retreat," Alerio instructed. Then to the veteran Centurion, he added. "Storax."

"What's that?"

"The maniac's name is Private Storax," Alerio declared. "and if it wasn't for him, you would have lost your left side as well as your right."

"I know that Sisera," the infantry officer affirmed. "I just didn't want it to go to your or that drunken would-be priest's head."

The box formed by the Legionaries began moving to the north. Within the square, Alerio fell in among the Tribunes.

"You can lose the shield, Centurion Sisera," one suggested. "I don't think you'll be fighting anymore today."

Alerio glanced down at the face of the shield. Through a horizontal gash, he could see the layers of oak that gave the scutum its shape and resilience. A slight discoloring between layers was the glue holding the slim sheets together. Ripped from the gouge but visible around the edges, were neat lines of the linen topping the layers of wood. Finally, the groove showed the outline of the goat skin cover that made the shield waterproof.

"No. I think I'll keep it for now," he replied.

In the absence of an enemy force, the formation divided into Centuries. Once in units, the pace increased, and they crossed the field quickly and entered the incomplete marching camp.

The infantry officers clustered around the Senior Tribune, but Alerio avoided Pompeius by veering off towards the ballistae. After a short search, he located the senior engineer.

"I thought you might want this," Alerio offered by holding out the infantry shield.

Bent over and distracted by the release mechanism on one of his bolt throwers, the engineer glanced back, noted what the Centurion was holding, and returned to the ballista.

"What do I want with an infantry shield?" he questioned.

"You can see what a bolt in flight does when it skims a shield," Alerio replied. He rotated his stiff and aching right shoulder and added. "Plus, I can tell you and your artillerymen how it feels to be on the receiving end."

"That would be interesting," the engineer agreed. "Let me fix this and we'll hold a meeting. Anything you need while you wait?"

"I could use a wineskin and a spot out of the sun," Alerio informed him.

"We can supply those," the engineer promised.

***

Cavalrymen entering the marching camp explained the reason for the Iberians' retreat. Megellus Legion North had arrived. Along with the three thousand fresh heavy infantrymen and eight hundred light, came General Postumius Megellus and Colonel Zenonis. The

266

commanders and their Tribunes trotted into camp and gathered around Senior Tribune Pompeius.

"Myrias, my friend, you saved my supplies and my ballistae," General Megellus boasted. His use of the Senior Tribune's first name confirmed the Consul's affection for Pompeius.

"Sir, I can't take all the credit," Pompeius replied. "My infantry officers reacted precisely to my orders. Together, we withstood the Iberian attack."

"Your courage and humility are touching," the General gushed. "I sent the Greek infantry from Syracuse to help Colonel Claudius. Let's go see how he fared without his trusty Senior Tribune."

The command staffs galloped off following the General northward. None paid any attention to the group of artillerymen sitting under a leather cover in a semicircle.

"Shouldn't you go with them, Centurion Sisera?" one of them inquired.

"A staff Centurion is as useless as a bolt on a thrower without torsion," Alerio responded. "It'll look dangerous and ready but has no power to launch."

"What was that you were saying about being hit?" the senior engineer urged.

"I said, when the bolt connected with my shield, it felt like I was kicked by two mules," Alerio explained.

The ballista crews laughed. They never received firsthand descriptions from people down range of their weapons. Mostly because, anyone they targeted died.

***

The contested land that witnessed Colonel Gaius Claudius' fighting retreat resembled a disorganized military parade. Thousands of Greek and Latian infantrymen moved over the fields in waves. Some watched the closed gates of Agrigento, others moved to help construct marching camps, and still more repositioned to temporary areas.

Alerio stepped down into the camp's ditch, crossed the bottom, and stepped up on the other side. Once on flat land, he dodged between units while peering around searching for familiar faces.

The sixteen thousand Legionaries from four Legions plus twenty thousand Greeks from Syracuse clustered on the south side. Only a few units had received orders to disperse around the besieged city.

"Centurion Sisera?" a Tribune sitting on a horse shouted. "Centurion Sisera?"

Alerio saw him on the far side of two converging Centuries. Losing the view as shields, javelins and armored bodies marched by, it took a moment to locate the noblemen when the last rank of infantrymen parted. Alerio raised his arms and flinched. His right shoulder cramped from the bolt's impact, and he settled for signaling with his left arm.

"Over here," Alerio called.

The mounted staff officer nudged his horse towards the Centurion. As he closed the distance, Alerio noted the Tribune held the reins for a second horse.

"Colonel Claudius sent me to collect you," the junior Tribune said while reaching down to hand Alerio the reins.

"Where is the Battle Commander?"

"The Generals and their Colonels are on the main road leading to Agrigento," the Tribune replied. "Trying to get the Qart Hadasht commander to come out and fight."

"How's that working out?" Alerio inquired as he leaped onto the animal's back.

"So far, a flight of arrows from the walls to back us off was the only reply."

"That is a pretty definitive answer," Alerio suggested as he guided the horse between moving units. "They aren't coming out to do battle."

***

"What does that mean, they aren't coming out?" Senior Tribune Pompeius demanded. "Is that from a mystical message from the Goddess Minerva or are you simply guessing?"

When Alerio and the junior Tribune reached the road, they fell in with Colonel Claudius' staff. As soon as Pompeius saw Alerio, he turned away and didn't acknowledge the staff Centurion.

"Colonel, Centurion Sisera reporting as ordered," Alerio announced as he pulled his horse to a stop. Then he attempted to salute but his right arm hung up on the bruised bone, sore tendons, and muscles from the bolt hit. His arm stopped painfully, locked up, and hovered in the air. It appeared as if he was making a fist in the direction of the Battle Commander.

"The Generals have sent messages to the city asking for battle or offering safe passage," the Colonel informed Alerio bringing him up to date on events. Then the Battle

Commander pointed at the clinched hand and asked. "Is that fist directed at me?"

"No sir, my arm seems to be stuck in mid salute. I caught a bolt and suffered some damage," Alerio offered. Then he said. "The Qart Hadasht forces aren't coming out to fight, sir."

That's when Senior Tribune Pompeius whipped his head around and questioned the staff officer.

"What do you mean, they aren't coming out?"

"I didn't receive any wisdom from the Goddess, Senior Tribune," Alerio explained. "I was in the city. They have warehouses full of food. Whether it was for staging in Sardinia on the campaign to attack the Republic, or a reaction to the Legions crossing Sicilia, I don't know. But I do know they have enough provisions to feed their people and soldiers for months."

"If they don't come out and fight, how can we negotiate for them to leave Sicilia?" Pompeius shot back. The outburst took everyone in the command staff by surprise. None more than Myrias Pompeius himself.

"Senior Tribune, the purpose of battle is to defeat the enemy," Gaius Claudius remarked. "The lives of our Legionaries are not to be thrown away simply to bring the enemy to a treaty tent. When we commit men to combat, it is to slay the foes of our Republic."

Infantrymen from the First Century guarding the Battle Commander nodded their heads in agreement. Before Claudius could say more or Pompeius had an opportunity to correct his affront to the God Mars for his weak words, the meeting between Consuls Postumius Megellus and Quintus Vitulus broke up. General Megellus and Colonel Zenonis trotted over to speak with the Colonel of Megellus Legion East.

"Gaius. The consensus is the Qart Hadasht Commander doesn't want to contest our presence," Postumius Megellus exclaimed. "Your opinion?"

Gaius Claudius pointed to Alerio. "Ignore the arm gesture, General, Centurion Sisera has an injury. He also has insight into the enemy."

"Sisera. You're the spy from Sardinia?"

"Yes, sir. The Qart Hadasht Commander's name is General Hannibal Gisco," Alerio informed the General. "Behind those walls he has approximately thirteen thousand Iberian heavy infantry and eight thousand light composed of northern Celts. Sir, if he does come out, it'll be more of an arrow's flight as opposed to him forming battle lines."

"Gaius. Your thoughts," General Megellus requested.

"The only time they engaged us was with overwhelming odds and from ambush," Colonel Claudius replied. "I believe we are in for a long siege, sir."

"Zenonis, Claudius, have the men break out their shovels," the General instructed his Battle Commanders. "If Hannibal Gisco won't come out at my beckoning, he sure as Hades isn't coming out on his own terms. I want a deep trench encircling this entire city."

"What about the Valley of Temples, General?" Colonel Zenonis inquired.

"Run the ditch between the town and the temples," Postumius Megellus stressed. "We'll keep the Gods on our side."

"As they should be," Pompeius declared.

"Speaking of Gods, Myrias, you should do a sacrifice to honor the Gods for making your first battle a success," General Megellus suggested. "Let the other staff members handle the ditch detail."

"Yes sir. Will you be attending?" the Senior Tribune asked.

"No. I'm quartering at the Temple of Asclepius," Megellus stated. "I visited the Valley once during a trade mission for my father. Of all the temples, the food at Asclepius was the best. And the accommodations the most comfortable. Everything was excellent as long as you disregarded the snakes."

"Sir, I'd like Centurion Sisera to accompany you," Claudius requested. "He's wounded. Maybe the healers can help him."

"The Temple of Asclepius is known for its healing arts," Megellus announced. "Come along, Sisera. Maybe the priest will let you hold one of the Aesculapian Snakes. I hear they grow to six feet."

"More like five one," Alerio mumbled thinking of Assistant Administrator Dosis. Then seeing the General was waiting for a reply, he said. "I look forward to seeing the snake, sir."

"Snakes, Centurion," Megellus corrected. "There is more than one snake at the temple."

"Yes, sir," Alerio agreed. "Probably a lot more than one."

Act 7

Chapter 28 – Healing Ills

The temple compounds looked different in the daylight from on top of a horse, surrounded by the General's staff, and while being escorted by the veterans of First Century. A lot different from when Alerio crept down the hill and hid in the bushes outside the walls.

"Have you ever seen anything so majestic?" the General inquired. He twisted around on his horse and indicated the temple dedicated to Castor and Pollux off to their right and the Temple of Asclepius coming up on their left.

"They are sights to behold, General," Alerio offered.

"If you think this is grand," Postumius Megellus suggested. "You should see them after dark with the braziers glowing softly along the top stoops."

"I imagine it's breath taking, sir," Alerio responded. "But I'll pass."

He had no intention of staying in the temple area overnight. It wasn't the thought of snakes, he assured himself. As a farm lad, one of his jobs was killing snakes in his father's fields. But there was something unsettling about being in a compound where snakes were bred and raised. As the General's party turned off the Street of the Gods and entered the long approach to the temple, Alerio rethought his emotions. As it turned out, it was the idea of sleeping in a compound full of snakes that bothered him.

***

An old cleric and an officer of the valley guard waited on the bottom step. Both bowed to the General as he reined in his horse.

"I am Consul Postumius Megellus of the Republic," he announced while slipping off his mount. "General of two Legions and a representative of the Roman Senate. And I require shelter in the compound of Asclepius for myself and my staff."

"General Megellus. At the healing Temple of Asclepius, your wellbeing is our only goal," the old priest replied. "I am Administrator Thalassa, and you, Postumius Megellus, shall have the use of a holistic house for as long as you desire."

"With or without the snakes?" Megellus inquired.

"The Aesculapians will be removed, and the floors scrubbed while we take refreshments in the temple," the ancient Rector promised. "If you'll follow me."

While the General ascended the steps with his host and four Legionary bodyguards, the Tribunes, and staff Centurions, including Alerio, slipped from their horses. A groan escaped from Alerio when his right arm delayed in responding and caught on the mount's back.

"Are you alright, Centurion?" inquired a veteran from First Century.

"A word of advice," Alerio offered while cuddling the arm in his left hand. "Never play catch with a ballista."

Alerio chuckled at the shrewd remark while he walked to the shade of a garden wall. Putting his back to it, he slid to the ground and closed his eyes.

In the ranks of the First Century, the Private who questioned Alerio snorted.

"He's a merda of a staff officer," the infantryman groused to the squad's Tesserarius. "Don't play catch with a bolt thrower, my hairy cōleī."

"So that's him," the NCO replied. "He doesn't look that tough."

The Private glanced over to where the staff officer sat sleeping against a wall.

"That's him, Corporal?"

"From what I heard, the artillerymen couldn't target the enemy because our infantry formation was between the bolt throwers and the Iberians," the Tesserarius explained. "They couldn't figure out how to put bolts into the main body of the enemy without killing our own men. They settled for aiming at a flanking squad."

"What's the mystery in that? Straight as a javelin flies," the Legionary offered.

"On one shot the Centurion caught the bolt with his shield and deflected it," the NCO reported. "Two squads had moved from the main body to attack the Legion's flank. The bolt, on a new course, pinned every one of them. That staff officer saved the entire left side of the Legion line."

"By playing catch with a ballista?" the Private reflected. "So, he wasn't kidding."

"Not according to the artillerymen who showed me the shield," the Corporal said. "We're going to find a well and rotate the squads for a break. Squad leaders on me."

While the NCO went to coordinate with his Decani, the Private jerked his scutum halfway into the air. He imagined an iron bolt flashing by and striking it. Then he recalled the power of a bolt in flight, cringed, and lowered the heavy shield.

"There is no way he ricocheted a bolt off his shield."

***

Alerio dreamed of being chased across his father's farm by snakes running on their tails and offering him wineskins. As a result, it didn't bother him when someone nudged him from the nightmare with the edge of an infantry shield.

"Yo, Centurion, your mother is looking for you," a Private sneered.

Opening his eyes, Alerio saw smirks on the faces of the veteran infantrymen. The Legionaries in First Century were all battle tested and they trained hard. To have a healer seeking you out when there was no blood or bone protruding from your skin, they saw as a sign of weakness.

Alerio balled his hands into fists and placed them on the ground by his sides. Then he pressed down attempting to stand. The left arm straightened, but the right folded before he could get his feet under him. Pain shot through his shoulder, and he collapsed into the dirt on his side. The impact sent more spasms up his arm and across his ribs. He groaned.

"This man is in distress," a Greek voice pleaded. "Help me get his armor off."

"There's no blood. And he rode in just fine," a Latian voice responded. "The Centurion can undress himself, Doc."

"Is there no one in charge of you reprobates?" the healer questioned. His voice grew more shrill with each word. "Can someone please help me with this man?"

"Hold on, Doc," the Corporal said attempting to prevent an incident. He pointed at two Legionaries. "Get the staff officer up and stripped."

Alerio was scooped out of the dirt and placed on his feet. Hands expertly unbuckled his armor and pulled the tunic over his head. At the sight of Alerio's naked torso, a collective gasp ran through the Tribunes, staff Centurions, and the veteran Legionaries.

As if the deep black and blue discoloring spread over his right arm, shoulder, and ribs weren't painful enough, Centurion Sisera's body was marred with battle scars. He might be a staff officer now, but it was apparent, the Centurion had seen an unfair share of combat.

"Can you walk?" the healer asked.

"Doc, it's my arm and side, not my knees," Alerio replied. Then he adjusted a band of black silk that circled his hips and urged the medic. "Lead on."

"What happened to him?" a Tribune inquired.

"That, sir, is the result of playing catch with a ballista," a Legionary answered.

"Catching a what? That's insane. He must be touched by Furor," the nobleman suggested.

"Maybe Nemesis, sir. If it was punishment for arrogance," the Private corrected. "But for sure, Centurion Sisera is familiar with Algea, the Goddess of pain."

***

Alerio cried out. A little from the pain, some from having the tendons stretched, and a lot from mental discomfort.

"She's one of our gentle ones," the healer explained as the shake curled around Alerio's arm and upper body. Under his armpit, the healer held the snake and she tightened. The flexing coils lifted the arm away from Alerio's ribs. "After the treatment, we'll wrap you in herbs and await the incubatio."

"The what?" Alerio questioned between clinched teeth. After the manipulation of his bruised body, all the muscles on his right side were taut and hurting.

"It's the temple sleep," the healer replied while dipping lengths of cloth in a pot filled with a thick pungent liquid. "As you sleep, you will be visited by the God Asclepius, or by his earthly representatives. In the morning, you will describe the dream to a senior Celebrant. From that, he will prescribe treatment."

Despite the pain, Alerio smiled. He already had a dream. At least the one he would report as having come during temple sleep. If the snakes, in the nightmare he had earlier, wanted him to have wineskins full of vino, who was he to argue.

***

In the middle of the night, Alerio attempted to stretch. But the restrictive cloth bindings woke him. His chest and arm were individually wrapped while an additional wrap fixed the arm against his side. Loose at first, as the balm infused cloth dried, it compressed his arm and chest. At least the strong aroma of peppermint, lemon, and other unidentified herbs had faded.

Shifting, Alerio tried for a more comfortable position by rolling over. Ending up on his right side, he caught his breath against the pain and rolled onto his back. Now wide awake, he stared up at the dark ceiling.

When the healer brought him to the holistic house, he gave Alerio fresh water. There were slices of orange floating in the pitcher, but none fell into the mug. A couple of healers wrapped him, helped him to a cot but, provided nothing solid to eat. In a Legion camp, someone was always coming off duty and cooking. For company and conversation, the Legionary would gladly share a meal. Thinking to find a cook house or a pantry, the wounded Centurion slung his legs over the side of the cot. Before standing, he ran his fingers under the bed frame and debated with himself. Deciding to leave the Golden Valley dagger in place, he stood but had to stifle a groan in the process.

Movement on the floor alerted him to the presences of Aesculapian Snakes. Several had been placed in his bed when the healers laid him down. Thankfully, none of the serpents remained in the cot. As the living embodiments of the God Asclepius, Alerio moved carefully to avoid offending the snakes. Stepping over a couple of long scaly bodies while slipping down the hallway, Alerio made his way silently to the front door.

The stealth paid off. The attendant sleeping in a chair beside the doorway never stirred when Alerio left the holistic house. An infantryman of the Republic prided himself on his strength, the ability to follow orders, and his hard-won martial skills. A less discussed talent was locating food or drink at any time of the day or night.

Alerio elevated his chin, let the night air drift by his nose before inhaling. After a second sniff, he headed towards the aroma of a cooking fire.

On the far side of a garden, Alerio gazed down a back street of the compound. In the distance were the embers of neatly arranged campfires. He assumed the First Century's bivouac rested close to the house where the General slept. Another sniff of the night air guided him to the left and around a pool of water. Through a row of hedges, Alerio spied a building separated from a few others. Smoke wafted into the air and the fragrance of fresh bread hung around the structure. To his joy, Centurion Sisera realized he had found the bakery for the temple complex.

Considering that he was a patient, Alerio didn't know if he was allowed to eat. Disregarding the idea of rules and regulations, he slipped from the bushes, crossed the open ground, and peered into the bakery through a window. Covering one entire wall was stacked brick ovens. Flame flickering out from the ovens highlighted wooden tables. On the tabletops in the center of the room, rounds of prepared dough rested, ready to be baked. Further back at the edge of the firelight and mostly in shadows was the reward for Alerio's midnight patrol. Floor to ceiling shelves of baked bread waiting to be distributed for breakfast. In the absence of a baker, Alerio bent as best he could against the healer's stiff wraps, lifted his leg, slipped it over the windowsill, and stumbled into the bakery. Then with a grin on his face, the hungry Centurion tiptoed to the shelves.

***

If he had two free hands, Alerio would have collected rounds of flat bread in both. Being restricted, he settled for grabbing three loaves before retreating to the window. He had just balanced the bread on the windowsill and lifted a leg to climb out when voices drifted through the doorway. They were muffled by the crackling of the burning wood in the ovens, the width of the room, and the exterior wall. Alerio wanted to take his prizes somewhere comfortable and eat them. He did, but he recognized one of the speakers and couldn't ignore the man.

"It's for the good of the temple," Assistant Administrator Dosis exclaimed. "When they regain control of the surrounding areas, what do you think they'll do?"

"Come to the temple for healing, just like everyone else," a second voice answered. "I have bread that needs tending."

"And I have a temple that I am trying to save," Dosis shot back. "The Qart Hadasht Empire can make life difficult for us when they discover we sheltered the Republic's General."

"The Temple of Asclepius offers the healing arts to everyone," the baker countered. "and fresh, unsoiled bread for all on which to break their fast. Take your evil elsewhere, Dosis. I'll not be part of your plan."

Alerio reached the doorway and looked out. In the moonlight, he saw the administrator facing a large man wearing an apron. The Legionary might have assaulted Dosis before demanding the return of his gladius rig except for the two men standing behind the priest. Although not in armor, sword belts equipped with

Hoplite swords and knives circled their waists. Realizing this was not a fight he could win, Alerio backed away from the doorway.

"No hard feelings," the baker offered. "You and the temple guards come in and have a loaf. Fresh and hot from the oven. What's not to like?"

The crunch of sandals on the walkway alerted Alerio that the four men were moving towards the building. With a burst of speed, the Legionary shot across the room, bent his knees at the last moment, and jumped at the window.

In midair, as his waist sailed over the sill, Alerio remembered he couldn't bend and roll to soften the landing. Plus, the bindings restricted his bound and prevented him from reaching the proper velocity to clear the opening.

The tops of his feet caught the inside of the sill and jerked him to a sudden stop. Then, as if a log was partially shoved out of a window, the stiffly wrapped Legionary cantilevered downward and impacted the soil with his face. Stunned and motionless for a heartbeat, his body bridged the distance from the earth to the sill. Finally, he legs rolled and his feet dropped from the window.

Alerio lingered with his face pressed to the grass while panting and waiting for the waves of pain to subside. When it became only deep throbbing, he shifted and used his left arm to gain his feet. Squatting, he looked up at the window. To his delight, the three loaves remained balanced on the windowsill. Despite the clumsy exit, his clandestine mission was successful. The Centurion raised up and clamped the stolen loaves of bread between his fingers.

"Now this batch has honey in them," the baker informed his company. "Later this morning, Dosis, we'll go see Rector Thalassa. I'm sure once he hears your argument, he'll make the wisest decision."

Alerio looked beyond his hand, passed his bread, through the window, and into the room. The valley guards stood on either side of the doorway nibbling on loaves. While they were stationary, Dosis followed the baker around the room. He didn't have a loaf in his hand nor was he chewing fresh bread. Instead, the temple's Assistant Administrator chewed the inside of his cheek as if nervous about something.

The two men walked from the shelves to the tables where Alerio lost sight of Dosis. The baker selected uncooked loaves from the tabletop then turned and carried them to the ovens. When he moved, the priest reappeared. This time, there was something in Dosis' hand.

***

Before Alerio could call out a warning, Dosis stepped behind the baker. Raising up on his toes, the priest slipped one hand over the baker's shoulder, gripped the man's jaw, and snapped his head back. With the neck exposed, he brought the knife around from the other side and drove it through the baker's throat. The large man fell, forward spewing blood onto the oven shelves before smashing his forehead on the brick face and crumpling to the floor. In response to the violent killing, the two valley guardsmen stepped away from the wall and, in a single file, marched out of the bakery. Dosis dropped the bloody knife beside the dead baker and followed them.

The knife was a broad bladed dagger, and its origin was unmistakable. Most Legion infantrymen carried a pugio as a third weapon or as a utility knife. With all the wounded and dead Legionaries from today's fighting, it wouldn't be difficult for Dosis to get his hands on one. And the message delivered by his dropping the pugio next to the body was clear. A Legionary brought into the temple compound by General Postumius Megellus had committed the murder.

Thinking to take the weapon and prevent the General's staff from being blamed, Alerio lifted a foot to the windowsill.

"Master. Master. Here's the extra honey you sent me for," a young lad's voice called from the other side of the building. "I was delayed because someone left a wineskin and a note of appreciation for your skills. The pantry attendant had a hard time locating it."

The apprentice raced through the doorway and stopped. With his mouth open he stared down at the body of the baker for several moments. Then, he began screaming. Alerio dropped his foot to the ground, spun in a half circle, and hobbled for the hedge row. In his flight, his stolen loaves of bread remained on the windowsill - forgotten.

Chapter 29 – Sweet, Gentle Polydeukes

"Centurion, it's time for your morning treatment," a healer called from the doorway. He stepped into the narrow sleeping chamber and gasped when the Legionary turned over. "You are, you are filthy?"

Alerio tilted his head, examined the soil and grass stains on the wraps, and with a surprised look on his face suggested, "It was a very active incubatio."

Even though he didn't need help, the healer assisted Alerio in getting out of the cot and hovered beside him as they walked down the hallway to a treatment room. There they were met by another healer and together the medical technicians unwound the dirty cloth.

Once free of the restrictive wraps, Alerio flexed with only a little pain. But when he attempted to raise his right arm above his head, it became too excruciating to go beyond shoulder height.

"We have just the Aesculapian for that," the medic said. He opened the lid on a woven basket, reached in, and using two hands, lifted out a snake almost five feet long. "He's a little aggressive but, he'll get those bones unstuck."

This time Alerio paid attention to the snake and the healer. Rather than the coils massaging aches and tender spots, the Legionary noted it was the hands of the healer manipulating the sore muscles and stretching the joints through a range of motion. He may have uncovered a secret of the Temple of Asclepius, but he didn't care. As long as the treatment got him healthy and back to the Legion.

Once the 'serpent' had loosened his injuries, the handler dipped clean cloth into more of the herb sauce. When his chest was partially wrapped, Alerio's stomach growled.

"When is breakfast?" he inquired.

"Your first full day at the temple is for cleansing," the medic informed him as he snugged up the first layer of the wrap. "Orange water and olive oil will accomplish it. After drinking, and of course being indisposed, you'll have a session with a cleric to discuss your dream."

"The breakfast sounds as unappetizing as it can be," Alerio complained. "But let's get on with it so I can meet the Doctor."

"Oh, the celebrant isn't a doctor, he's a priest and an interpreter of dreams."

"I'd like to discuss this nightmare therapy," Alerio mumbled. He indicated the tight herbal soaked bandages.

"What's that you said, sir?" the medic asked while immobilizing Alerio's right arm against his body.

"Nothing. Nothing important," Alerio responded. "Now, where are those delicious beverages?"

***

Alerio opened the door to the latrine and shuffled out to be greeted by an overly pleasant temple assistant.

"The body requires a cleansing to reset for health," the medic proclaimed.

The Legion officer's gut rumbled, and his right arm ached from being pinned against his side. After the uncomfortable morning, Alerio felt like taking his anguish out on the smiling snake handler by punching the man.

"It wasn't my stomach that caused me trouble. At least it wasn't until I got here. My problem came from catching a bolt from a ballista."

"Are you feeling alright, Centurion?"

Another choirs of rumbling from his lower regions triggered Alerio to turn and hurry back into the toilet facilities.

"No. I am not," he mumbled while closing the door.

After four trips to void his gut, the urge faded, and Alerio was no longer indisposed. But he was famished.

"Can I eat now?" he inquired of the two medics waiting for him.

"You must speak to the priest and tell him your dream first," one answered. "He will suggest food to accompany the treatment."

"Does he ever stipulate a beef and wine therapy?" Alerio asked hopefully.

"He has," the other medic replied as he fell in at Alerio's side. "But it's rare and usually for undersized sons of rich men."

"That leaves me out on both counts."

"Tell my companion about catching an artillery launched iron bolt," the first medic suggested. "I'm sure he'd be interested."

"I didn't actually catch it," Alerio described. "It grazed my shield, knocked me down, and left me bruised and hobbled."

"You didn't catch it in your hands?"

"No, that would be insane," Alerio assured them.

The two medics exchanged looks and the second one walked away. Before Alerio could question the action, they reached the steps to the temple.

"The priest is also an administrator for the temple," the handler warned. "His time is valuable. Walk in and sit down. When he enters don't stand. Simply tell him your dream."

"Like meeting the Colonel in his tent," Alerio replied. "Except for the sitting."

They climbed the steps, and the healer left him at the doorway to a small room. In the back was another entrance with a closed door. Alerio walked in and sat on a marble bench. After the cleansing, the cool stone felt good under his cūlus.

***

An internal debate raged in Alerio's mind. To whom and when should he bring up witnessing the murder of the baker. Because of the negative conversation concerning the Republic and the dropped pugio, informing the General or Colonel was paramount. On the other hand, the killing affected the temple's organization. That meant he could simply keep the incident to himself. But, seeing as he was waiting for a priest, he deliberated the idea of telling the dream interpreter. Then the rear door opened, and his thoughts slammed into a brick wall and his options ended.

"Alerio Sisera. I see you but not my apprentice," Assistant Administrator Dosis mentioned while walking into the small room. "I hope it was painless for the poor lad."

"He's not dead, Administrator," Alerio responded. He stood and glared at the cleric. "But he is in an uncomfortable situation with the city militia in Agrigento."

"You should know I have assistants and temple guards within shouting distance," Dosis warned.

"I'm in no position to threaten you," Alerio assured him.

Thinking the Legion officer referred to his wrapped and trapped right arm, Dosis nodded wisely and gestured to the marble bench.

"No, I don't suppose you are," the priest stated while pulling over a saddle chair and sitting. "Retake your seat, Centurion."

"Tell me. Why do you hate the Republic so much?" Alerio questioned as he settled gently onto the stone.

"My dear lad, I don't hate anyone. What I do is love the Temple of Asclepius more than anything," the cleric explained. "Your upstart Republic is here today and maybe for the next few months. Oh, you'll strut around like world conquerors but, eventually, the Qart Hadasht Empire will send a fleet. They'll land an army, and sweep you Latians, and your Greek allies, from the lands of Sicilia."

"That's wishful thinking, Administrator," Alerio suggested. "The Legions are very good at land warfare."

"And I am good at the politics of protecting the temple," Dosis boasted.

"Does that include cutting the throat of an unsuspecting baker?" Alerio challenged.

"How convenient. I was struggling with the most adventitious person to blame for the unfortunate demise of Polydeukes," the temple administrator confessed. Then he jumped up, circled behind the low chair as if to use it as a barrier, and shouted. "Guards. Guards."

A pair of Hoplites rushed into the room.

"You called Assistant Administrator?" one of the two sentries asked.

"This, this evil man has just admitted to murdering the baker," Dosis informed them. "Take him to a room near Rector Thalassa's officer. I'll send for him once I consult with the Head Administrator."

Alerio stood and used his free hand to lift the white patient's tunic to show he was unarmed and one handed. Despite the docile mannerism of the prisoner, the guards prodded the Legion officer out of the room with the tips of their spears. As soon as they cleared the doorway, the healer waiting for Alerio burst in.

"Assistant Administrator, what happened?"

"When the patient began telling me about his dream from the incubatio," Dosis described while lowering his head as if in prayer. "The God Asclepius reached into the Legionary's heart, took control of his mouth, and forced the truth from him. The truth that Alerio Sisera murdered sweet, gentle Polydeukes."

"It's a miracle," the healer cried. "I will go and spread the word."

"Before you alert the entire complex," Dosis insisted. "Run and fetch the baker's apprentice. Then go to the hostile house where Sisera is staying and ask the attendants about anything unusual. Have them all report to Rector Thalassa's office. Finally, locate the Captain of the Temple Guards and get the murder weapon. I'll need everything in the Rector's office as soon as possible."

The snake handler ran from the room and the Assistant Administrator smiled. At first, he worried the Roman General would hear about the tribunal when the brash young medic ran around boasting about the miracle. Now, with him busy collecting the evidence, Dosis relaxed. Sisera's life would be forfeited rapidly because justice on temple grounds was swift. After condemning the Centurion, all projected allegations against the Republic's forces would be accepted. Dosis' goal of protecting the temple was within reach.

***

When they shoved Alerio into the storage room there had only been two guards. When they took him out, two stood on either side of a door further down the hallway, two more were positioned on one end of the hall and two others stood post on the opposite end. Counting the two escorting him, the corridor held eight armored Valley of the Temple guardsmen. The presence of the Hoplites wasn't reassuring to the Legion staff officer.

"Go to the Rector's office," one of the guards instructed.

"Which way?" Alerio inquired. He stepped to his right and bumped the guard.

A spear shaft slammed into his sore right arm and Alerio stumbled away from the impact. Shuffling to keep his balance, the Centurion studied the faces of the two sentries at that end of the hallway.

"No. To your right," the other Hoplite said while delivering a nudge of his own.

Alerio lurched as he adjusted giving him a moment looked over the two sentries on the other end of the hallway. None were the guardsmen who accompanied Dosis during the killing. One thing became clear from the rough handling, the baker was a popular figure. He must

291

have been for his death to bring this much ire down on his accused killer.

With the prisoner taking small, controlled steps and making no quick movements, the two escorts relaxed and fell back. The situation became fluid at the door to the Rector's office.

Centurion Sisera planted his left foot. Then lifted and bent his right knee before driving it into the lower belly of a door guard. The man collapsed around the knee and the patella sank into his gut. Vomit projected into the hallway and the escort on the right stepped back to avoid the deluge. The left side Hoplite, however, raised his spear and clubbed Alerio in the back.

Propelled forward, Alerio expected to bounce off the wood. But the door opened, and he fell face down into the room. Waves of pain streaked up and down his arm and shoulder. Through the tears, he peered back at the doorway.

"Good to see you again, merda for brains," he sneered at the guard he had assaulted.

The guard on his knees in a puddle of his own puke stared at the Legion officer.

"Do I know you?"

"No. But I know you."

Numerous voices shouting came from within the room. All the voices fell silent after a moment and allowed one to be heard. It wasn't the loudest or most robust. In fact, the speaker's voice crackled as would the voice of any old man.

"Get him off the ground, and for mercy's sake, stop beating the accused."

"We're sorry, Rector Thalassa," the guards apologized at the same time. They reached down and lifted the one-armed Latian off the floor. When Alerio staggered as if injured from the strike by the spear shaft, one of the guards inquired. "Where do you want him, sir?"

"Place him on the couch in the corner," Thalassa instructed. "And if you can abstain from beating him further, one of you stay with him."

While a Hoplite positioned himself at the end of the couch, the other guard marched to the door, walked through, and closed it behind him.

With his chin resting on his chest, Alerio's head rolled back and forth. While his head movement was random, his eyes scanned the room as he tried to identify who was there. Priests, medics, and at least two military man, his Hoplite and another both from the temple guards, occupied the office. By the end of the search, he knew one other thing. There were no Legion officers present.

Chapter 30 – Connecting Point

"As he did each morning, Master Baker Polydeukes rose long before daylight," Dosis said in a voice that reverberated off the office walls. "With his apprentice by his side, the baker made bread, cakes, and fruit filled pastries for our compound. Then last night, while his loyal apprentice left to fetch supplies, Master Polydeukes was murdered."

The Assistant Administrator held up a pugio.

"This is the weapon that took our baker's life," he exclaimed while showing the wide Legion dagger to all sides of the room. "Sadly, his blood and fittingly grain, still cling to the blade. And make note, it is a knife of the Republic's military."

Dosis set the weapon on the corner of a big desk. Thalassa leaned from behind the desk and examined the dagger.

"Please continue," the Rector urged.

"Liris. Tell the Rector what you found when you returned from the pantry," Dosis instructed the baker's apprentice.

"Well sir, I had to wait for the supply man to find a letter addressed to Master Polydeukes and then fill the honey amphora," Liris stated. "I was gone much longer than I planned."

"Yes, yes, that's understandable," Dosis said. "But now, tell us what you found when you returned to the bakery."

"Master Polydeukes, dead, on the floor, sir."

"Was there blood? Was he cut? Bruised?" the Assistant Administrator asked in a rapid-fire fashion. "Give us details."

"His forehead was cut and his, his throat was sliced," Liris stammered. Then looking around, he added. "Like a gutted hog, sir. But only his neck. And he wasn't hung up to drain. Just lying on the floor in a pool of blood."

Dosis raised an arm, pointed to the ground as if the baker' body laid there, then to the apprentice, and finally he indicated Alerio.

"While his apprentice was away, Alerio Sisera stealthy left the holistic house, entered the bakery, and killed Master Polydeukes," the Assistant Administrator informed the room. "One of our house healers has Sisera's wraps from last night. Please show them to Rector Thalassa."

The snake handler, who first worked on Alerio, stood and from a leather bag pulled out the grass and soil tainted lengths of cloth and an equally stained white tunic.

"You can see the Legion officer left his room and, even if he denied it, we know he was alone on the temple grounds," Dosis professed. He pointed at the dirty wraps. "Thank you, medic. We have the means, the weapon, and can place the Legion officer near the bakery. In short, Alerio Sisera is guilty of homicide. Of killing our master baker in cold blood. I ask that Centurion Sisera be executed immediately as is the right of the healing temple."

"Sir?" one of the medics asked. "What about the miracle of the confession?"

"Ah, there already is a preponderance of evidence," the Assistance Administrator deflected. Then his eyes drilled into Thalassa's, and he demanded. "Senior Administrator, I ask that you do your duty in this matter. Order the strangulation. And, I might add, you should expel the Republic's General and his staff for the safety of everyone sheltered in the temple complex."

The Senior Administrator broke eye contact and cleared his throat as of to deliver a verdict.

"Don't I get to say anything in my defense?" Alerio asked from the corner. He swung his legs to the floor and grunted as the wraps pulled tight. "I was, after all, there when Master Polydeukes was murdered."

Cries demanding the Legion officer's death flowed from the lips of everyone in the room. He had just confessed, or had he? The smile on the Centurion's face confused several of the clerics attending the trial. It didn't appear to be the expression of a guilty man.

***

"Centurion Sisera, do you wish to question any of the assertions?" Thalassa asked.

"Yes, Rector, I do," Alerio said while standing.

The guardsman shifted as if to prevent the Legion officer from leaving the couch area. Thalassa waved him off.

"Please Centurion Sisera, it's your life in the balance. Continue."

"The Assistant Administrator claims I cut a large man's neck," Alerio offered while pointing at the wraps on his right side. "How is that possible with one arm?"

"I am not versed in the use of weapons," Dosis admitted. "But guard Lieutenant Eidos is an expert."

The Hoplite officer left his chair and walked to Thalassa's desk. He picked up the dagger and cut the air with the blade a few times to test the balance.

"Based on the limitations of the attacker," Eidos described while aiming the dagger's tip at the bandaged Alerio. "Centurion Sisera snuck up behind Polydeukes and kicked him into the brick ovens. That explains the cut on his forehead. Then Sisera stood over the dazed baker and holding the knife like this, he stabbed Polydeukes in the neck."

The Lieutenant held the dagger in his left hand with the blade protruding to the left. From a bent over position, he mimicked an awkward thrust low to the ground.

"After the butchery, he dropped the knife and fled."

"Thank you, Lieutenant," Dosis stated as the officer set the knife back on the desk. Then he questioned. "Your guilt seems obvious to us, but tell me Centurion, do you have other inquiries?"

"Yes, sir. Are there any blood stains on my dirty wraps?"

The cloth and tunic came out of the leather bag. After inspecting them the medic announced, "Grass and dirt stains, but no blood."

Alerio nodded then crossed the room to stand in front of the apprentice.

"Liris. Did you clean the ovens after the body was removed?" he inquired.

The apprentice swallowed and peered around the room.

"You may answer," Thalassa said.

"I did, sir. Master Polydeukes was keen on cleaning after he baked the last item. Any leftovers and ash had to be removed before he would use the ovens again," Liris exclaimed.

"Did you clean your Master's blood from the brick face?"

Dosis threw his arms in the air and stomped to Thalassa's desk.

"This is a stalling tactic by a condemned man," he exploded. "Enough of this rhetoric. Master Thalassa, order the execution."

"May I remind you, Assistant Administrator, that I may be old, but I am still the Senior Administrator of the Temple of Asclepius," Thalassa asserted. "Liris, answer the question."

"The ovens were a mess," the apprentice described. "His blood splashed from the top oven down to the bottom shelf. It took me all morning. But they are clean now and ready for the next…"

The apprentice baker began to cry as he remembered his master wouldn't be firing up the ovens in the morning or any morning ever.

"Thank you Liris," Alerio said. "One more question. Did you find anything on the windowsill while you were cleaning up?"

"Yes, sir," Liris whimpered between sniffles. "Three loafs left there to cool. By Master Polydeukes, I guess."

From the hallway outside the door, angry voices rose, there was a scuffle before the door flew open.

General Postumius Megellus and Colonel Gaius Claudius marched into the room. Following close behind came five First Century infantrymen.

"I am sorry to arrive unannounced, Master Thalassa. But I seem to be missing one of my staff officers," Megellus declared. Glancing around, he spotted Alerio. "There you are Centurion Sisera. Is there a problem?"

"No sir. I was just about to explain the death of a beloved baker," Alerio responded.

"Then by all means, don't let me stop you," the General said while he and the Colonel took seats.

The one Temple Guard in the room found himself crowded by Legion infantrymen pressing in from either side. If Alerio had fears before, he no longer worried about being strangled in the temple of healing. But he did want to set the record straight.

***

Alerio took a finger, placed it on the edge of the dagger, and flicked it. It began to spin and, in the silent room, the guard on the hilt created a grating noise as the weapon rotated.

"The loafs of bread on the windowsill were mine," he admitted. "After I witnessed the murder and Liris returned, I fell out of the window. In a panic, I fled and left behind the only reason for my visit to the bakery."

"You were at the bakery," Dosis proclaimed. "We no longer have to guess, Master Thalassa. The Legion officer by his own words places himself at the scene."

"I also stated that I witnessed the murder," Alerio insisted while reaching down and snatching the dagger from the desktop. "But I wasn't the only person in the bakery."

He gently tossed the dagger into the air. It twisted then fell hilt first. Alerio placed his hand under the falling weapon with his palm facing downward. The dagger remained balanced on the back of his hand while Alerio resumed his defense.

"One of my Legion titles is weapons instructor," he described while maintaining the balance with slight movements of his left arm. "I am an expert with a variety of edged weapons. The pugio has a wide double-sided blade and is capable of easily slicing a throat. But Master Polydeukes wasn't on his knees when he was cut. By Liris' description, we know spewing blood coated the face of the ovens from the top to the bottom. Only a man standing when cut could coat that much area."

Alerio flipped his hand over and for a moment balanced the dagger on his palm. Then he gripped the hilt, dropped his arm, and tossed the pugio underhanded behind his back. The blade flashed as it arched up and over his shoulder. It fell towards the floor and halted when the weapons instructor snatched it from the air.

"I could have held Polydeukes' head back or sliced his throat. But not both simultaneously," he stated. With a series of swipes at different angles with the dagger, Alerio demonstrated the dexterity of his left hand. "And I wouldn't need to reach over to his right side to cut him open."

"But you confessed," a medic shouted. "A celebrant of the Temple of Asclepius heard the God force you to admit your guilt."

All eyes in the room shifted from the Legion officer to Dosis. The Assistant Administrator sagged in his chair and dropped his eyes to the floor.

"Cleric Dosis, tell them the God spoke to you," the healer pleaded. "You told me…"

"I know what I told you," Dosis screamed while vaulting out of the chair and across the room to Thalassa's desk. "Don't you see what's happening here. We've declared the temple to be an ally of the Roman Republic. When General Hannibal Gisco charges from the walls of Agrigento or, the Empire lands an army on the beach and advances, they will drive these provincial rubes across Sicily and into the Messina strait. And our temple will be destroyed as revenge for aiding an enemy of the Qart Hadasht Empire."

"Did you betray the sacred trust of a dream interpreter?" Thalassa inquired softly as if it hurt to ask. "Did you lie?"

"For the best of reasons, I had to save the temple."

"The Temple of Asclepius has treated the ill of every persuasion for over four hundred years," Thalassa explained. "War Lords, paupers, Kings, and merchants have come to us for healing. That trust supersedes politics because of our adherence to the healing code. You have not saved the Temple. By your actions, you've threatened its very existence."

"I only…"

"Enough," Thalassa barked. "Centurion Sisera, finish your dissertation. I fear we know already, but please, tell us who killed the baker."

***

Two days later, Alerio extended his arms over his head and stretched his back muscles. The sun warmed his skin, and the vino warmed his body. Beside him, a brook from a spring trickled water along a stream meandering through the temple's garden. When a shadow fell over him, he opened his eyes expecting a healer.

"Colonel Claudius, sir," Alerio acknowledged upon recognizing the Battle Commander.

"Stay where you are," Gaius ordered while reaching down to take the wineskin. After a sip, the Colonel sank to the grass. "Are they treating you alright, Centurion Sisera?"

"Yes, sir. I'm accustomed to the snakes and the massages," Alerio replied. "I've full use of my arm and the shoulder only aches a little. I'm ready to return to duty."

"That's why I've come to see you privately," Gaius Claudius said with a laugh. The humor came from having a squad of infantrymen not ten feet away making the privacy concept ridiculous. "I want you to know what I'm doing is nothing personal."

"That sounds ominous, Colonel," Alerio remarked. "Am I to be the Legion's latrine officer?"

"I'd take you for that if I could, knowing the job would be done correctly. Like what you did for Senior Tribune Pompeius. I asked you to keep him alive and you did."

"Sir, I overstepped my position and half expected charges to be brought against me."

"Oh, Pompeius tried. He even went to the General with his complaint. But I interceded and nothing will come of it. Good job on your part."

"Sir, if you thought the Senior Tribune would hesitate, why didn't you send Senior Centurion Lembus with the detachment?"

"Because they're friends and the Senior Centurion would have waited to act out of respect," Gaius Claudius stated. "I knew you would do the right thing without regard to esteem as long as it saved Legionaries lives. You did and you saved Pompeius   professionally and probably his very life. Even with that, I have to reassign you for another reason."

"I'm not sure if I should ask about the new posting or what the other reason is," Alerio questioned.

"The other reason is you remind everyone of a murdered baker and a dead Assistant Administrator for the Temple of Asclepius," Gaius informed the staff Centurion. "As far as the new duty, it's as far from Agrigento as I can imagine."

"Where is that, sir?"

"For some reason, the Senate is asking for young bright Centurions to be transferred to Stifone."

"I've never heard of it, Colonel."

"It's a little village in hill country about a hundred miles up the Tiber."

"What's happening there?" Alerio asked hopefully. "Bandits, a revolt, something interesting?"

"It's deep in the heart of Umbrian territory and the tribes in that area have been at peace with the Republic for almost forty years," Claudius reported to the disappointed junior officer. "I'm afraid it'll be building duty. You know roads, barracks, bridges, and the like."

"I really wanted to be part of the Sicilia operation, Colonel," Alerio complained to the Battle Commander. Seeing no give in the Colonel's expression, Alerio asked. "When do I leave, sir?"

"Hiero II of Syracuse sent thousands of troops but only part of the supplies he promised. If he doesn't deliver more and something happens to our supply base, you'll be glad you're not here," Claudius suggested. "The General is sending an envoy to Syracuse. His cavalry escort leaves from Camp Favara tomorrow at midday. A horse and pack mule with your gear will be here at dawn. Enjoy your last night at the spa."

The Colonel took another sip and handed the wineskin to Alerio. He stood and the infantrymen came to attention. After the crowd of Legionaries trooped out of the garden, Alerio took a long pull of vino. Ritual required overindulgence on the last night of a posting. And who was he to break with Legion tradition.

***

Hungover and slouched on the horses back, Centurion Sisera guided the animal and the mule out of the Valley of Temples. Looking to his left, Alerio saw the gash of raw earth from the trench that surrounded the entire city of Agrigento. The Legionaries had completed the ditch in just a few days.

The channel prevented the Iberians and Celts from venturing beyond the walls for random attacks. Now they would need to come out in force and bridge the trench before engaging. If the Qart Hadasht mercenaries made a move, the forces of the Republic would have ample warning. Without a doubt, the unwanted siege of Agrigento had begun.

Off to his right, Alerio gazed over the ocean. A ship under sail slowly and majestically crossed the horizon. He watched until he developed a knot in his neck. Other than the trip to the Capital, his next duty station would be far removed from open water.

In his fuzzy state, he attempted to visualize anything interesting about a posting at a place named Stifone. Nothing came to mind as he nudged the horse out of the foothills and onto the path heading to the interior of Sicilia.

The End

Author Notes:

The old saying, history is written by the winners, is true. However, as we saw at the beginning of this book, *Polybius of Megalopolis*, a Greek Historian who was pro Carthage, and *Cassius Dio*, a Roman Historian who was pro Rome, both wrote history. Thankfully for a historical adventure writer, they wrote from different points of view that clashed on facts, motivations, and outcomes. From their contradictions, <u>Deceptive Valor</u> was born.

The treatment, other than using snakes for massages, in the Temple of Asclepius was close to accurate. As a wellness temple, they used dream interpretations to create treatment plans and believed in a holistic approach to health. Plus, they did have nonvenomous Aesculapian snakes in the treatment houses, some growing to over six feet in length.

A big thanks to Jeff S. and other readers who emailed me notices of typos. It's a big help for cleaning up errors in my earlier books.

Thank you for reading book #9 in the Clay Warriors Stories series. When we began this journey, Alerio Sisera was an undersized school lad with bully issues. Now he is an officer in the Legion seeking a home unit. In book #10, the first Punic War enters its third year, and if you didn't pick up on the hints, you'll discover the purpose of Stifone.

I appreciate you spending time with Alerio and me in our version of the Roman Republic. Until next time, be safe and don't stand in front of any loaded and cocked ballista.

J. Clifton Slater

Contact Information:

GalacticCouncilRealm@gmail.com

To sign up for my newsletter and to read blogs about ancient Rome, please visit my website.

www.JCliftonSlater.com

I write military adventure both future and ancient.
Books by J. Clifton Slater
Historical Adventure – *Clay Warrior Stories series*

#1 Clay Legionary	#2 Spilled Blood
#3 Bloody Water	#4 Reluctant Siege
#5 Brutal Diplomacy	#6 Fortune Reigns
#7 Fatal Obligation	#8 Infinite Courage
#9 Deceptive Valor	#10 Neptune's Fury
#11 Unjust Sacrifice	#12 Muted Implications
#13 Death Caller	#14 Rome's Tribune
#15 Deranged Sovereignty	
#16 Uncertain Honor	#17 Tribune's Oath
#18 Savage Birthright	#19 Abject Authority

Novels of the 2nd Punic War – *A Legion Archer series*

#1 Journey from Exile	#2 Pity the Rebellious
#3 Heritage of Threat	#4 A Legion Legacy

Military Science Fiction – *Call Sign Warlock series*

#1 Op File Revenge	#2 Op File Treason
#3 Op File Sanction	

Military Science Fiction – Galactic Council Realm series

#1 On Station	#2 On Duty
#3 On Guard	#4 On Point

Printed in Great Britain
by Amazon